YUGANTAR

The dream of Bharatavarsha takes shape 2300 years ago

RAGHAVAN SRINIVASAN

Leadstart
INKSTATE

ISBN 978-93-90463-68-8

First published in India 2020 by
An imprint of Leadstart Publishing Pvt Ltd

Sales Office:
Unit No.25/26, Building No.A/1,
Near Wadala RTO,
Wadala (East), Mumbai – 400037 India
Phone: +91 969933000
Email: info@leadstartcorp.com
www.leadstartcorp.com

Disclaimer: The views expressed in this book are those of the Author and do not pertain to be held by the Publisher.

Editor: Kavya Shree
Cover: Nimesh Pilla & Sunil Butola
Layouts: Victor Patali

Dedicated to my mother and father
for their love, patience and wisdom.

About the Author

Raghavan Srinivasan is a graduate in Chemical Engineering from Madras University and a post-graduate in MBA from McMaster University, Canada. At present, he is a professional consultant in the social development area. He lives in New Delhi. As a consultant he has written and edited a number of documents. He has also been editing a magazine called *ghadar jari hai* for several years now. It started as a print publication and is now an online magazine (http://ghadar.org.in/gjh_html/?nocahce). He has written several cover stories, articles and travelogues for print and online newspapers.

Raghavan is passionately interested in Indian literature, philosophy and history. He believes that the past of our sub-continent has many clues to help us find our way in these confusing times.

The author can be reached at raghavansrin@gmail.com.

ACKNOWLEDGEMENTS

As my first attempt at novel writing this has been a long and hard trek but a most enjoyable one. Though I had earlier edited books and written articles and journal papers, novel writing was a completely new experience. It was like moulding and chiselling a stone patiently and bit by bit into a presentable sculpture.

I thank all those who wished me well in this venture and enquired now and then about its progress with expectation and concern. Firstly, I profusely thank my friend and guide, Balle, for providing me with insights on how to interpret Indian history and thought from a peoples' perspective.

It is with a deep sense of gratitude that I thank my wife Vidya and my son Srinath for the constant understanding and support they gave when I sat glued to my table for days on end. They provided useful feedback on my initial drafts. Srinath's friend Nagarjuna, a post-graduate in history from JNU, gave me essential feedback in the initial phase. My close friend, Dr Shivanand Kanavi, Adjunct Faculty, National Institute of Advanced Studies, Bengaluru, and author-journalist encouraged me to no small extent by introducing me to various publishers. Taru Bahl, a colleague and friend, and an accomplished journalist introduced me to the fascinating world of publications. My friend, Subhasis Ganguly, with his extensive experience of the publishing industry gained through a long stint at Penguin, gave valuable support. Dr Surinder Mediratta who runs a YouTube channel called 'Legally Respectful for Women' gave me suitable tips for the project. My sister, Indra Srinivasan, showered me with profuse encouragements which kept my creative juices flowing. My wife's aunt Vijayalakshmi and my sister-in-law Bhuvana supported me with bubbling enthusiasm. It was so gladdening to note that this long list of well-wishers had so much faith in my writing abilities.

Copious thanks are due to Leadstart Publishing who guided me through the publishing process in a very professional, systematic and most of all, transparent way. The painstaking and meticulous editing done by Kavya Shree has improved the readability of the novel to no small extent. As a first-time novelist, I have greatly benefited from the gentle guidance provided by Pooja Dutt, Devanshi Doshi, Ananya Subramanian and others in the Leadstart team.

I also thank all the early readers who went through the entire novel or parts of it and gave me useful suggestions to make it a better read.

That king is more dead than alive in whose kingdom women are easily abducted from the midst of husbands and sons, uttering cries and groans of indignation and grief. The subjects should arm themselves to slay that king who does not protect them, who simply plunders their wealth, who confounds all distinctions, who is ever incapable of taking their lead, who is without compassion, and who is regarded as the most sinful of kings. That king who tells his people that he is their protector but who does not or is unable to protect them, should be slain by his combined subjects, like a dog that is affected with the rabies and has become mad.

Mahabharata, Vol xiii – Anushasana Parva, Chapter 61 (sacred-texts.com)

In the happiness of his subjects lies the king's happiness, in their welfare his welfare. He shall not consider as good only that which pleases him but treat as beneficial to him whatever pleases his subjects.

Arthashastra, 1.19.34 (Translation by L.N. Rangarajan)

MAP 1

Map of mahajanapadas of Bharatavarsha in 4th century BCE

MAP 2

Map of trade routes of Bharatavarsha in 4th century BCE

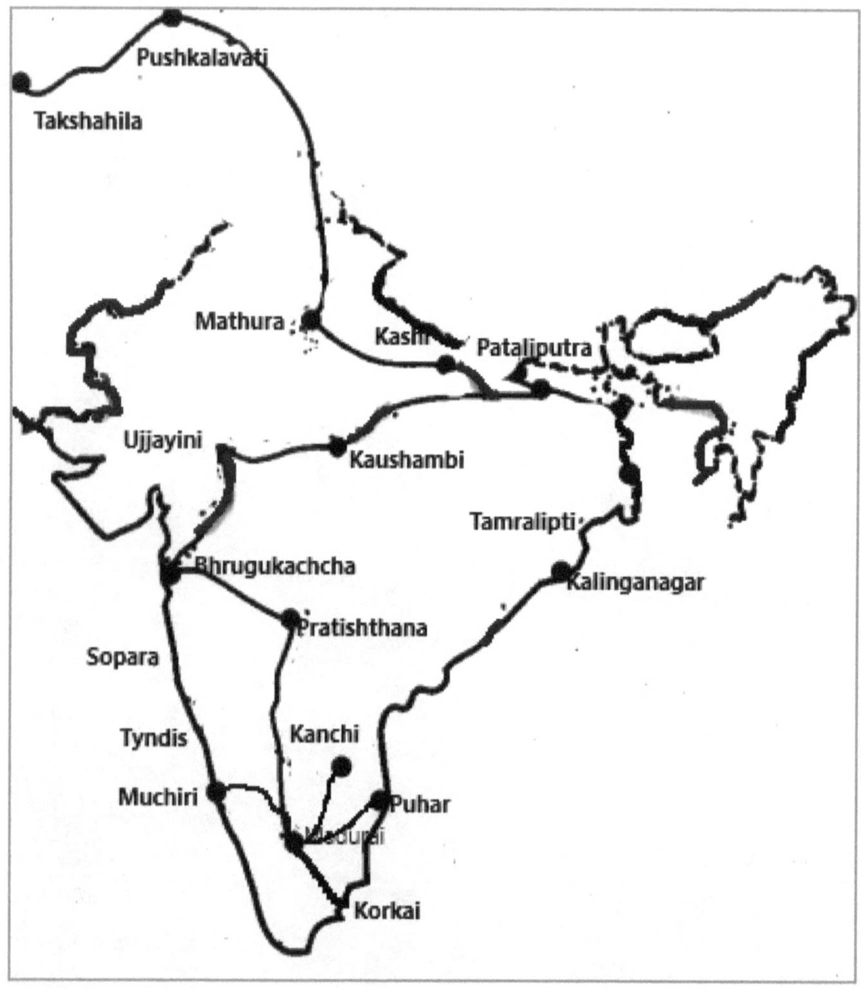

Source of map of Bharatavarsha on the cover: United States Library of Congress (https://commons.wikimedia.org/wiki/Library_of_Congress)'s Geography & Map Division (https://www.loc.gov/rr/geogmap/) under the digital ID g7651e.ct000605 (http://hdl.loc.gov/loc.gmd/g7651e.ct000605)

CONTENTS

PREFACE

As a student of history, but far from a scholar, I have felt that the past of our sub-continent has many clues to help us find our way in these confusing times. Our forefathers gave the concept of zero to the world. The various schools of philosophy, including the orthodox and the heterodox schools, have in them a breath-taking range of philosophies and world outlook. Indian thinkers were among the foremost in mathematics, sciences, economy and statecraft. Several epics, plays, scientific, legal and political documents have lasted the ravages of time.

The fourth century BCE, in which this novel is located, is a particularly interesting period to understand this past. It is a period full of dangers and opportunities. Old republics are giving way to large towns and cities. Empires are in the making, their huge armies sustained by back-breaking taxes.

Buddhism, Jainism and other heterodox sects are challenging the established varna system and Vedic orthodoxy. The intellectual life of India is bristling like new shoots after the monsoon.

The rising trading community resents the domination of the Kshatriyas and the Brahmanas. State power is up for grabs.

The Macedonians are at the gates of Hindukush with their massive army hoping to take advantage of the dissensions between kingdoms.

There is chaos, poverty and suffering everywhere.

This is the time when the people of India vanquished both external aggression and internal chaos. This is precisely when Bharatavarsha was forged. One of the world's largest empires, the Mauryan Empire, established a world-class administrative system at this juncture. It is in this period that India showed tremendous potential in trade, shipping, manufactures, technology, literature, philosophy and statecraft.

What led to the decline of the political, moral and economic fabric of the Indian sub-continent in the first place? Is it the varna system or the constant infighting or downright complacency with what has been achieved? And how did Indian society respond to this? What gave it the resilience to emerge stronger? I have tried to find answers to these questions in this novel and possibly succeeded only partially.

By studying the past we can perhaps find answers to the questions that have been haunting us for some centuries now, only by answering which we can go beyond the sandhi that the Indian sub-continent is stuck in today. It will be downright injustice to indiscriminately glorify the past or to blindly replicate thought systems from the ancient past. It will be even more criminal to sweep away our entire past as feudal and ancient. Those civilisations which have not settled scores with their past conscience cannot hope to lead the world.

Historical fiction is a good medium provided it is not lost in glorifying kings and empires. My effort has been to bring out the economic, cultural and political milieu from the viewpoint of the productive forces of society which gave rise to these kings and empires.

I have tried to weave the story around historical facts such as the second urbanisation in the Gangetic Plains, invasion of Sikandar, fall of the Magadhan empire, the Sangam period of the South and writing of the Arthashastra.

There are many grey areas in the chronology and documentation of events which happened 2300 years ago. Based on recent archaeological evidence and analysis of historical documents I have done some interpretations which have been presented in this novel.

Interpretation #1: There was no Aryan invasion from outside India. The earlier Indus civilisation disintegrated over several centuries due to various factors. By 330 BCE'—the period of this novel—there had been sufficient mixing of cultures, languages, religions, scripts and schools of thought which defined the concept of India.

Interpretation #2: The second urbanisation was very widespread. World class cities and ports developed both in the north and south. Excavations at Kodumanal and other sites in Tamilnadu have established archaeological evidence of international trade and a flourishing steel industry in that period.

Interpretation #3: Excavations at Keezhadi in Tamilnadu revealed that the Tamil Brahmi script is at least 2600 years old. Graffiti marks found in the region may have evolved from the Indus script and served as a precursor to the Tamil Brahmi script

Interpretation #4: Paurus was not defeated by Alexander at the Battle of Jhelum (or Hydaspes). The relationship between them and the retreat of Alexander after the battle points to a stalemate rather than a clear victory.

Interpretation #5: The Arthashastra was not the work of a single author. While the first part could have been written during the Mauryan period, there were later interpolations and remouldings. This accounts for a lot of contradictions within the document.

Interpretation #6: While the Periplus of the Erythraean Sea, written by an anonymous Egyptian Greek is the earliest surviving documentation on Indian Ocean trade routes, Indians must have been proficient in cartography given evidence of their international sea trade from the time of the Indus civilisation.

Interpretation #7: At this period, Vedic orthodoxy had not yet turned into a religion. Polytheist gods such as Indra, Varuna, Agni and Surya were yet to give way to one supreme god, the Vishnu, of whom all other gods were just emanations. This was the period when philosophies such as asceticism, materialism and scepticism were in full flow. So, I have looked at the clash between Vedic orthodoxy and the heterodox sects as a clash of philosophies and not a clash of religions.

I am sure these interpretations will not go uncontested. I have dared to provide these interpretations using the time-tested defence that this is a work of fiction. I hope that those who are better informed will help me to formulate these interpretations even more rigorously in the best Indian traditions of exchanging vada and prativada—thesis and counter-thesis.

PROLOGUE

Sayana – Pataliputra – 330 BCE

The priest Sayana looked out from the windswept balcony outside the rooms on the first floor of his fired brick and wooden house. A wooden palisade ran around the perimeter of the house to keep away dogs and cats from the dusty road outside and to keep in the couple of cows and buffaloes which his household reared. Far away he could see the faint outlines of the gates of Pataliputra, the capital of the Magadhan empire—Indra gate facing the south and the Brahma gate facing the north. His gurukul was in the forest range away from the city, where he spent a few months every year teaching students.

He liked the hustle and bustle of the city which was fast growing into the largest city among the host of cities that had mushroomed in the Gangetic Plain. But he was extremely distressed at the growing anarchy and violence in the empire thanks to Dhanananda's inept rule. *Inept is a mild word*. The king had acquired a formidable army and stinking wealth which were the talk of the town. He had an army of 20,000 cavalry, 200,000 infantry, 2000 chariots and anywhere from 3000 to 6000 elephants. This huge army was fed by back-breaking taxes forcibly enforced by the huge administrative apparatus.

Dhanananda's greed, his expansionist policy and brutal exploitation had taken his unpopularity ranking to a new high among the people. The king claimed to be from a lower caste and hence a common man. He balanced the hold of the brahmana priests over the Magadhan state by getting closer to their competitors, the shramanas. But this didn't seem to help him in the rankings. Sayana hoped that this unpopularity will soon get transformed into rebellion. He smiled with satisfaction at the thought that this is what he will be discussing with his companions soon today.

He leaned over the balustrade to check what is happening in the courtyard. His wife and daughter were tending to the cows. A maid was dusting the verandah and the wooden pillars that held up the ceiling of the house.

He resumed his thoughts with a chuckle. *What was it that made a priest like me get involved in politics?* The duty of a priest was to show the way to people to attain *moksha*, the ultimate freedom from all misery and the highest state of spiritual attainment. But Sayana did not accept this narrow definition of his profession. He had mastered the Vedic texts, the Upanishads and read through the epics. The gradual transition of the state from a tribal society to the republics and now to kingdoms and empires interested him immensely. That is where he thought his knowledge should be put to good use.

What was it that Bhishma said when he was lying on his deathbed of arrows piercing into his skin? He explained that the world has moved ahead from the stage where people were both the ruled and the ruler. Production of goods, trade and surplus obtained from them have become so enormous that those who possessed wealth required a king, an administration and a standing army to remain wealthy. This is exactly what happened, reminisced Sayana. Tribal societies were replaced by republics of a ruling clan. Now these republics themselves are being replaced by kingdoms and empires where it is not the clans which mattered but the class of exploiters. Anyway, Sayana consoled himself, the republics were really republics only for the ruling clans. There was no point in fretting about their downfall.

Sayana could have easily found a plum position in the elite Brahmana advisory council of the king. But he opted out of it. He could not tolerate the way the Council was stoking up Dhanananda's dream of becoming a 'chakravartin', the ruler of the world. Literally, this meant a ruler whose chariot wheels can keep rolling anywhere.

To become a chakravartin, a king had to command a huge army and unlimited resources. The Council had been dinning into the head of Dhanananda that among all the kings of Bharatavarsha, he was the one who was most qualified.

For this Dhanananda must perform the *ashwamedha yagna*, the horse sacrifice. After a lot of rituals, a horse accompanied by the king's warriors would be allowed to wander for a period of one year. All the territory it covered during this period would then become the property of the king unless challenged. If at the end of one year, no one had dared to capture the horse, then the poor animal would be ritually sacrificed and the king announced as the chakravartin. The *yagna* involved a lot of propaganda work and political manipulation. Generally, the horse would be guided to travel only to those kingdoms which have already accepted the suzerainty of the would-be chakravartin. Rituals and gifts would fatten the purses of priests.

Sayana let out a sigh. Things are going to become more and more difficult in this land. He hated the caste system and abhorred the rituals. He had many enemies in the Council. The king did not have any love or respect for him either.

He had woken up early and taken his morning bath. His wife called him from below reminding him of his breakfast. 'You said some visitors are coming today. Will they be having their lunch here?' she asked in a tone that conveyed that he should have kept her informed earlier.

'Yes!' he shouted back. 'They will be here till evening. Make a nice lunch for them.'

As he moved towards the steps, a beautiful rendering of Raag Lalit on the rudra veena came gliding towards him in the crisp morning air. A maestro was playing the instrument in the temple across the street during the usual morning rituals. As the artist played on the lower octaves of the raga, the refreshing shower of the melodious notes made Sayana shiver in excitement. He closed his eyes to awaken his inner eye. The artist built up the tempo gradually, a lingering step here and a hurried step there. He led the listener to a kind of nada yoga, the union of music and the spiritual mind. Like a consummate magician, the performer took his audience into confidence that he is leading them to a great secret path. He teased them with abandon. As he traversed the notes from the *shuddha* to the *teevra*, the endorsement of the listener was complete. Sayana waited till the composition was rendered completely and then let out a sigh of satisfaction.

He came down the steps slowly. In his youth he would have come down skipping two at a time. But he was nearing sixty now. He was thin, almost to the point of being frail, but he was steady on his feet. A few wrinkles were showing on his face. The back of his hands showed a web of veins. But he was healthy, both physically and mentally. He had many things to accomplish in life yet. *But then, life was always short of one's expectations.*

His son was busy with some reading. He had taken after his father in his profession. He was a pleasant youth of about twenty-five but a bit too solemn and grim to attract pretty girls. What cheered him most was when his aunt visited and had long discussions with him on philosophy. He looked up at him and wished him as Sayana sat down for breakfast. Sayana had noticed that he had begun to guess what his father was up to these days. He has to let him know soon.

❈ ❈ ❈

In Magadha, unlike Kaushambi and cities towards the west, Sayana had felt that brahmanical rituals were less imposing, and there was some free mixing in society. But that was only among the higher strata. Even the naastik sects which dismissed the Vedic rituals did not interfere too much with upsetting the fragile balance maintained by the ruling establishment. Debtors, slaves and soldiers were not yet welcome into the fold of the Buddhist and Jain sanghas though they claimed to be egalitarian. Women were being grudgingly allowed in and Sayana was happy about that. With gradual increase in trade and surplus, women had become commodities and had lost their earlier position at pre-historic times. But, the real history has now started.

After finishing his breakfast Sayana went back to his room on the terrace after giving instructions that the guests should be brought up when they arrive.

Sayana's office was a large rectangular room with walls made of fired brick with a coat of lime. Two windows looked out into the balcony. In the centre of the room was a round table carved from teak wood. A hand drawn map of Bharatavarsha or Jambudwipa or India, whatever it is known as, lay sprawled on the table. The map showed the mahajanapadas, the large kingdoms and the Magadhan empire. Rivers and trade routes criss-crossed the map. Even the south and Thamizhagam were represented on the map.

Peace in Bharatavarsha was in danger right from the time it started germinating in the womb of urbanisation. Huge forces were at work now, trying to gobble each other. Philosophical schools, the darshanas, were now transitioning into religions with their rigid rituals and restrictions. *We have to make the best use of the debates and discussions that are going on now before the right to conscience and the right to dissent vanish altogether.*

His attention was drawn to the creaking of the wooden fence door and the commotion downstairs. His guests had arrived.

Two Buddhist monks entered first and greeted Sayana. They were quite a contrasting pair—one was younger, tall, well-muscled and looked fresh while the second bhikshu was older and appeared a bit tired from the journey. The third visitor had the distinct aura of a medical professor. He looked glum and restless. The Jain monk was also tall and moved around before lithely settling down on the charpoy. The one with a turban and angavastram looked every bit a trader and seemed quite at home in meetings and conferences. The last visitor stood out from all of them. He had the accent of the north-western tribes and a long battle scar angled across his face from his right forehead to his cheek, getting lost in his bushy beard. He undid his scabbard and placed his sheathed sword on the side table.

Sayana greeted the visitors and quickly came to the subject. 'We don't have all day and I know you must be tired from the journey.' He paused and went towards the matki at one corner of the room and filled up the copper jug with cool water. He then filled the kulhar, terracotta cups, with it to pass around. 'We have been communicating with each other regularly. I will not be going into details now. So, let me get quickly to the crux of the matter.'

The guests were listening with attention. The room felt a bit warm. Sayana pulled out his peacock feather fan and fanned himself until he had gathered his thoughts.

'We have to build our shakhas everywhere. We have done that in a few northern cities, but that is not enough. We must visit all the major cities, including those in the south. We have to get familiar with the trade routes and establish connections at all transit points so that we can move quickly from one region to another,' he said with a tone of urgency.

The Jain monk interjected first. 'I understand we have very *little* time. I have already made plans to travel far and make acquaintances in some of the ports. We need the support of sailors and fishermen as well.'

The younger Buddhist monk added, 'The cities in the Gangetic doab have many artisans' guilds. Colonies of blacksmiths, coppersmiths, weavers, stone cutters, and many other professions have sprung up and they are organised into guilds. We need to spread our message there. Some progress has already been made.' He reported.

A smile played on the lips of the senior monk. 'Our work is expanding and soon we can expect the kings' spies to follow us. We have to keep our propaganda open but our organisation secret. We should be more careful about where and when we meet next.' He cautioned others but there was no hint of fear in his voice.

Sayana looked at the tribal warrior for his views who grinned and said, 'The north-west is going to be the hot spot. We need to keep moving towards it. I have a feeling that is where major events are going to happen which will have an impact everywhere.'

The trader nodded. 'I feel that whenever my caravan makes trips from Pataliputra to the east and north-west. Anyway, there are changes happening everywhere and we need to unite all the streams into one mighty river,' he said adjusting his angavastram and looking around in anticipation.

'We've got our work cut out,' observed Sayana. 'Let us spend some time in firming up our plans. That is why I have the map laid out on the table.'

It was later afternoon when the detailed planning came to an end.

Sayana concluded with, 'Let us reiterate *again* that we should not be judgemental and ignore any section of the people other than those who are wielding power to gratify their greed. We may outwardly belong to many religions or geographies, but we have the same goal. We are the Yugantar.'

The elderly Buddhist monk knew that Sayana meant it. When recruiting students in his gurukul, Sayana often used to tell this story from the Chandogya Upanishad to them.

The story went like this:

Once Satyakama wanted to join a gurukul.

He asked his mother, 'Ma, I want to be a student. What should I tell about my family?'

'I don't know your family, my dear,' she said. 'I had you in my youth when I travelled about a lot as a servant, and I just don't know! My name is Jabala and yours is Satyakama. So, say you are Satyakama Jabala.'

Satyakama went to Gautama Haridrumata who was running a well-known gurukul and said to him, 'I want to be your student, sir. May I join?'

'Can you tell me about your family, my friend?' Gautama asked.

'I don't know my family, sir,' he answered. 'I asked my mother. She said that she had me in her youth, when she used to travel about a lot as a servant. She said that as she was Jabala and I was Satyakama, I should give my name as Satyakama Jabala.'

'No one but a true Brahman would be so honest!' he said. 'Go and fetch twigs for my stove, my friend. I will initiate you for you have not swerved from the truth.'

The monk knew that Sayana used the story both to demonstrate the respect for women and the need to look beyond social status. He also knew that Sayana hated orthodoxy and rituals and abhorred gifts.

Sayana made the most important point at the end of the meeting. 'We all know that the Bhagavad Gita says,

परित्राणाय साधूनां विनाशाय च दुष्कृताम् ।
धर्मसंस्थापनार्थाय सम्भवामि युगे युगे ।।'

Sayana paused here. He was referring to Lord Krishna's revelation to Arjuna at the time of the Mahabharata war. It meant: *To protect the good, to annihilate the evil, and to reestablish the principles of dharma, I appear on this earth, age after age.*

'I don't want to sound pretentious. We and the people are the "I" mentioned in the Gita. We are the ones who have taken up the mission of reestablishing the principles of dharma. We are not against this or that individual but against evil which has taken hold of the system. We are not going to do it alone. The people of Bharatavarsha will be with us.'

The other members nodded in approval and left one by one.

Sayana slept peacefully that night.

Book One:
The Gathering Storm

1

REBELS RAID THE ARMOURY

Satya – Ujjayini – 330 BCE

A light shower pattered the cobbled street forming dark rivulets. Stars in the night sky had vanished, plunging the town streets in a pall of gloom. The mud walls and the wooden railings of the houses lined on either side of the street had a ghostly appearance. The four men moved slowly and stealthily towards the central square of the city which had the armoury in one of the side lanes. Their voices were muffled by the cloth mask they wore, their eyes glittering through a slit.

'Don't you think we are taking a big risk? Just the four of us to raid an armoury guarded by at least a dozen guards!' asked Bala through the wet mask which clung to his mouth, opening and closing like a mummy speaking through its wrapping.

'Nothing to worry. This is just a short foray to see how well the armoury is fortified. When the actual uprising starts, we won't need to waste time trying to find out whether the armoury is the real place where the arms are kept. No surprises at that time,' explained Satya, their leader, as he shrugged off the droplets of water gathering on his sleeves. The wet cotton shirt clung to his muscular upper arms giving them a chiselled contour. He carefully stepped around puddles of mud while maintaining a good pace with his long legs. His movement was graceful and quick. At this moment he looked solemn and guarded.

Bala wanted to keep asking questions. Not that he didn't know the answers. This kind of banter took his attention away from the cold wetness seeping through the clothes and the tingling fear coursing through his veins. This was not the season for rains. It was the month of Magha with the harvest festival, Makar Sankranti, just around the corner. But a festival was the last thing they had in mind tonight. Maitreya and Sajjalaka, the other two members of the rebel band kept to themselves. They were in no mood for talking on this sombre night and anyway it was difficult to compete with Bala in chitter-chatter. Satya seemed to be deep in thought, his hand firmly gripping the hilt of his longsword as he moved in front.

'How long is it going to take for the people of Avanti to rise up against this tyrant king and overthrow him?' asked Bala. This shook Satya out of his reverie.

'Looks like it will take some time,' he replied in a gruff tone. 'It is hard to believe that people of Avanti can tolerate a despot like King Palakavarma. He has been merciless in looting peasants, traders and artisans of the kingdom—those who are really producing the wealth which feeds these greedy pigs!' He continued in a slightly raised voice. 'That king who cannot protect his subjects and ensure that they have enough to eat and live, doesn't deserve to be a king! Even the Puranas say that. But the people have been brainwashed by the brahmanas that the king is the divine representative of the gods. Until the people are convinced that a rebellion is necessary and possible, we have to be patient.' Hoping that he made an impression on his comrades, he continued to walk at a brisk pace.

Can it get worse than this? Avanti had been a part of the second urbanisation that swept the entire Gangetic Plain. The earlier republics, the gana-sanghas, had given way to kingdoms and chieftains were replaced by kings. Power became concentrated in the ruling family and had to be legitimised. Emphasising the caste status of the king and regularising brahmanical rituals became the order of the day. Kingship became hereditary but it could be guaranteed only by the might of one's army. The rivalry for power between the brahmanas and kshatriyas continued fiercely, but they had to contend increasingly with the wealthy traders. Traders, farmers and moneylenders were grouped into the vaisya caste, the third in the caste hierarchy. So, the rulers, threatened by the growing influence of the wealthy traders, insisted on the varna hierarchy even more strongly.

The kingdom of Avanti co-existed with the kingdoms of Kashi, Kosala and Magadha whose fortunes ebbed and flowed depending on who had more control over the Ganges Plain and its river ports. From the time of the Mahabharata, the power centre had shifted south east, from Hastinapura to Mathura, Kaushambi and Pataliputra.

The Nandas had already overthrown the Shisunagas in Magadha and emerged the most powerful of the second urbanisation process. Avanti groaned under the jackboots of the Magadhan empire. So the people of Avanti had to cough up enough taxes to satisfy two despots.

When they neared the city square, the rebels quietened down. At this time of the night, already past the eleventh muhurta, there was no soul in the streets. The eeriness of the night had settled like a thick blanket of snow on the chauraha, the city square. Except for the pitter-patter and the rustling of leaves as the droplets slid down their shiny blades, there was silence.

It is high time we put an end to wars and mindless looting, but will the people of Bharatavarsha unite?

The city square was bathed in the dull glow of the oil lamps suspended on a long iron pole in all the four corners as well as in the central platform. Tiny droplets danced in a swirl of colours as they cut across the stream of light from the lamps making the whole square look like a psychedelic stage.

Satya gathered all his gang members together for a pre-armoury raid briefing.

'Let's not be adventurous. We are here just to get a good peek into the armoury so that it can help us in the future,' he whispered solemnly.

Bala was not thrilled with this restriction. 'You call this a raid but what good is it if we leave the armoury intact? Let's at least grab a few longswords and some katars. If we are lucky, we may even get a scabbard lined with gemstones.'

'Don't be foolish. You were the one who was just whining about the risk. In the armoury they keep arms for foot soldiers and cavalry. For a gemstone studded scabbard you will have to raid the Mahamatra's house!' retorted Satya in a tone chastising a kid.

Maitreya opened his mouth for the first time. 'Are we going to keep arguing all night? Why don't we listen to our leader? We can make better arms in our forge than what we would find here. Are we not the city's best blacksmiths?' he admonished.

Satya looked at his friends with affection. They were inseparable, like day from night, with an acute sense of each other's moods and emotions. A united Bharatavarsha was their common dream, fuelling all their activities. They all belonged to the Agaria tribe who had for centuries harnessed fire, aag, to make fine products out of smelted iron.

Satya had heard a lot about the history of his tribe from his father. He remembered sitting on his father's lap and demanding a story every night before going to sleep. One of the stories he remembered was that their tribe were the descendants of the 12 brothers of the mythical Lohasur, the iron demon. The gods of the shudras and tribals were not allowed to be a part of the pantheon of gods of the higher castes. A few centuries earlier, at the time of the Mahabharata, the Pandavas had routed the Agaria king, Longundi Raja, and forced him to take refuge in the jungles.

But forest life did not deter the Agarias from making iron products. The second urbanisation brought them back into the fold of civilisation. As demand for productive forces shot up, the state allowed shudras to settle down in colonies within the town and even initially exempted them from tax. Iron making was still a family enterprise and the nuances of the profession were handed down from generation to generation by word of mouth.

✳ ✳ ✳

As the rebels entered one of the roads branching away from the square which housed the armoury, Satya signalled his buddies to keep their mouth shut. Soon they could see the iron palisade, about 6 feet in height, going all around the armoury with pools of water under the railings. The rebels effortlessly hauled themselves over the palisade. Security guards were nowhere in sight. Perhaps they never expected intruders at this time of the night and had decided to drown themselves in the local mahua brew.

The armoury had several rooms, bolted on the outside with massive locks but with windows giving a peek into what was stored inside. Arms were kept segregated into mukta, weapons which were thrown such as arrowheads, bows, tridents, javelins, lances, chakras and iron-tipped spears. In the section containing the amukta weapons, those held in a warrior's grip such as longswords, scabbards with daggers, clubs, broadswords, pikes and maces were neatly stacked in sections.

It was too tempting to grab a few polished swords and scabbards. But when Satya tried to break one of the huge locks with a hammer, all hell broke loose. The guards groggily jumped to their feet and gathered their swords. It was now time for an orderly retreat, thought Satya.

'Our job is done, let's move!' he ordered brusquely making it clear that he expected quick action from his friends.

Bala was a bit disappointed. 'I will keep these pathetic jokers engaged!' he shouted. 'Let's leave with some trophies. Who would believe we raided the armoury if we went back empty handed?'

Satya grimaced. He was in no mood to prolong this adventure. Not that he could not keep the guards engaged, particularly when a couple of them were making a futile attempt to stand up. Another guard was gathering his waist cloth which had unfolded from the knot when he slid on the wet floor. The decision proved to be life-saving.

Just when they climbed over the palisade and landed on the road, they heard the clatter of horses' hooves, muffled by the mud, coming from the direction of the main square. This is trouble. Satya looked up with consternation.

2

A Patient Visits On A Festival Day

Madhavi – Madurai – 330 BCE

The city of Madurai was wearing a festive look. Colourful flags floated in waves from atop houses and shops. Rivers of people constantly flowed through the broad streets of the city, making small eddies around markets, parks and wandering minstrels. A royal procession passed through the streets led by elephants and heralded by the sound of conches and drumbeats. Chariots followed, drawn by black stallions of the finest breed.

Stall keepers at the markets were revelling in offering their wares. There were shops selling sweet cakes, others selling garlands of flowers, palm sugar, scented powder and betel quids called beeda. Men and women sellers were going from house to house selling bangles, trinkets, earrings and flowers. City guards on mounted horses trotted through the streets looking for trouble spots and drunken brawls to fill in their daily reports. Well-to-do traders and noblemen flaunted their white silk dhotis, brightly coloured shirts and white angavastrams whose edges were embroidered with gold. From balconies and turrets, women, men and children watched the festivities and whistled and cheered in approval.

One part of the market was abuzz with craftsmen working in their shops making bangles of conch shell, goldsmiths and silversmiths working on exquisite jewellery, cloth merchants rolling out silk sarees with the finest weave, coppersmiths, flower vendors, sandalwood factories and weavers working on their spindles. It seemed that their work increased during festival days for at other times their products lost their fascination.

An odd painter made portraits of fair maidens and couples giving a finer touch to what nature had in mind. A food court served mouth-watering dishes ranging from steamed rice cakes, mango pickles, sugar candy, fried balls of lentil dough, mutton kuzhambu, and watery buttermilk flavoured with ginger and coriander leaves. Outside the food court, beggars and dogs competed for the odd morsels thrown in their direction or into dustbins. A fairly large crowd of merry-makers gathered around toddy shops to gladden their hearts and spirit with pathaneer and toddy.

Bards and musicians were sought after by festival revellers as bumblebees seeking fresh flowers. A band of musicians roved around the market square armed with sound instruments which were hard to ignore. Kadamban beat a large bass-like drum, *kadamparai*, accompanied by another musician who blew lilting music through his long bamboo wind instrument, *kuzhal*. PaaNan, who was the centre-piece of the music band, sang songs in all *pann* tunes that reflected the mood of each landscape of Thamizhagam, the Tamil country. Their mastery with the *yaazh*, a stringed instrument with a wide frequency range, drew a standing ovation.

The doors of houses all along the streets were adorned with mango leaves. A pair of banana tree trunks decorated their gates on either side. People lined up in their verandahs to get a glimpse of the festivities. Every house sported an intricately drawn *kolam* in front of it.

Not all the town's residents participated in the festivities, though. The outer colonies housed many small artisans and peasants who just did not have the time nor the means to decorate their houses and roister in the revelry. Even further away from the centre of the city were the colonies of new immigrants who left their forest life to settle down in the city to pursue some occupation. Beggars, thieves, drunkards, prostitutes and mercenaries made up the other part of these colonies. Men roamed about the streets unwashed and unshaven, naked children frolicked around garbage dumps, and women and girls made a long beeline to the nearest water source.

Well beyond the outskirts of the city, a small hillock housed a colony of Siddhars. They were saints, doctors, alchemists and mystics though not all Siddhars can boast of even more than one skill. Their knowledge was handed over orally from one generation to the next until the development of the Brahmi script enabled them to capture all the knowledge onto palm leaf manuscripts. These manuscripts being fragile and susceptible to destruction by the elements, the Siddhars preserved them with the same obsession with which the Lord of Wealth, Kubera, preserved his treasury. Some of their researched works were penned into poems that would survive many millennia for their wit and philosophy.

Siddhars also practiced the martial art called Varmam which doubled as an art of self-defence and medical treatment at the same time. A trained Siddhar in Varmam can press specific spots on the human body with stupendous results. The same spot when pressed in different ways can disable an attacker in self-defence or balance a physical condition as a quick fix medical treatment.

As it happens in most cases, such talented sects get relegated to the outskirts of the city due to the peculiarities of their occupation and their unpredictable moods. Some of the Siddhars were downright dishonest. A few doctors duped their clients with promise of elixirs and aphrodisiacs in exchange of a hefty fee. Some of their alchemists convinced clients to invest in their laboratories which supposedly had cracked the secret of converting copper and iron into pure gold.

On a fairly steep hillock, in a small dwelling in the Siddhar colony, Madhavi was peering fondly at her impressive display of medicines and herbs. Dozens of pots covered with cloth were stacked neatly in one of the large shelves. Hundreds of stoppered vials lay in one corner of a roughly hewn worktable made of teak. Numerous jars of herbs labelled neatly by her peacock feather quill were lined up on another shelf.

Raw material for the medicines were piled up on one corner of the floor of the medicine room. The Siddhars used raw materials which were derived from plants—*Mooligai*; metals and minerals—*Thathu*; from animals—*Seevam*. There were further sub-divisions in these categories. Plant raw materials, for example, can come from roots, bark, leaves, fruits and flowers. Their knowledge of metals and minerals enabled them to convert these into their ionic forms which could then be digested by the human body. The raw materials were ground with herbal juices and processed under controlled temperatures for longer shelf life. In fact, it was believed that the potency of their drugs improved with time. Wonders could be expected even with microscopic doses.

Neatly segregated and heaped on a tightly woven bamboo mat spread on the floor were various herbs, plants and seeds such as vendhayam, vembu, vilvam and athimathuram.

✻ ✻ ✻

A knock interrupted Madhavi at her housekeeping efforts. She was not expecting any guests today of all days. But festival time is no guarantee for patients to forget their illnesses or to acquire new ones. She came reluctantly out of the medicine room and peeped out of the door.

'Came to wish you a good festival,' greeted Nandi in a cheerful tone, standing tentatively at the foot of the steps, expecting to be invited in. He looked very much like the enterprising trader that he was. His silk dhoti was sparkling white and tied around his waist with a silk band studded with emeralds. A sleeveless shirt with blue and orange stripes hugged his waist and chest. A golden arm band with intricately carved figures of snakes with ruby studded eyes coiled up and down in a tight grip around one of his biceps. His wristband was a chain of gold with a clasp studded with emeralds. A thin gold chain hung around his neck, half covered by his silk angavastram wrapped across his shoulder.

Well, here is my first patient for the day! 'Nandri,' replied Madhavi. 'You know that I don't have much of an appetite for festivals,' she smiled and made way for him to enter.

Nandi cast an appreciative glance at her. Madhavi was tall and exuded poise and confidence. The flower printed cotton sari and simple jewellery around her neck and wrists gave her a charming look. The red tilakam on her forehead made her face look rounder. A wisp of kohl under her eyelashes made her eyes more expressive and quizzical than they would normally be.

Nandi was one of Madhavi's regular patients, though she knew that his illnesses were mostly feigned and served as a ruse for visiting her. He hardly hid his interest in her but she brushed it away lightly. She was not yet ready for a relationship. No, not with her ageing father to take care of. Moreover, she had serious doubts about Nandi's idea of a relationship, given his wealth which drew maidens like flies. Nevertheless, she enjoyed his company for his easy-going conversation and knowledge of world affairs.

'What makes you come to this desolate part of the city when you could be having a feast at your friends' place?' she taunted him.

'How can a place where you live be desolate?' he replied with pretended shock. 'I am fed up with feasts. I think I have a slight indigestion. Could not sleep well yesterday,' he said, trying to manufacture some justification for his visit.

'Let's check what bothers you,' said Madhavi to make him feel at ease. She took him to the examination room and made him sit on a low bench while she herself stood next to him and took his right wrist to check his pulse. Generally, patients and visitors were not allowed into the medicine room for fear that the ingredients spread over the room, including the gory animal parts, will make them uneasy. Slit snails and amputated frogs are not a cheerful sight for grumbling patients.

'How is it you Siddhars can feel a person's pulse and find out their *aadi-andam*, their beginning and end?' he asked playfully adjusting his angavastram.

In one corner of the room was a long table, stretching all along the wall, on top of which hundreds of palm leaf manuscripts were stacked one above the other. He knew that all Siddhar households had such stacks of manuscripts handed down from generation to generation, which the doctors consulted often. He noticed that they were an endangered lot, with frayed edges which often disintegrated into powder. The room had the musty smell of a library housing manuscripts.

'Feeling a pulse tells me a lot,' Madhavi explained. 'My three fingers—the index, middle and ring finger—can feel the three humors in your body: vatham, *pitham* and kabam. In fact, a good practitioner can sense up to 32 different pulse qualities,' she continued while applying different pressures on his pulse.

'Adeyappa!' exclaimed Nandi. 'Maybe you will find 32 different complications with my health,' he joked. 'But that would mean that I would need to come more often for my medicines,' he added hopefully.

Madhavi ignored the joke and continued to give her patient a small lecture on her profession. 'In our medicine, we consider an individual as a microcosm of the universe. Every individual has a miniature universe within oneself,' she explained releasing Nandi's wrist. 'The whole universe, including man, is made of five primordial elements.'

'But how come my brother-in-law is such a fool compared to me,' joked Nandi, 'if we are all made of the same elements?' He laughed loudly to make sure that the joke was not lost on her.

Madhavi just smiled politely. 'Yes, all beings are made of panchabhootas, the five elements: earth, water, fire, air and space. But not in equal proportions.'

'I think I have more fire in my constitution,' observed Nandi.

'Looks like it,' agreed the doctor in a matter of fact tone. 'You have a slightly higher level of pitham because of your fiery constitution. That is one reason for your frequent stomach upsets,' she suggested.

Nandi didn't seem to be very happy. 'Which means that I have to live with indigestion all my life,' he complained.

I need a break. 'Let's talk about better things,' said Madhavi, changing the subject from the intricacies of her profession. She put away the low stool and inserted the palm leaf manuscript back into the right slot.

'Then why don't we walk to the city market?' suggested the trader. 'My indigestion will probably get better,' he said, already past the door and walking down the steps, leaving no choice for Madhavi.

They had no inkling that this visit will change their lives.

3

A Daring Escape

Satya – Ujjayini

The commotion that the security guards at the armoury made must have alerted the guards. *But this cannot be the city guards.* Satya knew the timing of the night rounds of the city guards very well. They were concentrated more around the city gates and gambling dens and ale houses in the poorer parts of the city. *This must be the Mahamatra's guards. But what is the Mahamatra doing at this time of the night outside his quarters?*

The swords of the rebels came out singing from their scabbards but there was no intention on their part to challenge the guards firmly ensconced on their saddles. That would have been suicide. Through the haze, the rebels could see the soldiers advancing towards them. Their thickly coiled turbans, the shirastrana, were secured with scarfs tied below their chins. Their coats extended as far as their heels. Above the waist, they wore an armour of bison leather, kept in place by a double band of cloth tied across their chest and waist. Their golden breastplates scattered the flickering light of the streetlamps into a thousand rays.

The gentle patter of the rains had turned into a loud drumming. It was stinging their eyes and they knew the horse-borne riders will be having a tougher time finding their way through the street. The royal guards had swords in their hands. One of them pulled out a long spear tipped with iron.

'Catch these thieves alive!' shouted the captain of the guards. 'I want to know who they are. After that we will skin them alive or throw them under the elephants!'

There is no time to waste.

'You three, disappear into the lanes in different directions!' barked Satya. 'I will draw them away into the galis.' His friends did not argue. They scattered in different directions and disappeared into the dark fathoms of the narrow city bylanes.

The leader of the guards had to think quickly. It was futile to chase the scums who were running in different directions.

'Don't go after those pigs. Let's get the leader of the gang and break him,' he commanded wiping away the pool of water collected where his crotch met the saddle. The mares whickered and charged towards Satya. The riders cursed the rain and the fleeing rebels.

Satya knew the city like the back of his hand. He kept ahead of the guards and taunted them through winding alleys. For the captain, this would be an important catch. For long there were rumours floating in the royal corridors that a rebellion was brewing in the kingdom. If only he can get this rebel. 'Faster, let's break his legs!' bellowed the captain as he spurred his guards on.

But the winding alleys of Ujjayini were not the right terrain for chasing rebels who seemed to sprint like a deer. Urbanisation was an integral part of the rise of large states and the expansion of Ujjayini had kept pace with the growth of Avanti and the growing trade in the region. As towns sprung up across the Gangetic Plains, their growth was determined by several factors which gave them their special features. Towns such as Rajgriha in Magadha, Shravasti in Kosala and Kaushambi in Vatsa gained importance as administrative and political centres. Religion propelled the growth of other towns such as Vaishali. Others grew out of markets. In case of Ujjayini, it was on a trade route between towns in the east and west. It was at the crossroads of the Uttarapatha to the north and the Dakshinapatha to the south. Its vantage location allowed it to control river traffic. With the growth of towns, urban planning became an important aspect of state administration. But the alleys of Ujjayini violated all norms of urban planning.

The chase was getting more and more frustrating for the guards. Satya was leading them into alleys which were getting increasingly narrower. The huge commotion created by the horses' hooves and the cursing and swearing must have woken up many people but no one stepped out. The city had strict restrictions for its residents. But they didn't apply to stray dogs, cows and pigs. The howling of dogs made the horses nervous and stray cows disturbed their rhythm. Finally, one of the guard's horses stepped on a sleeping dog and the ensuing howls thoroughly disoriented the mare and brought her to her knees, creating an avalanche of buckling horses and cursing men.

A couple of guards started chasing Satya on foot, their heavy breastplates slowing them down.

'Let's go back,' one of them panted.

The other younger guard didn't want to give up. 'This fool will slow down soon!' he shouted, urging his companion to run faster.

Satya deliberately led them towards the street in which tannery workers lived. The rain had made the street muddy and slippery with all the effluents of the tannery. Satya gingerly avoided the potholes and soon came to a wide gutter over which a narrow plank was laid for people to cross. He crossed the gutter with some effort.

The security guards didn't want to lose face. They held their hands and stepped on the plank. Satya waited until they had reached the middle of the plank with his stiletto in hand.

The canopy of a tanner's shop was bending low over the gutter weighed down by the water which had collected on its surface. It was supported by ropes stretching on either side and anchored by heavy stones. Satya cut one of the ropes with his stiletto and the entire canopy came crashing down on the guards who were tiptoeing over the plank making them lose their balance. Both fell with a big thud into the ditch. Satya moved away quickly but could hear their loud curses and rants for some time.

❋ ❋ ❋

He stayed in the shadows and watched the guards. They emerged out of the gutter stinking like corpses. Once he was sure that they had retreated like a bear stung by bees, he began to follow them. He had to find out why the Mahamatra's guards were out at this time of the night and whom were they escorting.

He followed them from a distance like a stealthy cat until they stopped in front of a large double-storeyed wooden building supported by iron pillars. A mantle of fragrance gently rested over the sprawling garden in front of the house. Intoxicating smells from chameli, rajnigandha and parijat wafted over the compound wall and the tall iron gates. The pillars on either side of the tall iron gates sported terracotta figurines of exquisitely shaped dancing women. A few horse-drawn carriages were parked outside the gates on the wide road, the drivers exchanging bawdy jokes while they waited patiently for their masters to return.

Satya knew the house. It was provocatively named Manorag, mind's passion. It belonged to the most famous courtesan in town, Vasantasena, known to be close to the highest corridors of power. Minsters, nobles and high-level officers frequented her house but not in such large numbers at the same time as was happening today. *These rogues have gathered here for some high-level confabulations.*

His heart bled for Madanika, his beloved, who worked in the den of vice owned by the courtesan. Vasantasena must be ordering around her maids and servants to serve food and wine to her guests. Madanika would be really cursing her fate to be ordered around by a courtesan, who clung to power mongers like a leech, and her lecherous and scheming guests. For all practical purposes she was a slave though not of the type prevailing in contemporary Athenian society.

In Ujjayini, or for that matter in other towns as well, there was no apparent distinction between freeman and slave in the sense that a slave could buy back his or her freedom and return to the caste in which she was born. The dasas were not untouchables, and therefore what was not immutable in Indian society was not freedom or slavery, but caste. Lower castes were less free than the upper castes, and the untouchables bordered on slavery.

She will probably have some interesting news to share when we meet next. Satya started walking back to his colony with many qualms.

4

A Chance Encounter

Madhavi – Madurai

It was late afternoon and the sun shone a little less fierce than in the morning. A slight breeze made Nandi's angavastram flutter a bit. Trees grew densely on the hillock on which Madhavi's colony rested, giving the appearance of a small forest. Down below she could see the river Vaigai flow placidly with small streams branching off into paddy fields. Thatched roofs were clustered along the shore of the river, occupied by families of fishermen and boatmen. A wooden pier jutted into the river at an angle. There were some boats tied to the pier and many floating along the river. Thin tendrils of smoke were rising from some of the houses, indicating that they were from cookeries which fed the other families.

Far away, the golden kalasams atop the temple tower, shaped like inverted pots with a spike on top, glittered here and there. Madhavi went down the hill path brushing her fingers against the rough barks of the mango, tamarind, jackfruit and fig trees. She took enough care not to get too close to the beehives. The Siddhars required a lot of honey for their preparations.

The market, angadi, was close to the centre of the city. The morning bazaar, nalangadi, was being wound up and the evening bazaar, allangadi, was getting ready to display its wares.

Madhavi observed the contrasting scenes in the streets of Madurai. The market footpaths were lined with beggars. Small unclothed children were running behind the carriages of the rich, with the city guard trying to shoo them off. But the markets had a cosmopolitan character which few cities in the world could boast of. Traders from northern kingdoms from as far away as Kalinga and Magadha came to sell their merchandise wholesale. Madurai was not a port but the yavanars—Romans and Egyptians—frequented its streets to look for a good bargain in diamonds, jewellery, pearls, sapphires and coral beads. Carriages of wealthy merchants and nobles waited outside the gates of courtesans. Taverns overflowed with jubilant customers. She recalled a poet's candid observation about the womenfolk in these affluent households:

My garment smells of ghee and frying curry,

and is stained with dirt and lampblack.

My shoulders stink with the sweat of the child

whom I carry upon them and feed at my breast.

I cannot face my lord, who, in gay attire,

rides in his car to the streets of harlots.

The king declares that this a festival of the people but is it?

(Translation of a verse from 'Eight Anthologies' by A.L. Basham)

'Why is there so much poverty amidst plenty?' Madhavi asked Nandi in a dejected tone. 'Foreigners come here from thousands of kadams away to buy the most exotic precious stones and pearls. But what image of Thamizhagam they will take along with them?'

'Madhavi, do you seriously think that these Romans and Greeks have no rich and poor among them?' asked Nandi as he inspected a heap of paddy in one of the shops in the grain merchants' street. Sacks of pepper, millet, gram, peas and sesame seeds were stacked neatly along the front side of the shops. A customer could easily inspect the quality of the goods before purchase. 'There are rich and poor in their societies too. Even worse, they have slaves whose lives belong to their masters. Wherever there is wealth there is bound to be poverty,' he quipped.

An intoxicating aroma made them breathless when they entered the flower street. It had a row of shops where garlands of flowers, sandalwood powder, fragrant pastes, incense sticks, and benzoin resin could be bought at wholesale prices.

'Why should the Pandya, Chola and Chera kingdoms keep fighting with each other? All of us eat the same rice pudding and celebrate the harvest festival. Why should we look at each other as enemies?' she asked as she manoeuvred around a young seller trying to get her interested with his assortment of earrings and bangles. He carried a long pole from which these items hung on nails fixed at different heights.

'It is like three siblings fighting for a share of the family heirloom; we are not under any foreign rule here,' said Nandi trying to lighten the conversation. When he saw that his comments made no impression, he added a bit triumphantly, 'Our kingdom may have its faults but we don't have the obscurantist varna system of the northern kingdoms. Here everyone is a Tamilian and that's it.'

'What good is it to be a Tamilian if one cannot afford even a cup of *kanji*. Look at the women in their tattered saris cleaning those pots,' she pointed towards the backside of an eatery. 'Our artisans who make jewellery, our divers who fathom the ocean for pearls, our peasants who produce the tastiest of millets—why should they live without any idea how their future will pan out?'

* * *

Lost in their conversation they noticed that the sun had set behind the high wall of the city and shopkeepers had hung their lanterns from a hook fixed to the front of the sloping awning of their shop. They had not noticed a pair of shadows following them at a distance.

As they turned into a sparsely lit alley, Nandi changed the subject of their conversation. 'Madhavi, only a few yavanars come to the markets in Madurai. In Poompuhar you can see hundreds of them. Hundreds of ships bring all kinds of exotic stuff to our shores and take back our manufactures to faraway places. I will be visiting the port after two or three months. Will you come with me? It is an awesome port. Even though it belongs to the Cholas, I prefer to go there than to Korkai, which is the Pandyan port.'

Madhavi's face brightened. She had heard a lot about the large port city, one of the world's large thriving ports, and had really been looking for an opportunity and here it came knocking. 'I will certainly come,' she replied instantly, hardly hiding her excitement. 'I have to make arrangements for someone to look after my dispensary, but that can be done. Give me enough notice.' Then, looking around she added, 'It is getting dark; I think we should return now.' She had hardly completed her sentence when a rough hand grabbed one of her arms in a painful grip from behind. She yelled and struggled to turn around to see who had the temerity to hurt a woman in the city known for its respect for women.

In the fading light, she realised that her captor had a companion whose scarred face and shoulders were faintly visible. His scarred features did not make much of an impression on her but the small curved dagger, the kuthuvaal, did. The dagger was close to shaving off a good part of Nandi's right ear and cheek. 'Hand over all your gold and money, otherwise neither you nor your girlfriend will have a face worth carrying on your shoulders,' he threatened in a gruff voice that meant business.

Nandi had a terrified look on his face and the possibility that he may not have a face at all made it even more grotesque. He wailed, 'Take what you want and leave us alone. But remember that the city guards are not far away.'

'Oh, we will make sure that the city guards know nothing about this,' said the scarred guy nonchalantly easing his blade a bit away from Nandi's face.

Fortunes changed dramatically in the next few seconds. The rough edge of one end of a thick bamboo pole landed on the scarred thief's wrist with such force that the dagger flew away like a pigeon released from a cage. At the same instant, Madhavi turned around slightly and with her index and middle fingers of her free hand gave a sharp jab on her captor's abdomen which made him yell and wiggle in pain. Once her other hand was freed, she gave him another jab on the neck which made him buckle down and pass out.

While Nandi looked around in wild wonder, Madhavi thanked the Jain monk who owned the bamboo pole and had appeared from nowhere. 'I thought Jain monks were nonviolent,' she enquired sweetly after she and Nandi regained their composure. The scarred thief quietly slipped away while the conversation was on.

'Yes, we generally abhor violence, but dravya-himsa is justified when you have to act in self-defence or protect others from violence,' replied the monk gauging the two of them with his sharp eyes.

'You certainly intervened at the right time. Where are you from?' asked Madhavi rubbing her left hand which was still smarting from the rough grip of her now unconscious tormentor lying sprawled on the dusty street.

The monk relaxed and smiled warmly. All three of them started walking towards the end of the alley which fortuitously had brought them together.

'I am from Pataliputra. Your city Madurai is well known there. Many Jain monks have come here before me. I have heard the evil claws of the varna system has not yet gouged this society. There is much to learn from your culture, trade, medicine and industry. I have always wondered what makes traders from the north and east and yavanars from thousands of kadams away flock to this place,' said the monk in an earnest tone.

'You have come to the right place and met the right people,' said Madhavi with a laugh. 'Let us meet some time soon. I want to learn about Pataliputra too and about your religion.' *Something tells me that I am going to meet you again.*

Nandi liked the way the evening ended. He could have been lying unconscious in that dingy alley stripped to the bone but here he was, chatting happily with Madhavi and a stranger. What made the evening interesting was this being the first time that he had witnessed Madhavi employ her nerve-numbing skill.

But Madhavi had a fitful sleep that night. The confrontation with the city vermin stirred her sub-conscious memories. She was travelling in a cart resting her head on her mother's lap. Her mother's soft hands were on her shoulders, patting her gently. Her younger brother was sleeping, curled into a ball, behind them. The steady sounds of the bullock's hooves on the dry mud road lulled her to sleep. Her father in the driver's seat was occasionally shouting *'hai, hai'* spurring the bullocks to move faster. A whiff of scent from a jasmine grove on one side of the road floated in making her smile in her sleep. Suddenly, the lantern hanging at the front of the cart shattered, plunging them into darkness. She gripped her mother's wrists and wailed. She remembered her brother, desperately felt around with her arms, but could not find him. The more she cried and wailed, the more her mother's arms started slipping away. A mist rose in front of her and a few black figures with sickles in their hands moved around like ghosts. One of them stood over her and raised his sickle when she let out a loud cry.

Madhavi woke up with a start. It was the same nightmare once again. She wiped her sweating forehead, drank a cup of water from the copper jug and strode out of the house into the cool forest.

5

REBELS MEET IN THE PARK

Satya – Ujjayini – 330BCE

The festival of Vasanta Panchami was in full swing in Ujjayini. It marked the transition from winter to spring. In another 40 days, the people of the city would be celebrating Holika, which would acknowledge the real advent of spring. This day, besides being a milestone in the progress of seasons, had other reasons to be celebrated. It is the birthday of Saraswati, the goddess of knowledge, language, music and art when the young are initiated into writing. The ripe yellow mustard fields lend their dash of colour to the garments people wear on that day.

The Pushpakaranda park in the city was brimming with revelers and the forlorn alike. Young shoots bristled on tree branches. Bees swarmed around blossoms, eager to collect their honey like a tax collector collecting his toll. Creepers clung and climbed up the trees as if they meant to pluck the flowers and fruits of their host. Watchmen guarded them with the same authority as loving wives would embrace their men.

Around the park, lofty trees stooped a bit burdened with their heavy fruits and blossoms. A carpet of flowers lay at their feet. Hanging from the leafy tree-top bowers, monkeys swayed from branch to branch like the breadfruit bobbing in the breeze.

Ujjayini was a city of flowers and trees. The palace was surrounded by beautiful parks. Wealthy nobles and merchants had huge gardens around their houses. They spent their weekends drinking and dozing lazily in even larger private parks in the suburbs of the city. The farmhouses of the rich boasted of artificial lakes and pools, often with fountains, and with steps leading them down to bathing.

Pushpakaranda park, however, welcomed the rich and poor alike. One side of the park was lined with artificial hillocks, the kridasaila. The park had several small lakes which served as quiet getaways for the city dwellers.

An expanse of water was almost an essential feature of gardens in the city. A machine operating a revolving spray, the variyantra, constantly watered its lawns. There were bathing pools which had few takers at this time of the season. The park also had a subterranean chamber at one end of the bathing tank, cooled by water surrounding it on all sides, where tired bathers would retire in the hot summer months. At one corner were swings which were the delight of both children and adults. The park was watered by channels which wound their way from the main tank to the trees and flower beds.

There was fragrance and colour all around. The Asoka trees stood erect bearing a mass of lovely scarlet and orange blossoms. The trees were believed to start flowering only when kicked by a beautiful woman as vouched by a poet.

Other favourites of park visitors were the tall, pale-flowered sirisa, the fragrant organge flowered kadamba, and the red kimsuka. Equally popular were bushes and creepers, especially the jasmine, with its many varieties, and the white atimukta. A number of champaka trees, with very fragrant yellow flowers, and the hibiscus lent further colour to the park.

The most breathtaking were the range of water lilies and the lotus flowers, which floated on the small lakes, supported by large shiny leaves.

Satya was seated on a low-lying rock in one corner of the park talking animatedly to his friends. He slowly surveyed the co-habitants of the park. *People of Bharatavarsha love fun. Look at them flying kites with abandon when their chulha has not been fired for days.* 'Yesterday a group of peasants had come to give a petition to the king to lower the taxes and write off their debts. But he refused to even give them an audience and commanded his guards to drive them away with lathis,' he said with disgust. 'Our king, his family members, nobles, administrators and tax collectors have emptied our treasury. So why would he lower the taxes?'

'Our king has four wives, and countless concubines and children. So do our worthy nobles. In these days of rising prices, don't they need all the panas they collect as taxes,' sneered Bala. 'We need to sympathise with their needs also.'

The other three laughed. 'Yes, instead of the king ensuring our prosperity we are ensuring the prosperity of his entire family. May his kith and kin keep expanding as we slog more and more,' Maitreya spat out. A monkey made a sudden swing to another branch upsetting a raven which had comfortably perched itself, drawing a loud caw from it in protest.

'The greedy merchants and traders take away whatever is left with us. They buy our products at a bargain and sell us stuff at a huge margin,' complained Sajjalaka.

Three children had climbed one on top of the other onto a swing and were squealing with laughter as it went up higher and higher. After a pause, Satya resumed the conversation. 'The people are fed up and boiling with rage. A small spark may ignite a forest fire. The entire kingdom may erupt in rebellion any time. But we don't have a leader who can show us a way to stop this fleecing of the people.'

Sajjalaka who looked engrossed with the gymnastics of the monkeys turned his attention to the discussion. 'They say the Magadhan empire is the richest empire in the world today. Even Sikandar has his eye on Magadha's gold. Will our lot not be better if our kingdom becomes a province under the empire?' he queried tentatively.

Bala reacted rather heatedly. 'The people of Magadha are even more oppressed than us because their empire maintains a huge army fed on taxes and tolls. So, it will be like jumping from a hot oven into the fire if Avanti is taken over by Magadha,' he said emphatically. 'That cannot be a solution. The people of Avanti have to find their own solution.'

A group of Buddhist bhikshus were washing their clothes and cleaning their eating bowls for their next round of alms. They were splashing water at each other and making loud jokes. *Look at them. They don't seem to have any wants.* But just at that time a security guard pounced on them. 'Don't make a mess here,' he growled. 'Get going.'

Satya went back to the history of the kingdom. 'At one time,' he said, 'Avanti was a gana, a republic. There was a restriction on the king's powers. He could not take any decision without consulting a council.'

'Wasn't the republic better than the current janapada where the king is the monarch, and he can do what he wants?' asked Bala.

Satya took some time to gather his thoughts. 'The republic had a council which advised the king and took all the decisions. But, only members of aristocratic families could be council members. Ordinary people had no powers,' he explained. 'But the republics have been dying one after another because of the rise of janapadas and mahajanapadas, the kingdoms and empires. With trade expanding and the economy growing, they required supreme power in the hands of one individual, the king, who could be passed off as god's representative on earth. The time for republics of the old type is over. We cannot go back in time now.'

A couple of drunkards who were stretched out on the grass near the shrubs blabbered something as if offering their own views in the debate.

❋ ❋ ❋

Bala noticed Satya often giving a wistful glance at the entrance to the park. 'Are you expecting someone?' he asked, unable to control his curiosity.

'Madanika should have been here long back,' he said a bit sheepishly.

The friends made a big hurrah. 'It's time we scoot. Our friend will not have time now for discussing politics,' mocked Bala.

'I haven't called her for a duet,' glowered Satya at his friends. He lowered his voice. 'It has been some time since we went on the raid. We still don't have a clue what was happening at Vasantasena's party.'

At that moment Madanika breezed into the park. She wore a long blue skirt with a matching orange blouse that fit snugly over her well-proportioned bust and shoulders. A white embroidered scarf wound around her neck and reached gracefully to her midriff. Her large eyes accentuated by her long black eye lashes darted left and right in anticipation. When she spotted them, her eyes brightened and a thin smile flitted over her soft red lips. She made long graceful strides towards the section of the park where the friends had been having a serious discussion.

Satya and his friends greeted her and showed her a place to sit on another low-lying rock. 'Sorry for being late,' she apologized. 'I had to wait until my madam left the house on some business. It's been a long time since we met.' Her last comment was particularly directed towards where Satya sat.

Satya acknowledged with a slight tilt of his head. 'A couple of weeks back there was a night-long party at your madam's house, looks like?' he enquired.

Madanika raised her eyebrows and looked at him with surprise. 'Looks like our streets have nocturnal strollers,' she commented. 'Yes, in fact, lots of things happened that night. That's why I wanted to meet you at the earliest,' she added making the men sit up. 'The Mahamatra had organised a secret meeting of some nobles and military officers. Vasantasena's place was chosen because it will not raise suspicions.'

The rebels got interested. 'What really happened there?' asked Sajjalaka.

'Don't be so impatient,' Madanika rebuked mildly. She knew this is something they wouldn't like to miss. She narrated what she heard in some detail. 'The Mahamatra reported that Sikandar had sacked Persepolis and burnt its palace in revenge for the burning of the Acropolis at Athens by the Persians at some earlier time. The library housing a number of documents written on cow skins was also torched. There is some doubt whether it was revenge or an accident, but it is clear the Macedonian army and their mercenaries are not very far away from our gates and they will be ruthless.'

'How does it concern Avanti?' Satya asked though he partly knew the answer.

Madanika shifted a bit on the rock which was not a comfortable place to sit and discuss such global events. 'The Mahamatra and some of his generals think that Sikandar's army is unstoppable and the day is not far when he defeats the border kingdoms one by one and enters Avanti and Magadha.'

Bala could not hold himself back. 'They say that Magadha's army is invincible. So he should be more worried about the Magadhan empire making Avanti a vassal state rather than worry about Sikandar entering Ujjayini,' he interjected.

An orange-violet glow from the setting sun gently settled on the park giving its trees with their shiny leaves and colourful blossoms a hallucinatory shroud. Shouts and squeals from the frolicking children seemed to suddenly soften. The rasping warnings of the park guards that the gates will be soon shut cut through the still evening air. Satya and his friends were bent over in conversation. They could not have noticed a shadowy figure moving stealthily towards a nearby spot to overhear.

Madanika felt a slight chill and tightened her scarf over her shoulders. 'One or two generals asked the same question. The Mahamatra was not too pleased. *"Tomorrow or day after the Magadhans will invade us. Should we wait and watch? If they get Avanti into their grip, then they will appoint a governor who will make sure that we all hang first. Is that what you want?"* He had bellowed. *"The north-western states are sure to make a deal with Sikandar. So why not we reach out to him as an ally? That will leave us out of the war. If the Macedonian and Magadhan armies clash, then both of them will get weaker. Do we want one large empire lording over us or two spent armies who would have had enough of fighting?"* This is his plan,' narrated Madanika and peered at her audience, trying to figure out their expressions in the fading light.

'Things are moving even faster than I imagined,' spat out Satya. 'Our kingdom is in great danger and so is Bharatavarsha. The rulers of all other mahajanapadas are putting their own interests at the centre of their calculations. They are least bothered about the people. If there is a war on the soil of Bharatavarsha it is the ordinary people and soldiers who will be sacrificing their lives. These rogues will sell themselves to the victor,' he declared bitterly.

The friends sat there silently deep in thought. The screech of the monkeys and the chirping of birds had died down. The group of children playing on the swing started leaving one by one. The bhikshus had gathered their wet clothes and begging bowls and were now starting back towards their vihara.

Bala broke the silence. 'Dhanananda will not send the Magadhan army in aid of the kingdoms in the northwest. His calculation will also be that if Sikandar enters Bharatavarsha it is better to meet him when his army is weakened in overcoming each one of the frontier armies which are bound to put up a stiff fight. Moreover, his army will have an upper hand in the familiar terrain of the Gangetic Plains than in the frontier provinces,' he surmised.

A breeze swept through the park making the leaves shiver as if they would like to huddle closer and prepare themselves for the dark night. The guards were completing one more round of the park making sure that vagabonds, tipplers and lovers did not make the park their home for the night.

Bala stood up and the others looked like they will follow suit. 'I have not come to the end yet,' announced Madanika a bit dramatically. 'They were getting more and more drunk and the arguments were getting louder but the Mahamatra finally stood up and shut everyone up. He said, "*Listen, you fools! If Magadha decides to overrun us, we will have no chance. If we want to checkmate them, we have to make truce with*

Sikandar. We need to send a representative to meet him before he enters Hindukush. We also need to find out which frontier king thinks the same way we do and make alliances with them. We have very little time. But for all this we need to remove a major obstacle." At this point in time, the captain of the Mahamatra's guard entered and requested permission to talk to him. I could not make out much but I heard him talk about the armoury and some rebels,' she said. 'Were you people up to something on that night?' she asked suspiciously. 'Otherwise, how would you know there was a meeting at Vasantasena's?'

Satya was a bit startled but brushed away her question with a smile. Though, a worried look descended on his face. 'We too have very little time. If we want to do something to prevent the bloodshed of ordinary people, we have to move fast.'

'What did the Mahamatra mean when he said that a major obstacle has to be removed?' asked Madanika as they all got up to leave the park.

'I would not be surprised if he is plotting to remove the king,' commented Bala. The five of them started walking away, followed by the shadowy figure at a distance.

6

CONVERSATION WITH THE JAIN MONK

Madhavi – Paravar colony – 330 BCE

Madhavi sat hunched over a roughly hewn trestle table whose top was overflowing with medicine vials and herbs. She had not slept well the previous night. This time in her nightmare she could hear her father yelling at her to run. She ran and ran through bushes of thorn and narrow stony paths, her sole bleeding and clothes torn. She plunged into a river and that is when she woke up.

'Why are you hiding your pregnancy from your parents?' she asked the young girl after examining her pulse. She did not mean to be harsh, but it must have been so since the girl looked startled.

'I didn't mean to,' she said, 'but they were not on talking terms with each other for months. I didn't want to add to their problems.'

'But that doesn't mean you should have neglected your health,' chided Madhavi, this time with a soft expression. 'Now take this medicine twice a day regularly and no spicy stuff,' she warned.

A bright streak of sunlight lit up the entire Paravar colony on the southern bank of the Vaigai river. She wended her way through the rows of residents who had squatted down waiting for their turn to meet the doctor. A couple of senior doctors had accompanied her to the camp, but there were some juniors too who required supervision. Siddhars were experimental with their medicines and so the juniors had to be kept on leash.

Madhavi had gone about her regular work like a zombie on many days. There was a never-ending stream of patients who predominantly paid their fees through blessings for a long life and wishing her a happy marriage. Older people wished her in traditional style by keeping their right hand on her head and saying 'pathinarum pettru peru vazhvu vazhga' which meant 'have a great life after acquiring sixteen'. The sixteen could have meant children or more practically, could have meant the number of virtues to be acquired over one's lifetime. Her dreams were, however, filled with travel to distant places, visits to magnificent ports and cities and discussions with the most learned. Her life in the Siddhar colony was getting to be a drag. She wanted to be free like a soaring eagle for whom scaling mountains and crossing seas is child's play. She longed to see the rest of the subcontinent and understand the lives and beliefs of other people.

The Siddhars had set up their monthly health camp among the Paravars who were mostly fishermen, seamen and maritime traders. They harvested pearl oysters and chank when the season allowed. There was a thriving export market for pearls and seashells. A little away from the colony were large saltwater pans to produce salt thanks to the year-long sunny climate. Though the community was left to govern itself, it had to pay regular taxes on their produce to the Pandyan king. They were not very welcome inside the capital city so they had pitched their thatched huts at a respectable distance from the city.

It was the middle of the month of Aadi when the sun starts moving south from the Tropic of Cancer to the Tropic of Capricorn. Copious waters flowed in the Vaigai river, the daughter of the sky, the favourite on the tongues of poets in southern Thamizhagam. Swirls and eddies sparkled under the bright sun as she danced around rocks and boulders like a resplendent maiden. As she moved with her delightful gait of over 250 kadams, a carpet of flowers from the date tree, the white kadamba, the orange fruit of the gamboges, iridescent jasmines, fragrant yellow and white champak flowers covered her willowy shoulders.

Poets described the river in ecstatic verses. Her dress is woven from a hundred different flowers, they imagined. The sand banks, edged by trees in blossom, are her youthful breasts. Her red lips are the trees that spread their red petals along the shore. Her lovely teeth are wild jasmine buds floating in the stream. Her long eyes are the carp, which playing in the water, appear and vanish like a wink. Her tresses are the flowing waters filled with petals.

She starts her long trek from the eastern slope of the Western Ghats as a mountainous offshoot. As she flows along, she grows in strength, gathering into her lap numerous rivulets and tributaries. The Suriliyar and Theniar join Vaigai along with the Varattar, Nagalar, Varahanadhi, Manjalar, Marudhanadhi, Sirumaliar, and Sathaiyar rivers originating in the Palani and Azhagar hills.

The pantheon of orthodox Vedic gods and their rituals had so far kept away from the land of Thamizhagam. On this day, the shores of Vaigai were crowded with families, with people offering prayers. Young girls laughed and prattled as they made offerings of kaadholai, the earrings made of palm leaf. To this were added karugamani, black beads, and the sweet kaapparisi made of hand pounded rice and jaggery. Their parents had brought them to participate in the fertility ritual so that they will be blessed with good husbands and children.

Hundreds of bamboo coracles, the parisals, spun around on the Vaigai carrying squealing children and happy parents. Boats laden with flowers, fruits and other goods were making their way towards Keezhadi and Azhagankulam, the international Pandya port.

Folk dancers lined the shores playing their songs while women danced the Kummi. A host of families had come for a picnic prepared with different kinds of flavoured rice which they ate on banana leaves.

By noon, the Siddhars had almost attended to all the waiting patients. They will soon wind up their camp and return to their colony in the city. Madhavi decided to take a stroll along the riverbank where the city revelers were having a lively discussion seated on the smooth weather-beaten rocks or taking a dip in the river. She could see vendors from the Paravar colony spread out along the shore to sell their wares. A few stalls selling fried fish and oysters spread the familiar aroma of sea food. Urchins gathered around these stalls waiting for scraps of food or the occasional coin.

Just when she was about to turn back, she spotted the Jain monk who, she remembered, made a dramatic entry in a dingy street on another festival day earlier to save her from thugs. He seemed to be thoroughly enjoying the pranks of visitors who had taken a plunge into the serene river. He looked considerably darker, tanned by the warm sun, since she last met him. But then, she had only seen him under the streetlights in the night.

The Vaigai river inspired different people in different ways, for good or bad. Poets or would-be poets experienced a sudden bolt of inspiration to take their poetry to new heights. The river brought clarity to the confused minds of besotted lovers and made them commit to the next crucial step. Those who had already taken the crucial step came to the riverbank in search of peace. Philosophers reflected on the ever-changing, ever-flowing river and came to the conclusion that nothing on this earth is absolute and unchanging. As she walked towards the monk, Madhavi wondered what kind of impact the river had on him.

When he spotted her, a smile of recognition lit up his face.

'It's been a long time since we last met,' she said. He acknowledged with a nod.

'Is your partner not here?' he enquired.

'No, I came here to attend to a health camp with my fellow doctors,' she replied. Her dark black tresses tumbled about her face in the gentle river breeze. 'Have you been in Madurai all this time?' she enquired.

The Jain monk sat down on a rock and motioned for her to follow him.

'I have actually been travelling all over south,' he said in a pleased tone. 'There is so much to see and absorb here. There is so much of activity going on here that we northerners are scarcely aware of. An occasional trader brings news about the south but there are so many fascinating things here which can only be experienced directly. No hearsay can give the real feel.'

Lucky guy, he gets to travel so much! Madhavi nodded in agreement. Happy that there was a willing listener, the monk continued. 'I think the yavanars know more about your country than people in our own cities like Magadha or Kosala or Kashi. I have come across hundreds of yavanars in the cities and ports. They seem to be regular visitors. They love your pearls, gems, ivory and carnelian beads.'

He paused as a family passed by with their picnic bags packed. The sand on the riverbed stuck to their wet clothes and wet feet. Children ran around noisily kicking up a spray of sand.

The monk suddenly remembered that they had not been properly introduced to each other. 'By the way, my name is Vallabh. I became a monk four years back. Since then I have been travelling across Bharatavarsha,' he said holding up the edge of his robe to keep away the sand spray from his eyes.

'I am Madhavi. I have hardly travelled a few kadams away from Madurai, though I would love to,' she responded.

The monk continued, 'I have travelled across the Pandya, Chola and the Chera kingdoms in these few months. You people speak almost the same language, use the same script, yet you keep constantly warring with each other. So much of your wealth is frittered away in wars. But then,' he carried on, 'the north is no different. Magadha is at war with Avanti, Anga and Kalinga. The big fish eat the small fish and become empires. There is prosperity at one pole and poverty at another.'

Madhavi looked at the monk with admiration. On political affairs she had relied on the experience of Nandi, but this monk seemed to be much better informed about world affairs. 'Is our kingdom really so different from yours?' she said with a faint smile playing on her lips.

'Yes and no,' he said emphatically. 'The biggest difference is that your society is not divided into the four varnas. There is, of course, the difference between rich and poor but you don't have people slotted into castes and treated like outcasts and untouchables for their entire life.'

Madhavi doubted whether the Paravars are any better than outcasts. But she knew that they could mingle with others in the markets and visit temples, and their local councils were recognized by the king.

The monk was not sure whether Madhavi understood what the varna system meant. 'The priests have an upper hand. People have to follow rituals and give gifts to the brahmanas. Otherwise the belief is that they will be born as a mongrel or a donkey in their next life. The more they follow rituals the more they have a chance to be better in the next life than what they are in this life. But whatever they do, they cannot change their caste in this life.'

Madhavi twirled her necklace with her index finger trying to absorb what Vallabh said. *It must be hell for people of the lower castes.*

'This system can never thrive here,' she said with a confident sway of her right hand. 'We are god-fearing but there is no place for rituals. We love our language and our bards. The Tamil Sangam includes everyone. There is no bar on anyone.'

'I know,' the monk agreed. 'But don't be so sure that the varna system will not make inroads into your country. It has reached the north-west frontier provinces and has Kalinga under its grip.'

'You said there is a connection between the north and the south. What is that?'

Vallabh looked around at the groups of visitors who had started putting back their stuff into their bamboo baskets. The sun's rays had mellowed, spreading a large sheet of orange across the expanse of the river. 'When I travelled from place to place in your country I came across a lot of graffiti done in your Tamil Brahmi script which looked very similar to the Indus Valley script. I saw that in Keezhadi, very near from here. Shows that you were linked to the north even many centuries ago.'

'But how come we are cut off from the north now?' asked Madhavi wondering herself where the connection broke.

'Well,' Vallabh replied matter-of-factly. 'So many things happen over time. It seems that there were great cities in the northwest at one point in time built by the people of the Indus civilisation. They slowly disintegrated and now we have cities and states coming up again in the Gangetic Plains."

'Shall we start moving towards the city?' asked Madhavi realizing that dusk was approaching. 'I have to make sure that all our leftover medicines are packed neatly. We can continue our conversation on our way back.'

Vallabh nodded. Madhavi made quick strides to the camp and consulted her colleagues on whether they can take leave from the Paravars. After ascertaining that the last of the patients has been attended to, she walked back towards Vallabh who had been patiently peering at the rocks along the riverbed.

'I am ready to leave,' she announced. 'The others will be coming soon.' This discussion is exciting.

❋ ❋ ❋

The two of them got into a parisal. As the coracle set in motion, a muster of white storks glided lazily across the evening sky. The river was dotted with cormorants, egrets and pond herons looking for food. Vallabh and Madhavi could feel the calm motion of the river as the coracle smoothly wound around river bends. It fell to a steady pace as the river straightened out, approaching the city.

'I can see that you hate the varna system which treats shudras like animals. How is your religion different?' asked Madhavi as she put out her right hand and splashed around the glassy water. She could see a shoal of fish winding their way under the coracle.

'Actually, ours is not a religion. It is just a way of thinking and a way of life. We do not differentiate between people. Members of all castes can enter our sanghas. Of course, to become a monk or a nun, one has to renounce all relationships and come with an empty hand. They have to take the five great vows.' He looked at her to check whether she was still interested. After ascertaining that she was, he continued, 'The first is not to injure any living being, *ahimsa*. The second is not to utter any lies, *satya*. One should not steal, *asteya*. That is the third vow. The last two are very difficult and differentiates a monk from a lay devotee. The fourth is to lead a celibate life, *brahmacharya*, and the fifth, to call nothing as one's own, *aparigraha*.'

Why do they make it so complicated? 'I will fail in the very first attempt,' Madhavi giggled jestingly. 'I cannot sacrifice my fish curry and crab toast. But I don't cheat anyone, even when a patient tries to outsmart me.'

Vallabh laughed at her frank remarks. 'Ahimsa is very important for us. At one time even brahmanas ate beef and meat. But conditions must have changed and the cow became a venerable animal since animal sacrifice had almost wiped out the bovine population. But our sect has gone to the other extreme. We cannot even hurt a fly or stomp on an insect.'

'These conditions are so harsh. They must be keeping out most people. How does your religion prosper?' Madhavi said in a tone bordering rebuke.

'Yes, it does keep out people. That is why we are called the shramanas, those who exert themselves to seek the truth and live an austere life. Kshatriyas keep away because a warrior has to fight in wars. It keeps out farmers, craftsmen, metalsmiths, hunters and doctors since their profession may hurt some animals. Finally, that leaves the traders, financiers and the like who generally prefer peace and don't have to deal with animals in their profession,' the monk explained.

That seemed incredulous to Madhavi. 'How can a nation survive with only traders?' she asked with astonishment.

'Not everyone would join a sangha and renounce everything. Only those who have conquered their self can be a conqueror, a jina.

Those who have mastered knowledge to build a ford to cross the stream of life can become a tirthankara, like our Mahavira,' Vallabh added a bit dramatically.

'Let me quote a verse from Mahavira in his conversation with Gautama, one of his beloved disciples,' he said and continued without waiting for approval.

> *'As the dead leaf when its time is up*
> *Falls from the tree to the ground,*
> *So is the life of man,*
> *Gautama, always be watchful!*
> *As the dewdrop that sways on a blade of grass*
> *Lasts but a moment,*
> *So is the life of man,*
> *Gautama, always be watchful!'*

Madhavi was curious about the social roots of the founders of this sect. 'If your sect doesn't accept the authority of Vedic orthodoxy then do you allow brahmanas into your sangha?' she asked.

The monk raised his eyebrows in wonder. 'That's a smart question. Looks like you are interested in a lot more than what is in your medical manuscripts,' he commented.

'My father encouraged me to read from a young age. We Siddhars are a well-read and enquiring community. We are poets, philosophers, alchemists, physiologists and doctors. Sometimes people think we are a crazy lot.'

Vallabh laughed. He really liked the relaxed and candid observations of Madhavi. As they neared the city gates, sounds and smells of the city slowly drifted towards them. The heady fragrance of the sandal paste and other perfumes from vendors outside the city gates wafted towards them like a toddler reaching out to its mother. The faint outline of the city palace and multistoried buildings appeared in the dim evening light. Sounds of conches and drums crossed over the city walls and welcomed the strollers back.

'All the naastik sects, that is those who do not believe in sacrifices, rituals and a supreme god, were founded by kshatriyas or brahmanas because they were the most influential and thinking sections of the population. Mahavira himself was a kshatriya prince and many of his most trusted followers were brahmanas. So, we are not against brahmanas. In a way, we feel that we are the true brahmanas. I will tell you a story if you have the patience,' Vallabh entreated.

'Sure, I am enjoying this conversation,' Madhavi responded with a nod.

The parisal avoided the regular boat jetties outside the city gates and made its way to a shallow spot to deposit its customers. The monk climbed up to the bank and gave Madhavi a helping hand. As they made their way towards the imposing city gates, he started on his story.

'There was once a famous brahmana named Jayagosha who had joined the Jain sangha and renounced all the worldly pleasures and property. He wandered from town to town spreading his thoughts. During the course of his travel, he reached the city of Kashi and fasted for a month. After completing his fast he reached the house of a brahmana called Vijayagosha, who was a great Vedic scholar and approached him for alms. Vijayagosha was performing a sacrifice, a yagna, at that time and was enraged that a mendicant had the temerity to disturb him in this all-important task. He rudely asked the monk to get lost. The monk was unperturbed and started a discourse on the meaning of brahmanhood and varna. He made fun of Vijayagosha's false claim to knowledge, his arrogance, mindless rituals, fake sacrifices, his comfortable way of life, his greed for gifts, and his continuing attachment to kith and kin.

'Jayagosha finally concluded by saying one does not become a shramana by shaving one's head, nor a brahmana by chanting Om, nor a muni by living in the woods, nor a tapasa by wearing clothes made of kusha grass and bark. One becomes a shramana by equanimity, a brahmana by chastity, a muni by knowledge and a tapasa by penance.'

As they entered through the city gates and walked on the paved streets, the monk fell into a pensive mood. Madhavi slowly digested all that she heard from the monk. It was quite a handful and very thought-provoking.

As they neared the footpath uphill to her colony, she asked 'Are you planning to be in the region for some more time?'

'Yes, my investigations are far from over. I will be travelling in the region for a while. When I return to Madurai, I will get in touch with you. I enjoyed the conversation,' replied the monk oblivious to the fact that the conversation was mostly one-sided. 'Should I accompany you to your place?' he asked with genuine concern. 'It is getting dark.'

'My friends are here and we live nearby. Don't worry. There is more than one nerve paralyser in our colony,' she laughed.

'My sympathies to those who dare to lay a hand on you people,' said the monk and wished her goodbye.

As she walked up the slope of the hill, Madhavi wondered whether her meeting with Vallabh was accidental or pre-planned. When she first met him in a dark alley in Madurai, she had a hunch that this would not be the last meeting. It turned out to be true. Did the Jain monk want something from her, she was not sure. He seemed to be very honest in his conversation. In fact, she enjoyed every bit of the conversation and looked forward to meeting him again. She did not believe in fate. But she knew that accidents and coincidences happen, and at that time one is given a small window of time to seize the turning point and take up the next higher challenge in life.

She would soon inform Nandi about the meeting with Vallabh and the conversation she had. He would be surprised and worried at the same time. He was a typical trader, conservative in his thoughts and actions. He would caution her. Perhaps that is what she needed at this time.

By the time she finished her household chores and spread out the jute sleeping mat on the floor, she had made up her mind that she would take a break from her routine work and find time to learn more about the world.

7

THE CARAVAN TO KAUSHAMBI

Sudjata – Pataliputra – 330 BCE

Leaving Pataliputra was not too difficult. The king's guards stood at the gates and took the usual king's toll as well as theirs. The head of the traders in Sudjata's caravan knew the guards by name. So they were given a concession.

The caravan was made up of 50 bullock carts laden with supplies for Kaushambi and Mathura. There were bolts of white linen, exquisite silk which had been brought from the eastern Ganga port of Tamralipti up the river to the city of Champa and then to Pataliputra, chests of medicines, bags of rice and iron ploughshares and sickles. Teams of bullocks pulled the caravans. Some of the traders and helpers sat on a dozen donkeys. Sudjata preferred the rocking wagons to the unpredictable sway of the mules.

He would have liked to sleep away the long ride but his compatriots had other ideas. They seemed to be a boisterous lot, making useless talk and guffawing at bad jokes. As they made their plodding way past rice and barley fields and pastureland, Sudjata could only hope that this trip gets done as fast as possible. He was a junior trader under a *setthi* who had bargained him into this travel with the promise of a *decent* commission if the goods get sold for a good price. There was no guarantee of the commission being decent but he had no choice. His parents were dependent on him. He was already twenty-eight and wished to get married soon and settle down.

Twenty wagons belonged to the *setthi* while the remaining were shared by a few other rich merchants. A caravan of 50 wagons was considered to be a modest one. Large caravans having 500 to 1000 wagons were not very infrequent in those times. War or peace, trade was multiplying. There seemed to be a never-ending demand for goods across Bharatavarsha and beyond. The long caravans and busy roads served the booming cities strewn all over the vast plains of the Ganga and Yamuna.

'Is that a real sword or a play sword that you are carrying?' nettled a stocky trader directing his question at a rather gaunt-looking trader friend of his.

'I have not sliced anyone's head with this but I don't mind trying this on you,' replied the other, a bit irritated. A roar of laughter came from the five other occupants of the wagon.

'He has brought it to cut the ropes tied around the bales,' said another hoping the conversation will keep them engaged for some more time.

The caravan route stretched from Pataliputra through Varanasi to Kaushambi. From there a road branched off to Bhrgukachha on the mouth of the Narmada making its way through Vidisha and Ujjayini. From Kaushambi, the main trunk road wound its way through the south bank of the Yamuna river to the city of Mathura from where it went north-west to the frontier kingdoms. It would cross the five rivers of the Punjab to the north-west city of Takshashila, from where it will stretch further west to Kabul valley and then onto central Asia.

The roads were deteriorating under the apathetic Dhanananda regime. The large rivers which criss-crossed these roads were not bridged. Engineering in the Magadhan and neighbouring janapadas, though very competent, had somehow not ventured into bridging wide rivers. Important crossings were served by regular ferry services.

Sudjata hoped that they could make it back before the monsoon starts. Once the rain starts it would be impossible to travel on these roads or cross rivers using ferries. Even monks and mendicants stopped travelling during this time. Buddhist and Jain sanghas had an express rule that monks should spend the monsoon months in viharas or at an upasaka's house. The hot summer months, the jaistha, were again to be avoided, but many ventured out. The most comfortable months were the months between the end of the rainy season and the beginning of hot summer, when the stars shone brilliantly under the cloudless sky. During these months, long caravans of rumbling carts drawn by oxen, asses, mules and camels travelled long distances.

It is not just the roads which had deteriorated but security as well. Road patrols were more frequent nearer cities and as the distance increased, security provided for traders in return for road taxes, decreased considerably. Roads passed through dense jungles and hills where dacoits made their homes. There were villages which prospered from looting caravans carrying goods as well as their passengers. The Jataka tales even talked about demons in certain parts.

Sudjata's *setthi* normally sent a convoy of at least 25 wagons with a few professional guards provided by the merchant's guild. At other times he would hire professional caravan guards, who were more mercenaries than professionals. A certain amount of insurance was built into the prices of goods. The guild compensated the *setthi* to an extent if things went wrong. So, for the *setthi*, a raid here and there by dacoits was built into his business risk, but for commission agents like Sudjata, an aborted trade meant a huge loss.

While Sudjata was lost in thought, his caravan mates were continuing their boisterous conversation. They were veteran gamblers and Sudjata often heard fairly large sums being mentioned. They used a four-sided dice and one could hear shouts of '*krta, treta, dvapara and kali*' depending on whether the dice showed four, three, two or one. Gambling was an important part of their life, as for most people in Magadha, the four terms also meaning four periods, the yuga, of the aeon itself.

They woke up as soon as the fledgling sun peeped above the horizon with dull orange eyes. The caravan travellers had their quick bath in nearby streams or lakes. One of the caravans carried cooking vessels, spices, rice, pulses, vegetables and meat accompanied by a couple of cooks who fired a make-shift stove and prepared a simple but filling meal for the travellers. The smell of ghee and oil heated up on pans would draw the weary travellers around at food time. The travellers ate chapatis accompanied by meat and vegetables seasoned with curry and completed their meal with curd or an occasional kheer made with rice boiled in milk and spiced with saffron.

As soon as the sun's rays dipped to the west, they would set up their camp again and have their evening meal. The men took turns to watch in the night. The professional guards mounted on their horses made a foray outwards to make sure they don't get surprised by bandits in the night. Camps were set up in open places so that a surprise attack would not be possible.

When they travelled on the main road, they met returning caravans who gave them news about the condition of roads ahead and recommended taverns for wine and ale. The road was also used by folks travelling to nearby places or farmers delivering their produce to markets. Some drove farm wagons laden with rice and pulses. Others walked along with their mules weighed down with fruits and vegetables for the market. The more well-to-do travelled in horse driven chariots or in palanquins carried by bearers. The caravan was often obstructed by herds of cattle, flocks of sheep or tribes of goats crossing their path in search of pasture. There were odd smiths pushing their wheelbarrows equipped with hammers and tongs travelling from village to village selling ironware or fixing iron doors and fences.

The road ran along the fertile plains of the Ganga. On either side were huge stretches of lush farms, green woodlands and crowded villages. The latter had an energetic communal life. Often, caravan travellers came across villagers who had come out rather early with their knives, axes and crowbars to roll away stones from the highways or cut down trees whose low branches caught the axles of carts. They filled up potholes on the roads, built embankments and dug tanks.

Sudjata sometimes stopped to trade with large villages. He observed that most villagers were free peasants and they owned the land collectively for all practical purposes, though the king claimed its ultimate ownership. Displacement of villages by the king's administration was unheard of. Peasants had to toil hard but poverty and indebtedness were not as backbreaking as one would imagine. In times of bad rains and a good king, taxes were withdrawn. The king attended to public works when pressurised by village councils. Most peasant holdings were small and the family worked on them. A few large farmsteads hired labour. The king and his ministers and higher-level officers hired serfs and labourers to cultivate their land, in exchange for one and one quarter pana per month. City dwelling merchants hired sharecroppers in return for a certain percentage of the crop. In times like these, heavy taxes and failure of administration, small peasants were driven to landlessness.

Many of those on the road carried small arms; some carried short swords, daggers and dirks. Farmers carried scythes. Many had bamboo sticks or short staff made from tree branches.

✳ ✳ ✳

On one of the evenings they stopped at a tavern for a drink. For the travellers it was an event to look forward to since caravans avoided taverns for obvious reasons. Though there were strict laws governing the running of state-run as well as private taverns, in these days of growing crimes and lawlessness, they had become favourite haunts of criminals. The king's spy network did not have a reach into many of them.

Liquor drinking was not allowed off premises but when a caravan visits a tavern, rules were flouted. Generally, taverns were prohibited from being close to each other to prevent drunken brawls getting out of hand. With the influence of sects which prohibited drinking, the state recognised drinking as a necessary evil over which a strict watch had to be exercised.

The tavern was well furnished and comfortable. The tavern-keeper welcomed the sarthavahaa Chandaka, the leader of the caravan, warmly. Sudjata was on friendly terms with Chandaka and could appreciate the bonhomie between him and the tavern-keeper as the upshot of scores of trade trips in this route.

Sudjata sat near a side table observing the inn's occupants. Chandaka soon joined him. He was at least ten years older than Sudjata and that much more informed and higher up in the trading ladder. He had led many caravan trips for his *setthi* who happened to be the same as Sudjata's.

The tavern had a choice of liquors to suit the taste of the parched travellers. The inn keeper announced the menu with a flourish. He was proud of his collection.

'There is rice beer, medaka, and for those whose palate craves aroma, there is a spiced beer made of flour, prasanna,' he announced in a sing-song voice.

Noticing that his customers were not impressed, he continued, 'If you prefer a fruity taste, you can have the exotic wine made from wood-apple, the asava,' he offered hopefully.

There was still no response from the traders. A liquor made of raw sugar stood in a large barrel with a tap at the corner. One of the liquor servers filled the liquor in a tankard and went towards the tables.

'Well then,' he said with renewed vigour, 'we have the house special made from the bark of the mesaringa tree spiced with pepper. It is simply out of the world.'

He also went on to acquaint them with the popular mango wine, shakarasura, and a connoisseur's wine made from grapes from the North-West for wealthy merchants. The inn-keeper was showing traces of irritation now. He could not understand why people took such as long time to decide on a flavour. Most customers he knew would stop caring about the flavour within an hour. Either they would be too drunk or too engrossed in their conversation.

Sudjata felt that his knowledge of liquor had suddenly increased manifold within a few minutes. Finally, to the inn-keeper's relief, they ordered for the house special.

It was a large tavern with enough space for about a hundred travellers. The benches in the tavern were crowded with townsfolk, farmers and traders. Taverns, in a way, were true levellers where even rich merchants rubbed shoulders with blacksmiths and farmers. Except for monks and priests, it attracted all sections of society. Women, of course, generally sat behind a screen. A row of huge wooden kegs sat on the floor. Serving boys and girls attended to customers for food orders, while the inn-keeper and his wife served the liquor. A couple of customers looked shifty, but Sudjata dismissed the thought as his imagination.

'Interest rates are getting higher and higher,' Chandaka complained. 'In these troubled times, our *setthi* has to pay two percent per month for the advance he took from the guild for stuffing his wagons.'

Sudjata nodded in understanding. With increasing lawlessness on the roads, interest rates on goods have to go up.

Both of them had ordered for rice beer which was served in a terracotta matka. They sipped at it eagerly. The day had been hot and the cool beer had a soothing effect on them.

'Higher interest rates would mean that we have to bargain for higher prices. But who has the money? The government is collecting octroi, taxes and tolls wherever it can. Our market is now getting restricted to luxury goods and high-flying buyers. Even the markets for rice and barley are now only in the markets of Kaushambi, Ujjayini and Mathura,' he added.

A bard was going from table to table requesting for an audience and getting turned down. Sudjata's stout caravan companion made a disparaging joke at the bard and others joined him in raucous laughter.

Chandaka asked the bard to get on with his story. To the accompaniment of his flute, the bard sang a story from the Jataka tales, one of the many stories of the Bodhisatta about an honest and a greedy trader where honesty is rewarded at the end. The Jataka tales were popular among the people for in these times of affluence, avarice and inequity, the tales lauded honesty and charity.

The merriment continued late into the night. The travellers returned to their camp a bit away from the tavern and fell into blissful sleep.

Sleep eluded Sudjata. He was tired of his routine work. There was nothing predictable in his profession. Prices went up and down.

Markets for some products expanded while for others it contracted. Traders like him, the honest ones, were buggered every day by taxes, the administration and the vicissitudes of the market. It was time that he found something more exciting. But what could a helpless trader like him do? How can he aspire for something beyond his reach? *Something will turn up, I know.*

The night watchmen made a desperate attempt to keep their eyes open with hands on the hilt of their swords. The scouts wandered around the camp for a while until drowsiness forced them to join the night watchmen.

The dacoits attacked when the camp sounded peaceful.

8

Visitors From Kamboja

Satya – Ujjayini – 329 BCE

As the four riders turned their horses with a gentle prod towards the gates of Ujjayini, the sun was out and the roads were bustling with activity. The waters of the Kshipra river dazzled under its strong fierce rays. Oxen carts, horse riders and people on foot poured in and out of the city's gates like swarms of locusts searching for their day's food. The warm sun made the riders sweat all the more because of their leather jackets and thick vests. The horses, however, trotted majestically, unmindful of the chaos of mud and shouting guards and traders as they passed under the portcullis whose latticed grill made of wood and metal had been drawn up to open up the city for the day's traffic.

The river not only provided an in-land trade route, it also provided livelihood for the numerous poets of Avanti. Thanks to its elegant flow and rich lore, the river elevated gifted poets to the position of court poets. Other wannabe poets sat long hours on its banks expecting a bolt of inspiration to strike them at any time. Even fishermen sang folk songs about the river while pulling their oars.

'Where the wind from the Kshipra river prolongs the shrill melodious cry of the cranes,
Fragrant at early dawn from the scent of the opening lotus,
And, like a lover with flattering requests,
Dispels the morning languor of women, and refreshes their limbs.'[i]

The riders from Kamboja had been on the road for several weeks now, coming down from Marakanda along the Uttarapatha to sell their excellently bred horses to dealers in several cities along the way. Kamboja was known far and wide for its excellent breed of horses. The janapada produced remarkable horsemen who were sought after by cavalries of other kingdoms. The kingdom also made considerable income by supplying its cavalry troopers to other kingdoms at times of war often tilting their fortunes favourably. Precisely for their supreme horse-riding skills, the Kambojans were often called Ashvakas, the horsemen.

'How are we going to find our friend in this big city?' asked one of the riders turning around on his horse to the tallest of the riders who was obviously their leader.

Suvala, their leader, had a long face and even longer brown hair. He was in his mid-thirties but his closely trimmed beard, grey in parts, made him look older. He had dark grey eyes which at times looked soft like the mist over the Kshipra river and at times steely like the long sword he was wearing at his side. He looked like a man who knew much more about the world than his age would have allowed him to.

'We have to do it quietly,' replied the leader. 'No need for the entire city to know about our mission, especially the king and his officers.'

'Let us then get into a tavern and make some discreet enquiries,' said the third rider. 'We can also refresh ourselves and have something to eat and drink,' he added hopefully.

The leader seemed to be weighing the option seriously. After few minutes he shrugged and said, 'OK, let's do that. But we have to get going with our business soon after. We don't have much time to waste.'

It was a while before they could get the location of Satya's house in the blacksmith's colony. The horse riders made their way through the crowded streets and markets looking back now and then to make sure no one took any special interest in their destination.

The riders had to go through the market to reach the blacksmith's colony. The market had several rows of shops, each specialising in a particular commodity. One row had shops which sold terracotta pots and cups and figurines of all shapes and sizes. Another row specialized in fired brick rings and platforms. Another had shops selling fine muslin and dyed dress materials. That part of the market which had jewellery and silverware shops boasted of cleaner streets and better dressed customers.

As they progressed into the more congested sections of the market, it became more difficult to guide the horses through the throngs of people. A girl, hardly 8 years old, was walking on a tight rope tied between two poles and balancing a wooden staff precariously. At 20 feet above ground level, it was a risky performance. But the crowd was roaring in anticipation as she struggled to bring her left foot forward. A horde of barefoot children was running between the poles hooting and jumping all the time but the girl was used to such dangers and didn't seem worried that one of the poles may get uprooted any time.

Close to this thrilling performance, a group of urchins was pretending to be dueling with swords using thin birches of wood. They had a gang of admirers who cheered them on while other pedestrians cursed them. One of the mothers of the urchins rushed in with a cane and gave a sharp blow on the back of her ward, who howled and cursed at her. But that was enough to put an end to the duel fight.

The street where vegetable and fruit vendors plied their wares was the worst. The horses whickered and whinnied in discomfort as they maneuvered carefully on the slippery road with a thick coat of vegetable peels and rotting fruits. Shouts of *'sweetest mangoes almost free'* and *'the best grapes in the world'* came from farmers standing near their cartload of goods.

The horse riders turned right and came to the foot of the path winding upwards on a steep hill. The blacksmith's colony started right from the foot of the slope and stretched all the way upwards.

❊ ❊ ❊

'This colony is dominated by the Agaria tribe,' remarked the leader as he assessed the row of forges and workers working on the steel products. 'Some consider them as the world's best steelmakers,' he added.

'The iron technology must have really spurred the economy and expanded trade in this region,' said one of the riders observing the vast colony buzzing like a honeycomb.

'Without a doubt,' said the leader emphatically. 'Look at the kind of iron products here—vessels, nails, ploughshares, rods and the like. Every industry and construction needs iron and steel. These people have really mastered the use of the new technology at extremely high temperatures. They say that iron axes made it easier to clear forests so that land could be made ready for cultivation. The iron hoe has improved efficiency in agriculture. And look at the iron ploughshare. It is more efficient in heavy soil as it can plough deeper than a wooden share. Our drives can definitely benefit from all this technology.'

'That's why we have come here, I suppose,' observed Shakuni, one of the riders.

'But can we attribute the growth of so many cities in the Ganges

Plain to better iron technology alone?' asked Pushkara, another one.

'No, iron technology is only one of the driving forces. But as these communities learnt to handle the technology, they found its use in other fields also. The technology has revolutionized the making of items from bone, glass, ivory, semi-precious stones and shell. Look at some of the houses here. The way we have learnt to work with stone structures, these people use wood for making beams for their ceilings. Their chariots and carts are of high quality. They make powerful ships to carry their goods on river and sea routes. But most importantly, their craftsmanship in making swords, daggers and spears is superb. Whoever has superior arms wins the war and expands his territory. So, the arms industry has been the biggest engine of economic growth. Since agriculture and other crafts have also developed, the kings can collect large amount of taxes from producers and traders to fund their war efforts.'

'Well, if iron technology has made warfare efficient and spurred economic growth, we have come to the right place to learn,' quipped a rider.

There were rows of blacksmiths working on open forges. Stacks of sickles, rods, plates and ploughshares were piled up on the side at various points on the road. Several carts were loading the finished steel products or unloading the iron ore. One part of the colony was occupied by vendors selling their iron ware from loaded carts.

As they climbed a bit more, they came across small factories built with fired bricks and mud, having a wide entrance and a backyard for storing the steel products. It was not tough to find Satya's forge and house. He seemed to be extremely popular in the colony.

When Satya came out of the forge to find out about the commotion outside, the leader introduced himself. 'I am Suvala from the city of Pushkalavati in the janapada of Kamboja. These are my friends, Hotak,

Shakuni, and Pushkara. We have come a long way and we need to talk quite a bit.'

Satya wondered why they have come this distance to meet him. He wiped his quizzical look with a smile and welcomed the visitors into the room next to the forge. Even though the room was separated from the forge by a thick wall, the visitors removed their thick jackets and footwear. Satya offered them a cool lemon drink and some fried corn and salted nuts. Bala and Sajjalaka also joined the company.

'We have come here on a crucial mission,' started Suvala a bit dramatically. 'Our janapada is in great danger now. Sikandar and his marauding army have been razing and burning cities on the way to Bharatavarsha. His life's ideal seems to be the capturing of this vast region since he believes that Bharatavarsha is the end of the world. So, if he captures all the kingdoms here, then he would have brought the entire world to its knees.'

He paused here and had a sip of the lemon drink. Satya and his friends waited in anticipation.

'Our tribes are valiant. We are the best horse riders in the world. But how can we stop this juggernaut if we don't have weapons?' He looked at Satya as if he expected an answer.

'We have to buy arms but even better, we need people who can manufacture arms from the raw material available at our place. We just don't have the knowhow for that,' continued Suvala hoping that he is making his point.

'If your king has sent you to scout for blacksmiths then why don't you talk to our king?' asked Satya.

Suvala glanced knowingly at his friends, who all had a grin on their faces. 'Well, it is not that simple,' he replied. 'We don't trust our king. He may make a deal with Sikandar. Our kingdom was conquered by kings from Ayodhya long back, they say. It was then conquered by the Achaemenid empire, by Cyrus the Great. So, we will not be surprised if our king ditches the Achaemenids and joins the Macedonians if he is offered to head the satrapy.'

'So you are not really a government delegation?' asked Bala. 'Looks like you have your own plans,' he added cheekily.

Suvala grinned. 'Yes, we are a rebel group who want to keep out Sikandar. At the same time, we don't want to get stomped by another empire. That's why we are not approaching your king or the kings of Magadha or the Chedis or the Mallas. We are contacting like-minded groups in these kingdoms who want a strong Bharatavarsha—strong not in terms of a huge army and a cruel king, but strong in terms of people having decision-making power in their hands.'

Satya looked at Bala and his friends with a glint in his eye.

'Can you mobilise some blacksmiths to come to our country and help us in manufacturing arms? That will be a great contribution. Not only that, we request more from you. Can you spread the message in your city among the people that Bharatavarsha is under threat but our kings are fighting with each other and calculating on which side they will get the biggest pie?'

There are people like us in other kingdoms too. It looks like there is a possibility to build an alternative to these monarchs who act only in their self-interest.

'This is very exciting. It is good to know that there are people everywhere looking for change. What is happening in your kingdom is also happening here. Our king wants to sell Avanti to the Magadhan empire and our minister wants to align with Sikandar and his Indian allies. But we are pitted against two big armies.'

'It is not a question of how big the armies are or how much the kings have in their treasury to finance wars. Ultimately it is the ordinary soldiers who fight their battles and sacrifice their lives. We have to convince them to fight to unite Bharatavarsha and not for installing despots and tyrants,' said Suvala earnestly.

✳ ✳ ✳

'I will take you around our forge,' suggested Satya and led them to the adjoining forge.

The forge room was sweltering hot but the visitors were very curious about the iron-making process. A tall terracotta figurine of Lohasur, the iron god, stood in one corner of the forge. Many men and women were busy preparing the raw material, cleaning the furnace and getting the air bellows ready.

The furnace was above ground level with a circular cross-section. The thick furnace wall was constructed from alumina-rich clay mixed with a small percentage of iron ore fines.[ii]

Satya pointed to the taper of the furnace supported by four sticks fixed along the wall. 'We have been using this technology for centuries. At one time our tribes used to build such furnaces even in forests.'

The charge had been fed through a sliding platform made of bamboo sticks covered with clay. The sizzling hot molten slag was now being tapped from the slag hole at the bottom, just below the iron bloom. The trumpet-shaped clay tuyere through which air had been pumped in using bellows protruded at an angle from the furnace.

'We first layer the furnace at the bottom with paddy chaff and clay mixed with charcoal powder. Following that, iron ore and charcoal are mixed in a particular ration and charged into the furnace in alternate layers,' explained Satya. 'The front wall is then built to the required height and the tuyere is fixed at an appropriate angle. The manhole in front is then closed using the same mixture of clay and charcoal. A moist piece of raw hide serves as the valve in the bellows, and the green bamboo piece you see here acts as a spring to blow in the air when the bellows are pressed by foot. The iron smelting process started a few hours back and now you see the results,' he said pointing at the molten slag.

Feeling comfortable with the strangers, Bala continued, 'Poisonous gases are produced during the process. They are ignited as soon as they emerge from the top.'

Suvala and his compatriots were sufficiently impressed. Here was a machine which made it possible to make sophisticated arms and spur economic growth in the region. Luckily, there was no monopoly over the technology nor did it require huge capital.

When the sun had set, the visitors sat down for dinner. 'We have hardly any time now. Satya, you would have heard that after defeating Darius III, Sikandar ransacked his capital city, Persepolis. His army pillaged, raped and looted the city. He was such a barbarian that after looting the city's treasures he systematically burnt down the palace and the city. He has destroyed the entire library containing documents and artworks worth hundreds of years' of labour. So much for the Macedonians bringing civilization to the east.'

Satya and Bala were horrified. Suvala continued, 'After that, Sikandar captured Bactria and crossed the Oxus river on the way to Marakanda. But just when he thought that he is on top of the situation, the Sogdian tribes under their leader Spitamenes, besieged Maraknada.' Here Suvala paused and looked around at his newfound friends.

'We have to learn from Spitamenes. He has an efficient army of horse-mounted archers and can roam around the plains and forests with speed. Sikandar's men are much slower and so they have become easy prey for the valiant tribal people. Sikandar sent an army of mercenaries to wipe them out but they were completely wiped out instead. This shows that he is not invincible. If only all our tribes and kingdoms were united, then we can easily drive his army back.'

'How can we concretely help?' asked Satya eager to step into the action.

Suvala replied in a firm tone, 'Like I said, mobilise as many blacksmiths as possible for our cause and spread the word that there is going to be a rebellion throughout Bharatavarsha against the enemy at our gates, and the enemy within. Our struggle doesn't stop with driving the external aggressors. We need to deal with our brutal and greedy monarchs as well.'

'I cannot agree with you more,' said Satya. 'We have made Ujjayini famous with our excellent iron products. But look at how we are treated. We are literally tax paying outcasts. The government refuses to provide sewerage or drinking water to our colony. We have to fight every inch for our basic necessities. We are with you. But how do we keep in touch?'

'We are visiting many cities in the region. I heard that merchants from here regularly travel to Bhrgukachha for exporting their goods. Why don't you bring a few cartloads of weapons to the port from where we can send them across to our friends in the northwest? Let's meet after 3 months. Is that OK?'

Satya looked at his friends expectantly. They all nodded in acceptance. 'Done!' he replied triumphantly.

That night, Satya tossed and turned on his cot trying to get some sleep. He was wondering whether he was a bit hasty in agreeing to supply the weapons to Suvala. But he had consulted his friends and they felt that something drastic needed to be done at this crucial moment. He was aware that many dangers lurked ahead. Working against the establishment meant a lot of sacrifices. He was worried about his friends, about Madanika and about his tribe. But then, one has to die sometime. It is better to give up one's life for a cause rather than wait till old age until one's bones disintegrate, the flesh shrivels and the mind rambles.

The next day when the visitors bid farewell to the Agaria colony, a sly figure followed them to the gate and then hurried towards the Mahamatra's palace.

9

Breath-Taking Puhar

Madhavi – Puhar – 329 BCE

A few months after she met the Jain monk, Madhavi's wish to travel around the world started taking shape. One cannot start on a world tour if you don't visit nearby cities first. So, when Nandi offered to take her to Poompuhar, shortly called Puhar, the world-renowned port of the Cholas, she became excited like a young girl looking forward to her first saree.

Preparations took time. The cart had to be loaded with provisions for the long journey. Its wheels and hub had to be inspected and repaired for frayed edges and small cracks. Nandi had maintained the cart in good condition. The wheels and the wagon box had been painted bright blue and red. The oxen had painted red horns contrasting sharply with their shiny black skin.

Nandi rode the cart himself. He had brought it early morning right up to the foothills of the Siddhar colony waiting for Madhavi to descend the footpath. He was dressed in an ordinary light cotton dhoti that was more suitable for the dusty roads.

'There you are, at last!' he exclaimed as he spotted her coming from behind a tree. 'Let's get moving so that we can cover quite a bit before it gets very warm.'

'I am all set,' she said happily, settling down in the narrow space for a passenger between the driver and the section of the wagon containing provisions and goods for the market. 'Luckily, we don't have to wait for an auspicious muhurtam to start our journey. The Jain monk had described a calendar of good and bad moments that the pandits in the north have developed. It seems that wealthy merchants consulted pandits for the right time to start their caravan and even sacrificed a goat's head to make sure that their trip was profitable.'

Madhavi had described her conversation with the Jain monk and Nandi took it quietly. She noticed a shadow of concern flit across his face that there was a new admirer for Madhavi now, though he was in a monk's clothes.

Both had a cotton shawl draped over their shoulders. There was a slight nip in the morning air. As they crested a low ridge, she asked him, 'What will I do in Puhar when you are busy with your customers?'

'I will not be away for long,' he laughed. 'I have no objection if you come along to the markets. You have never travelled away from Madurai, right?'

A smile appeared on her lips. 'Yes, my foster father was very scared of taking me out on trips after he saw my parents butchered by wayside robbers on the highway.' No point in telling you about my nightmares. 'He is not pleased with this trip. But after I met Vallabh, I have decided that I should take off now and then from my job and get to know the world better.'

Two fingers of light pierced the dawn, slowly lifting the misty curtain over the landscape. A wide plain spread out before them with a few small hills here and there. On either side of the road, lush fields got greener with the rising sun. They had left Vaigai behind and were making their way northeast towards the Cauvery river.

A toll booth stood at border between the Pandya and the Chola kingdoms. In peace times, people could travel between kingdoms without much hassle. Traders had to pay an outgoing duty as well as an incoming duty when they crossed borders. For all practical purposes, people on either side of the borders spoke the same language and celebrated the same festivals.

In times of war, which was not too infrequent, travellers had to be prepared for the worst. During those times, caravans of salt, paddy and linen make difficult journeys, their precious goods laden on bullock carts, equipped with both plenty of provisions for sustenance and bows and spears for protection.

Past the mountainous range of Sirumalai, they reached the Vellar river the next day. Though the river was shallow, Nandi did not take chances. He loaded Madhavi and a few heavy bags onto a Kattumaram, a flat bamboo raft, whose oarsman guided the vessel close to the cart as they both crossed the calm river.

Occasionally, they went past a palace of one of the vassals or ministers of the kings, who had their own territory supported by an elaborate security establishment. When the figures on pennons attached to the poles erected on the winding ramparts of the palaces changed from the fish to the tiger, they knew that they had entered the Chola territory.

'I don't know when war will break out again,' said Nandi as he observed the palace and standards of one of the chieftains on the highway. 'The Pandyas and Cholas are equally matched. They say that each one of them has 500 elephants, 10,000 horses and 20,000 carts. What a waste it will be if they decide to go to war. Both sides will get wiped out. The king from Lanka or Chera will get the upper hand.'

'I heard that the Pandya king is preparing for a great Sangam in Madurai. I hope he pays more attention to it than going to war with his neighbour,' she said hopefully.

✳ ✳ ✳

At last on the third day they reached the imposing gates of the city of Puhar. The city was divided into two districts, the Maruvurpakkam facing the sea and Pattinappakkam to its west. These two districts were separated by a stretch of gardens and orchards where daily markets were held under the shade of the trees.

The sun had dipped and the moon slowly came out from behind the clouds like a tremulous queen coming out of her chambers after seeing her despot king off. The travellers were tired as they reached an inn in Pattinappakkam. The inn-keeper nodded at the familiar face of Nandi while he raised his speculative eyebrow in the direction of Madhavi. Nandi made arrangements for separate rooms and a hot dinner for the two of them. The inn-keeper shouted instructions at the helper boy to unhinge the oxen from the cart and feed them.

They would visit the markets tomorrow. There was a day market called the naalangadi where an array of shops sold goods fit for buying during the day such as rice and other cereals, tamarind, curry powders, terracotta jars and cups, and iron ploughshares, shovels and so on. The night market, allangadi, specialised in flowers, sandal paste, betel leaves, and wine.

Cries of birds and vendors woke them up early. The cart had been cleaned up and when Nandi and Madhavi came down to the common area, a number of morning visitors were streaming in. They had a quick breakfast and left with the cart towards the seaport.

As they traversed the Pattinappakkam sector of the city, they could see that it was the operational part housing the palace and the mansions of nobles and rich merchants, the army cantonment, and professional establishments such as hospitals, administrative buildings, cultural centres, and the like. Many tall mansions outlined the city's skyline. They were surrounded by platforms which could be reached by tall ladders. These mansions had many apartments accessed by doorways, large and small, which led to wide hallways and corridors.

Various well-cared for gardens such as the Elavanthikaicholai and Kaveravanam adorned the city. The streets were busy with carts, chariots, horse riders and elephants transporting logs of wood and sacks of rice.

The second part of the city, the Maruvurpakkam, had a more business mien. Alongside terraced mansions owned by big traders there were warehouses. This part of the city had a big migrant population. Shops and vendors catered to a sizeable foreign population, the yavanars from Egypt, Greece, Africa and the south-east. Rows and rows of weavers, silk merchants, fish and meat sellers, potters, grain merchants, jewellers and diamond cutters lined the markets.

Many of the yavanars made Thamizhagam their home. They were employed as bodyguards by kings and nobles. They were hired as engineers, for their advanced knowledge of siege craft and construction of war engines for which there was no lack of demand. Fugitives from foreign shores found the southern cities very hospitable.

As they neared the port, Madhavi was struck by the grandeur of a floating city made up of big ships, boats and catamarans, hundreds of them on the move or waiting to gain entry. Right at that moment, a big ship was entering the port without slacking sail and made its way into the large dockyard. On a vast platform were poured out wooden cartons and cloth covered bales of precious merchandise brought from overseas. Several ships were already berthed on the quayside emptying out their goods. Overlooking them was an impressively tall lighthouse.

Nandi pointed to the ships which were equipped with steadying outriggers and steered by large oars. 'Madhavi can you see the difference between our ships and that of the yavanars?'

Madhavi was clueless. She shook her head.

'You will notice that in our ships the timbers are not nailed or riveted but lashed together with coir ropes. Sewn or lashed timbers are more resilient than nailed ones and can stand up better to the kind of fierce storms we have during the monsoon period. They can also negotiate the treacherous coral reefs of our oceans,' he explained earnestly.

Madhavi could see that Nandi had a very high opinion of the ports of the Tamil land. *Why not, if traders come here from thousands of kadams away, then it is definitely something to be proud of.*

Nandi was effusive in his description of the port. 'Ships come here from all corners of the earth. From the river Champa in the Ganga basin, ships sail down to the sea and along the coast to the south and Lanka. From Tamralipti in the east, ships not only sail to Lanka but to south-east Asia and Suvarnadvipa as well. These yavanars you see here would have also visited the ports of Korkai, the Pandyan port and Musiri, the Chera port.'

Madhavi was impressed. 'I think the Tamil kings have done a lot to develop their harbours and encourage sea-trade.'

Several customs officials were busy on the wharfs inspecting the discharged merchandise and stamping them with the king's seal. Multiple carts were lined up to take the custom approved goods to warehouses near the seafront.

Sacks of spices, boxes of perfumes, bales of fine linen, an intricately carved brass box carrying exquisitely designed jewellery, another containing the choicest pearls, beryls and semi-precious stones, figurines carved out of ivory, and jars containing dyestuffs, were all being loaded onto a Greek galley by the headload workers in the harbour.

'Are we exporting birds and animals too?' asked Madhavi in astonishment when she noticed some cages being loaded onto the ship.

Nandi laughed. 'Our monkeys, parrots and peacocks are a big hit with wealthy Roman ladies. Smaller animals can be taken by sea. We also export elephants and oxen, which have to be transported by land.'

'OK, we sell our monkeys, jewellery and spices. What do we get in return?'

'We get some wine and other stuff. Do you see those large Roman amphorae jars?' he pointed out to one corner of the wharf. 'They are filled with vintage wine which only our kings and nobles can afford. But it is raw gold and gold coins that we import a lot and turn them into bangles, earrings, pendants, arm bands and what not. I heard from one of the Greek merchants here that their politicians were complaining that we are draining away all the gold from their countries! We also import good steeds from Persia and pepper from Muziris. Sandalwood comes from the Kudda hills and gems from the Himalayas.'

It was a great experience for Madhavi. The port looked very busy with hundreds of people milling around. Sailors, workers, merchants and taxmen went about their work, giving each other space. Goods entering and leaving the port had to go through custom check posts, the sungachavadis, manned by efficient customs collectors. The goods were weighed in and the weights recorded along with the type of goods and tax collected. Nandi had told her that the daily trade in the port was high enough to warrant a regular workforce and a merchant guild. She could see ships carrying flags indicating their origin as well as the type of goods they carried.

A bit inland into the dockyard, a large shipbuilding platform spread out before them. Workers were busy assembling the frame and ribs of a ship, the kappal. A host of smaller crafts such as the ambi, padagu, odam and the thoni were also in various stages of completion.

'Siddhar amma, what are you doing here?' called out someone forcing Madhavi to turn around sharply. A lean, tall man with a familiar face was waving to her with his angavastram. Madhavi recognised him as one of her patients in the Paravar colony near Madurai.

'I should be asking you the same question, Vengayyan,' replied Madhavi with a smile of recognition.

Vengayyan was delighted when she could recall his name. 'There is a large Paravar colony here. Just as we do in Madurai, they fish and make salt and toddy. Some of them also do pearl diving and have even become big merchants. Pearl diving is lucrative. So once in a while, I come here with some of our colony mates,' explained Vengayyan.

Nandi went around mobilising some workers to help him take his cart of goods through customs and unload them at the wharf, where some known traders met him. The inspection, bargaining and the final clinching of the sale took some time. Vengayyan hung around and helped Nandi until the cart was empty.

'Why don't you both come to our colony here? My friends will be excited to see visitors from Madurai. You are welcome to stay for dinner too,' Vengayyan offered.

Madhavi felt some hesitation in Nandi but convinced him to join them.

❋ ❋ ❋

The Paravar colony was well inside the city. The evening market, the allangadi was being set up. As they approached the colony, Madhavi noticed houses made of burnt bricks with wooden palisades give way to mud-brick houses with thatched roofs. Streets narrowed down and streetlamps disappeared. Soak pit wells with terracotta rings gave way to open and overflowing sewers.

As they entered the colony a group of naked children surrounded them crying and heckling for coins. A mother with a shrunken face and tattered clothes begged for some food for her baby who hung motionless over her shoulder and looked with dull eyes at the strangers. Footpath vendors selling stale fish, rotten vegetables and flimsy terracotta pots and cups made the narrow roads even more difficult to negotiate.

> *'The hearth has forgotten cooking;*
> *It is overgrown with moss and mould,*
> *The woman, thin with hunger,*
> *has breasts like wrinkled bladders,*
> *Their nipples are quite dry,*
> *but the child chews them, weeping,*
> *She looks down at his face*
> *and tears hang on her lashes.'*

'On the one side we are draining the world's gold and gems to make exotic jewellery and getting wines from wineries several thousand kadams away. On the other side, here are naked children and dying babies waiting for morsels of food. What is the point of all this!' blurted out Madhavi in a tone mixed with disgust and sadness.

Vengayyan took them to a small house with a verandah in front and a kitchen at the back from where mixed odours of fried fish and prawns floated their way. They received a warm welcome since the Siddhars of Madurai were known far and wide for their dedication and service.

The meal was frugal but succeeded in tickling their palate. Rice made of rye tasted wonderful with the prawn curry and fish fry.

❊ ❊ ❊

As they returned to their inn, the evening market was in full swing. The splendour of the market and the poverty of its workers and craftsmen struck Madhavi.

'Is the Pandyan king organising the Sangam to invite poets to sing in his praise or to really enlighten the people of Thamizhagam?' she said as her lips pursed in despair. 'They say our language is among the most highly developed in the world today. We already have a grammar that has set rules for prose and poetry. Our poets are world renowned. Which other poet has the imagination to connect the environment to the moods of people. Poets in other regions describe their heroes and heroines as if they determine their environment. But our poets set the moods of their characters according to the ecological zone they live, the five thinais.'

Nandi was not sure where this conversation was leading to. 'I too think our poets are doing a great job,' he said sounding as if he had read their anthologies.

'Yes, they are great poets. They are great when they write their verses about love and passion in their agam poems. They are equally great when they sing about war and gore in their puram poems. Have you heard of poets in any other region who had such passion for classifying what they are going to sing about?' she asked.

'Not that I know of,' Nandi replied again sounding knowledgeable, though he had no clue about poets from other regions.

Madhavi continued with passion. 'They are so sensitive to ecology and environment, they have even further classified their works into five thinais: they sing ecstatically about hills in the kurinji; they handle the melancholy of the dry land in their palai; they boldly venture into jungles and woodland in mullai; they rejoice about cultivated lands in marudam; and finally they tackle the fury and storm of the coast in neydal. Is that not simply marvellous?'

Nandi continued to look at her with wonderstruck eyes. Her description of the poets was simply terrific.

'And finally, our poets connected the ecology to the strata and moods of our people. In the hill poems on hunters, they sung about hunters and tender love and cattle raiding. The dry land poems on pastoralists are full of lover's separation for long periods and ravages of the war in the countryside. The jungle poems are about forest dwellers, about lovers separated for brief periods and about raids on the plains.'

'Now, who is left out?' asked Nandi which made Madhavi throw him an irritated glare.

'The farmer poems, the ones on cultivated lands and on rivers, switch to love after marriage, on the wiles of courtesans—which is understandable—and on wars and laying siege.'

'Where do fishermen like our Vengayyan fit in?' asked Nandi helpfully.

'Oh yes, our poets don't leave out anyone. The seacoast poems are about them, on the pathos of fishermen sailing away from their families not sure whether they will return, and on pitched battles and gruesome killings.'

Nandi was astounded. 'You have analysed our Thamizhagam and its poets so well. Let the Pandyan king not forget to invite you to his Sangam or he is going to be in big trouble,' he joked.

'This is a serious matter!' she said disapproving Nandi's banter. 'But our poets are coming under the pressure of kings and nobles to sing paeans for them. Most poems are now about how their king went around killing for the glory of his kingdom. They say that women have ruled the Pandya kingdom several times. But do the poets talk about ordinary women who raise their families?' she said not really expecting Nandi to respond.

He nodded sympathetically but search as he may, no intelligent response appeared in his head. 'Maybe you should discuss this with your Jain friend and see if he has an answer,' was all he could say.

'Yes, Vallabh would have many things to say about our kingdoms and poets and people. Hope we meet him soon in Madurai,' she added, putting an emphatic end to the conversation.

Little did they know that they would be meeting Vallabh sooner than anticipated and discussing more than poetry and seasons.

10

TRIP TO BHRGUKACHHA

Satya – Bhrgukachha – 329 BCE

Under the early morning sun a million golden specks of light burst out from the Kshipra river giving its waters a gleaming shine. People from the city and travellers through the city had come out in large numbers to perform their morning oblations to the Sun God. Many threw coins into the river following tradition. A group of urchins dived into the river to retrieve the coins as much as they could. Many of them had collected punch marked coins showing the Ujjayini symbol of a junction at the crossroads or that of Rudra, the god of destruction. Ujjayini lay at the crossroads of major trading routes, the one going from Pataliputra in the east, Shravasti in Kosala, to seaports in Sopara and Bhrgukachha in the west, and the other called the Dakshinapatha, connecting Takshashila and Mathura to cities in the south.

Satya and his friends had made meticulous preparation for the trip to Bhrgukachha. They had acquired enough material for ten cartloads of weapons. While there was no restriction to trading iron implements once levies were paid, Satya took care to keep other iron implements like the ploughshare and steel sheets on top of the weapons so that they don't attract undue attention from the guards at the gate. Since they had undertaken many such trips loaded with iron implements, they did not have much of a problem in getting out of the city gates and joining the Dakshinapatha road.

As the carts lumbered along the bank of the river, a big flock of white stork rose like a giant winged curtain from the still waters. Grey francolins called loudly from the scrubland on the northern bank of the river as they pecked at grains and insects. Chestnut-tailed starlings looked at the caravan of carts from atop branches of trees lined along the river. A row of flamingos stood on their long thin legs along the shallow part of the river with their necks bent and their black-tipped bills buried under water. They used their long legs and webbed feet to stir up the water so that tasty morsels of sea food gets trapped in their bills.

Horns blew from ships as they moved away from the shore down the river. A few people standing alongside the bank cheered at the passengers on the ships wishing them a safe voyage. As their sails unwound like flowers blossoming under a clear sky, the ships picked up speed. A row of oars rent the water as boats glided gracefully carrying a load of fruits, flowers and fish. A group of washermen unloaded the pile of unwashed clothes from the back of their donkeys and settled down near their favourite stones to wash them.

The caravan did not attract much attention except for some urchins chasing the oxen for a while and shouting at the riders for coins. They soon joined a stream of caravans, horse riders, soldiers, students, teachers, ascetics and peasants. Bharatavarsha was on the move. The huge amount of traffic and the highways dotted with inns and taverns spoke of the booming production and trade and expansion of global contacts. As the caravan crossed from one kingdom to another, customs officials, the kammikas, levied taxes on their merchandise. The custom posts carried boards detailing the levies in Aramaic and Brahmi scripts to keep both foreign and internal traders informed. The rajabhatas, king's soldiers, criss-crossed the roads to ensure the safety of travellers from brigands and robbers who tried to waylay them.

Satya noticed a burly tall Buddhist monk travelling on a mule along with a younger monk. They hardly talked to each other. The elder monk glanced once in a while towards Satya and his caravan as if to make sure they don't get lost, which was a moot possibility since there were no other confusing forks or turns on the highway.

The most popular language among the travellers was Prakrit, particularly its western variant called Shauraseni. The language of the Buddhists, Pali, was also gradually evolving into a popular language in the region.

Bala glanced at Satya who was riding alongside in a pensive mood. To get some conversation going he ventured, 'When are you planning to marry Madanika?'

Satya did not expect this direct question, certainly not at this time when they were going on a serious mission. 'How can I even think of it when we have many important things to do?' he reacted dolefully. 'She has to be first released from the clutches of that bitch Vasantasena. I don't know how long it is going to take.'

'Why not try kidnapping her?' he suggested with a naughty grin. 'I heard that it is allowed as a legitimate form of marriage in the Dharmasutras.'

'The Dharmasutras are only for the upper castes. For us tribals, marriage is an option only when you pay off all the debts, buy your way out of slavery and give gifts to the brahmanas who will refuse even to enter our colony,' spat out Satya in a bitter tone.

'Well, let's find a way out soon, otherwise you will both keep looking at each other in the park and die as lovers. You are from the gothiar clan and she is from the kuri. I don't see any problem within our community. So, make a plan.'

Satya had also been thinking about settling down with Madanika and raising a family but there were too many things happening now to make a commitment. A voice of caution whispered to him that he should wait until the future was certain. But one never knew when this will happen in these uncertain times. Life seemed to have gotten on a roller-coaster. 'Let me talk to her when we get back,' promised Satya. What he did not suspect was that a plan will be forced upon the lovers very soon.

*** *** ***

When the sun set and it became difficult to negotiate the road, they decided to stop at a wayside inn for food and rest. They selected an inn large enough to accommodate most of the cart drivers. Satya and his friends selected a charpai to sit where they were served with food and drinks.

'How do we identify Suvala in that big port? Did he specify any location to meet?' queried Sajjalaka.

'He didn't specify any meeting spot. We are going there at the time he had indicated. I guess he will know a way to find us. We are a big caravan,' surmised Satya.

At that time, the tall monk and his companion entered the inn and walked straight towards them. Satya noticed that the monk had a gaunt face with a scar on the forehead. He was well built for his height and walked with assurance. He addressed Satya, 'I am Ananda from the monastery in Vidisha and here is my companion, Visabha. Can we join you for dinner?'

'Yes, surely,' offered Satya and drew up another cot nearby. The monks sat on the cot and ordered their food. There was a moment of silence when each group sized up the other.

Ananda broke the silence. 'We are friends of Suvala,' he said.

Satya and his friends lifted their heads from their dinner plates in astonishment.

'We were told that you would be traveling to Bhrgukachha with a large caravan on this day and we should accompany you to make sure that you reach your destination safely,' said Ananda while having a bite of a roti made from millets.

'We generally know our way. We were just wondering how to find Suvala after reaching Bhrgukachha,' reacted Satya.

'No, it is not only about meeting Suvala. You are being followed. Don't turn your heads but there is a short guy sitting near the entrance to the inn wearing a blue turban and a cream coloured kurta. He is a spy hired by the Mahamatra to follow your caravan. Apparently, his spies have informed him about your rebel activities, meetings in the park and the visit by Suvala and his companions.' Here he paused to take another bite and taste the pickle. Satya and his friends were surprised and worried that their actions have come to the notice of the most powerful general in the kingdom.

'I don't know what exactly his briefing is, but we should not take chances. He can poison you and your mates. Or he can get a band of bandits to raid your caravan at the right time. No point in waiting for the danger to pounce on us. It is better to find a way to avoid it.'

'But the Mahamatra could have stopped us at the gates or arrested us on the highway,' said Satya wondering about the spy.

'No, at this point he doesn't want to directly confront you without proof. Moreover, you are popular among your tribe and with traders.

So, that's too much to tackle. If it can be shown as an accident, then people around you will not suspect anything. In fact, you yourself would not have if I had not warned you.'

'OK, what should we do now?' asked Bala, a bit anxious. 'Shall we take him to the hilltop and throw him down. That will make sure that no one can find him.'

'That is too drastic and we will invite the wrath of the Mahamatra right away,' cautioned Ananda. 'I have an idea. About a kos from here there are some unoccupied barns. When we reach that place, I will go into one of the barns and Satya should follow me after some time. This will raise the suspicion of the spy who will follow us into the barn. When he reaches the darker interiors, we will grab and blindfold him and then tie him up and leave him there. Some local will find him there after a day or two, by then we would have reached our destination.'

The rebels, having no better idea, readily agreed. The next day after executing their plan to perfection, the enlarged band of rebels with the monks added, lumbered their way towards Bhrgukachha with the heavily laden carts.

❋ ❋ ❋

As they approached the city, the whitewashed walls of fired brick and mud rose before them. There were watch towers all along the gates to the city. The caravan entered the gates under the watchful eyes of spearmen standing security at either end of the gates. The city was relatively clean compared to Ujjayini. Wide and straight cobbled streets led into an inner square from where streets branched out hosting thriving markets of a tremendous variety of merchandise.

The Gulf of Bhrgukachha was a navigator's nightmare. It was hard and narrow to navigate for ships entering from the Indian Ocean. Even if the ships managed to enter the gulf safely, the mouth of the

Narmada river could be found only with difficulty for the shore was very low and could not be seen until one came quite close to it. To make life easier for the navigators, the port administration had hired a host of pilots going around the sea. They scoured the sea with their large boats called Tappaga and Cotymba, travelling up the coast and from there piloted the vessels to Bhrgukachha. None of this adventure deterred ships from Africa, Greece, Rome, Persia, Lanka, Burma, Indonesia and other foreign lands. Neither did it discourage ships from different ports of Bharatavarsha such as Poompuhar, Korkai and Muziris and from the Indus basin in the north.

The vast harbour had an inner and outer jetty divided by a long wall. The outer harbour was larger but the inner harbour offered better anchorage and facilities for loading and unloading the ships.

As the travelers from Ujjayini reached the quay, they could see ships sporting different coloured hulls and sails lined up along the wharf. The dockside wharves were swarming with sailors, traders and workers. A clutter of small boats was tied up at the far end, nearer to the fish market, from where the catch of the day can be unloaded and taken up to the market easily. The hoarse cries of fishwives floated in from the market.

A ship had just arrived. It was tied up to the end of a weathered wooden pier in the outer harbour. The crew fastened her to the pilings and lowered the gang plank for the crew and passengers to come on shore. A pair of customs officials immediately clambered aboard to meet the captain, inspect the hold and collect the duties.

After leaving the carts outside the customs office at the quay, they proceeded into the city. The road from the customs office led inside to a cobbled square. A fountain at the center of the square spewed water from atop a stone statue of three elephants raising their trunks to greet visitors.

The square was teeming with vendors and customers on this bright afternoon. Beneath arches of creepers of madhumalati, scribes, money changers, insurers and translators had set up their business. A few fruit and vegetable vendors were selling their ware from wooden barrows.

The markets were segregated into wholesale and retail sections for spices, perfumes, jewels, ivory and fine textiles. There were also shops for lesser luxuries such as sugar, rice and ghee.

Indian iron was much esteemed for its purity and hardness, and dyestuffs such as lac and indigo were also in great demand abroad. One section of the market had live animals and birds which could be bought for export. Smaller animals such as monkeys, parrots, golden pheasant and peacocks found their way to countries in the West.

Ananda explained that while India exported a variety of goods, its major import was gold. A small amount of pottery and glassware found their way in. There was some demand for wine, and the western traders also brought in tin, lead and slave girls. But the balance of trade was very unfavorable to the West and resulted in a serious drain of gold from their coffers.

'I think Sikandar is broke and he badly needs some gold back; that's why he is taking this big risk of crossing the Sindhu,' joked Bala.

The market streets had almost as many foreigners as locals, a corroboration of the international status of the port. There were the black yavanars from Africa and the pale yavanars from Macedonia and Persia. Each spoke in their language but trade carried on merrily. Silver and gold punch marked coins of Magadha and Avanti were in vogue as much as the Roman coins.

Ananda, noticing the wonder in Satya's eyes, said, 'Isn't Bharatavarsha spectacular? Every city from Pataliputra to Mathura to Ujjayini to Bhrgukachha is so full of charm and wealth. That's why foreigners flock to our cities and ports to buy the most exotic stuff available anywhere in the world. But the rulers have kept us apart for their own selfish interests. To the foreign traders we are one but for our rulers we are all divided into kingdoms.'

Ananda led them into a decrepit dingy inn. Inside the place time must have stood still for ages. The wooden beams holding the ceiling were stained with black and soot. The tiles on the floor had crumbled long ago into hard packed earth. The flickering oil lamps gave off more smoke than light. The inn had a large dining and drinking area with many nooks and shadowy alcoves where sinful acts and audacious conspiracies could be done.

As the visitors settled down, the benches began to fill with sailors, dock workers and traders. Suvala appeared from nowhere and joined them. They all wished each other. 'I chose this place so that we don't attract attention,' he explained.

'Yes, no spy in his right mind would expect us to choose this place,' commented Bala a bit caustically, chewing on a hard piece of roti.

Suvala came to the point immediately. 'Have you brought the stuff I requested? And how is the progress on mobilization?'

Satya narrated that they had been pretty successful in getting in cartloads of weapons. He had also identified a score of blacksmiths who would like to travel to the north and lend a hand in setting up iron forges there. Regular supply of iron ore has to be arranged.

'Next time it is going to be more difficult since the Mahamatra is after us. I should perhaps send the wagons and people through Mathura and Indraprastha,' he volunteered.

'Let us meet soon at Vidisha,' said Ananda as he sipped on a cup of hot porridge, holding it with both his palms. 'I heard that you have been organising a band of rebels in your town. I too have done some good work in and around my monastery. Let's discus preparations for an uprising.' Though he had lowered his voice they were in no danger of being overheard in the din caused by the raucous and drunk customers.

Having accomplished what they came for, Satya and his friends stayed a day more at the port to fill in their wagons with goods for the Ujjayini market. Ananda accompanied their caravan at a distance and after leaving his friends at the gates of Ujjayini, made his way towards Vidisha. Satya now felt that he and his friends have taken a decisive step which they cannot retrace. They have to now double their mobilization efforts and keep a watchful eye on the Mahamatra. His thoughts invariably turned towards Madanika. He had to leave her behind much against her protests. It was important for her to continue to get information from Vasantasena's cesspool of intrigue.

11

AT THE SEASHORE

Madhavi – Puhar – 329 BCE

Nandi was busy over the next two days, settling accounts and buying stuff to take back to Madurai. He had made many trips to Puhar and knew his way around the city as well as the markets. He went about his work in his usual breezy way, making witty remarks whenever a trader tried to get the better of him.

Madhavi watched with interest when he dealt with the sly traders.

'I heard you made a big killing in the Madurai market with the ponni rice that I supplied you last time,' one trader reminded him.

'Not so much as you made with me,' quipped Nandi. 'At least this time I expect a better deal.'

'Anna, you know that I would do anything for you. You are my most trusted customer. But what to do, there is less water in the Kaveri river now. But I will give it to you for almost the same price even though I will make a loss,' the trader assured him.

'That is not what I heard from your friend in the next street. It seems there is less demand this season and you guys are planning to make the same profit by hiking up the price,' Nandi replied smoothly.

'Anna, you know that my tongue will rot and fall away if I lie to you. The going has been bad. Let me get these sacks loaded on your cart.'

The haggling went on for a while and Nandi succeeded in getting a ten percent discount on the earlier price.

The streets of Puhar awed Madhavi. There were hawkers everywhere selling paints, bathing powders, cool pastes, flowers, incense, fragrant scents and a host of other stuff that can transform a crow into a beautiful maiden. Nandi took her into the manufacturing quarters where weavers were working with fine fabric of silk, fur and cotton. Some streets were full of shops offering the finest silks, corals, sandalwood and myrrh. Some of them specialised in rare ornaments, and the purest of pearls, gems and gold.

Other streets were not as fragrant or glamorous. Grain dealers heaped their grains in front of their shops. There were bakeries selling fresh mouth-watering muffins. Wine sellers displayed their finest wines in bottles and amphorae. There were fish mongers, mutton vendors, oil merchants, dealers in bronze and copper artifacts. Broad built blacksmiths mingled with sculptors, potters, goldsmiths, jewellers, tailors and cobblers. In the evenings, musicians armed with flutes, lutes and drums entertained the shoppers.

In the periphery of the city were quarters occupied by cavalrymen with swift horses, elephant trainers, charioteers and infantrymen.

Between the two parts of the city was an open area as vast as a battlefield where temporary shops and bazars sprang up at specific times of the day and night.

***

It was the seashore that fascinated Madhavi. As they sat and watched the sea on a stretch of white sand, they could see the dancing lights from the burning lamps of shops along the market near the harbour. Beacon lights shone from above guiding ships into the harbour. As the boats wobbled on the sea, light from the lamps carried by fishermen danced up and down. The moon and the stars looked down grudgingly on this festival of lights.

Madhavi recalled a verse describing how the water lily blossoms at night at the sight of the white conch bracelets and pearls worn by women on the beaches, mistaking them for the moon and the constellation of stars.[iii] A smile danced on her slender lips.

Nandi was enthralled by the smile. She is the very embodiment of the moon, he thought to himself, not yet having the courage to tell her directly. Her round face is the moon on which eyes have been painted like the fish, brows like a bow made by an extraordinary craftsman, and curls of hair resembling the dark misty clouds. He agreed with the poet who asked, 'Has the moon left the wide sky in fear of the serpent Rahu gobbling her up, and came down quietly to this little hamlet of fishermen?'

'How did you get into the medical profession?' Nandi asked hoping to get a good conversation going. He knew that Madhavi loved to talk about her profession.

'That was one good thing that happened after I lost my family in the highway robbery,' she mused looking at the approaching waves which gently caressed her feet and retreated. 'I think my guardian father saw that I had interest in medicine along with a strong heart to tend to bloody wounds and tumours.'

Waves stretched into the sands and grabbed garlands strewn around the beach of white jasmine and red lilies as if it demanded something in return for the precious pearls removed from their bosom by the pearl divers.

'There was some resistance in my community, I believe,' she resumed. 'They are a very closed community and very possessive about their knowledge. They questioned whether I could be considered as one of theirs.'

'What happened then?' asked Nandi.

'My father stood by my side. He just pooh-poohed away any opposition that an outsider, that too a girl, should not be taught medicine. He was very progressive that way. For us, our community bonding is so very important. Other communities look at us as a weird one experimenting with all kinds of things and having loose social norms.' She reflected and then added, 'You have been a good friend considering all the horror stories about us.'

Nandi was moved. This was the first time that she had expressed gratitude for the friendship. But he knew that he valued the friendship even more. His mother had passed away when he was young. He did not have a good relationship with his father who was always expecting him to climb up the social ladder and get married into an elite family.

Nandi moved a bit closer to Madhavi intent on continuing the conversation. He desired to take her hand and interlock his fingers with hers. The nearest he had come to holding hands with her was when she held his wrist and checked for his pulse. She must have often wondered why his rate was abnormal but had never disclosed his heartbeat count. He now was desperate to move beyond the doctor-patient relationship. The gentle sea breeze ruffled a few strands of her curly hair making them dance around her cheeks. The squawking of gulls, peals of laughter of children and the steady rhythm of the waves livened up the ambience. A radiant glow had descended on Madhavi's face. Just when Nandi stretched out his hand, they were disrupted in their peaceful retreat at the seashore.

Vengayyan came running to them and announced breathlessly, 'The Jain monk Vallabh has been arrested!'

12

BANDITS ATTACK THE CARAVAN

Sudjata – On the way to Kaushambi – 329 BCE

The night's peace was shattered by a shrill cry from one of the security guards sent to scout up the top of a nearby ridge, 'Bandits, bandits!'

For several seconds, there was no movement. The caravan riders were stunned to silence and numbness. Chandaka was the first to react. 'Security guards! Gather your swords and get onto your horses!' he shouted in a frenzy.

Sudjata woke up with a start. He immediately got up and went for his sword and dagger, which he always carried on these trips. He was not good with either of them but it may help slow down the bandits.

Everyone around him was running to reach their weapons or mount their horses or in the worst case, hide behind the carts. They could faintly hear hoofbeats approaching them.

The scout came running towards the caravan breathless and

blabbered, 'There are about ten or more of them. They must have followed us for a while and looked for an opportunity to attack us.'

One of the traders, a thin man in his forties with his dhoti half fastened around his waist, started fretting. 'I knew this was going to happen. We should not have got drunk in the tavern. Cannot we stay without wine for even a few days?'

The head of the security guards, Revata, was already mounted with his fingers curved around the hilt of his long sword. He had put on his leather vest. 'Get up on your horses quickly, you torpid nitwits!' he shouted at his companions. Some of them were still struggling with putting on their vests and nervously fiddling around with their baldric and scabbards.

Chandaka, Sudjata and the other traders gathered near the carts armed with whatever they could lay their hands on—swords, axes, hammers, clubs and iron rods.

The bandit riders were soon upon them. They were not a large force and could not have planned to cart away all the wagons by themselves. But they could make short work of getting away with some expensive items. They seemed to be a quiet lot with masks around their faces. They didn't want to waste time giving the victims any long speech about the purpose of their raid or about their antecedents. Their clothes and armour were nothing much to speak of, indicating that they hadn't succeeded in a good raid for quite a while.

For a moment, Sudjata wanted to leap out with his sword and pounce on one of the raiders but he let the excitement pass and crouched behind one of the wagons.

There were screams, loud whickering of frightened horses, clash of swords and shouts and cries everywhere.

Revata spurred his horse forward and went straight for the leader of the gang while giving instructions to some of his men to keep close to him and cover him. A deadly fight ensued. Horses and riders kicked up a storm of dust through which the traders could see only blurred figures and the glint of metal under the dull moonlight.

Some of the bandits broke away from the fighting and came towards the wagons, smelling their booty. The traders were dead scared to confront them with their flimsy swords and daggers. The brigands broke open the sealed boxes in the carts and pulled out whatever appeared to them as valuable.

But the breakup in the ranks of the bandits cost them a lot. Revata attacked the flank of the bandits ferociously. He slashed at the back of a knee of one of the bandits with his sword, causing the raider to cry out in pain. Another security guard plunged his sword into a horse's throat. The animal screamed and collapsed, bleeding profusely, causing the rider to lurch on its side. Revata caught him unguarded and plunged his sword into the bandit's throat as blood gurgled out like water would from a partly blocked tap. Both master and animal lay spread on the ground with their throats slit and life ebbing away.

One of the carts raiding bandits came hurtling towards Sudjata's cart, keen to carry away some booty before it was too late. Sudjata's heart sank. Why should he select his cart of all carts? The bandit was a tall and heavy bloke who looked ferocious with a big scar on his forehead visible above the mask.

Chandaka took Sudjata by the arm and whispered to him to keep his head down. But Sudjata didn't want to part with his precious goods. What if they tied the bullocks to the cart and ferreted it away entirely with its goods? That would be the end of his career. The horror of going back to report to his *setthi* with no cart gave him courage. He stood up and raised his sword as if the bandit will be chastened by it.

'Sudjata, don't be a fool!' shouted Chandaka.

But Sudjata took a step forward with intense belief in his prowess with the sword. Another bandit took advantage of Sudjata's engagement in another direction and started ransacking his cart. In his hurry, Sudjata stumbled over a stone and fell right in front of the heavy bandit who raised his sword to cut him into two or more pieces. Just when Sudjata tried to evade his strike with a desperate kick, the bandit turned back to stop a rider charging at him with a blood curdling cry. He was not quick enough. Revata came from behind and landed a mighty blow on the bandit's shoulder with his sword. He emitted a horrendous cry and slumped to the ground.

Some of the bandits had already left with their loot not wanting to stay till the outcome of the duel was clear. It was a ragtag team not bound by any loyalty or principles. Two brigands were lying sprawled, blood pouring from stab wounds. They were thin, their clothes ragged and weapons rusted. Clearly it was a do or die battle for them. One security guard had lost his life in the short battle.

Sudjata thanked Revata profusely. His cart had been ransacked but his life was intact.

✳ ✳ ✳

The sun had broken out by the time the security guards washed their weapons and faces in a nearby stream. They were more vigilant now with their daggers jutting out from their belts and axes and spears strapped to their saddles. The traders harnessed their bullocks to their carts and the caravan started moving towards Kaushambi.

Towards noon they saw a long parapet wall of stone climbing a steep hill, revealing battlements and army reinforcements. As the road narrowed on top, a watchtower rose majestically. The caravan riders could see some movements on the watch towers. The rocky slopes would deter any enemy attack from advancing from the sides of the hill. This was an outpost fort of the Magadhan empire.

From here stretched the most fertile plains of the doab, the area between the banks of the converging Yamuna and the Ganges rivers. This was the centre of the second urbanization when great cities and kingdoms sprouted all over the area like mushrooms in autumn. The carts trundled through tranquil land, at least for the time being, on whose rich black soil grew many varieties of cereals and millets well-fed from the waters of the rivers through tributaries and channels. Hundreds of lakes shone like diamonds under surya's penetrating rays.

Tall flat-topped mountains of the Vindhya range overlooked the rivers, the lakes, the highway and the Gangetic Plains. Travelers could see rivers and falls flowing down the ranges like silver necklaces adorning a stony bosom.

Traders, mendicants and peasants who were part of the caravan spoke less now. They wanted to reach Kaushambi as soon as possible without any more mishaps. Sudjata spent more time with Chandaka and Revata during their rest hours. They discussed life in Pataliputra, the risks that traders and security guards had to take to make a decent living, the mounting corruption and the possibility of a civil war. It was going to be a tough job for them to explain the loss of goods to their *setthi*. But, as yet, they didn't want to think about it.

The night before the caravan reached Kaushambi, the three of them talked about the changing world around them. Chandaka started the conversation. 'Our king, Dhanananda, has been making massive investments in expanding his army—one reason why we all have to pay more taxes. He wants to subjugate Vatsa, Anga and Kalinga, but that's going to take a big toll on people.'

'That's very worrying,' responded Sudjata with concern. 'When kings decide to expand their empire, it is traders, peasants and artisans who get hurt most. First they pay for the war and then they pay again for post-war reconstruction.'

'Wars also help kings to put down internal rebellions and quell any dissent,' continued Chandaka in agreement. 'That's why in spite of having the biggest army among all the mahajanapadas, Dhanananda's greed is not satisfied.'

Revata also joined the discussion. 'There is so much seething discontent in the empire that Dhanananda has to rely on the support of both the Brahmin and Buddhist establishments.'

'How come?' asked Sudjata. 'The brahmana priests had called him the fallen kshatriya because he was supposedly born in the barber community.'

'He doesn't appreciate that title at all but it is important for him to keep the brahmana high priests happy. The priests also don't have a choice because the Buddhist establishment is getting closer to the king,' explained Chandaka.

'That's very much there,' seconded Revata. 'Look at how many traders are joining the Buddhist sangha. For them it is an upward movement from their reviled shudra status.'

'How long will traders and artisans be at the bottom rung of the caste system!' spat Sudjata. 'As they get more educated and prosperous they are looking for an escape from rituals and gift giving.'

'In fact, many wealthy traders like our *setthi* are trying to get recognized by the sangha by giving generous donations,' said Chandaka.

'Hope that doesn't corrupt Buddhism and introduce rituals and gift giving into it,' reacted Sudjata with a tone of foreboding.

'I know the head of the Buddhist sangha in Kaushambi. He is a very learned and practical man. In these times so full of uncertainties it will be a good idea to meet him and get some gyan from him,' suggested Chandaka.

Revata and Sudjata nodded vigorously. 'Yes, we should,' they concurred.

Sudjata had trouble sleeping that night. The encounter with the brigands lasted just a few minutes but he remembered every bit of the assault. It was a surprise to him that he was not terrorized by the raid, the way many other traders were. He acted courageously and wasn't afraid to pick up the sword. Traders were reviled for being spineless but he was certainly not one of them. Chandaka also proved that he was a leader who boldly came out to protect his folk without worrying about the consequences to himself. Revata too turned out to be a warrior with his heart in the right place, not a self-serving mercenary. He felt he can trust them. With that decision, he slept peacefully.

13

FROM THE BRINK OF DEATH

Susmila – Kaushambi – 329 BCE

Susmila got up before the dawn pushed away the darkness that enveloped the village and forest lands nearby. If she didn't wake up this early and finish her work, there would be no end to her mother-in-law's taunts till the next dawn. If everything goes well, all that she can expect is some peace in the house. She never looked forward to a few good words of praise; that never happened.

She went around tending to the cows, goats and pigs. After that, she gathered twigs, branches and forest wood for the oven and the hearth. Lifting buckets of water from the well was the most strenuous. The screeching sound of the water pulley went on and on until all the pots were filled. The sun had come out and the village markets were astir when she heard a Buddhist monk at her door asking for alms. 'Mai, bhiksham dehi.' He had a wooden bowl in his right hand and a wooden staff in the left. As Susmila approached him, he lowered his eyes in deference, as most bikshus do. But when she turned around to get some rice for him, her mother-in-law, Mahishi, shoved her aside.

'Let me handle this; go and do your work,' she said gruffly. Her words fell like a lash on Susmila. Mahishi turned towards the young bhikshu and invited him to sit on the low bench just inside the door. He entered hesitantly and sat where she pointed.

'Get some water, Susmila. Why are you waddling slowly like a goose, hurry up!' she shouted.

When Susmila returned with a cup of water, Mahishi snatched it from her. 'I will give the water! A widow should keep a distance from holy men,' she announced, adding a new rule in the already large dos and don'ts compilation that existed for widows.

Mahishi then started complaining to the bhikshu as if he were a family member. He had come very recently to the vihara near the village and had visited quite a few times but had not shown any special interest so far in knowing their family matters. But Mahishi needed a listening ear, particularly today.

'I don't know what I did in my previous karma,' she started in a melancholic tone just short of a wail. 'I have lost my beloved son when he had just been married and now I am saddled with his widow. I don't know whether it is because of my sin or the sin of this wretch who was the cause for Yama snatching away my son.'

Charudatta, the bhikshu, did not know what to do. Every time he had come to this house, he had heard Mahishi yell at her daughter-in-law. But today she was intent on pouring out all her heartaches to him. He pitied Susmila who seemed to be living quite literally in hell.

He tried to calm down Mahishi and said, 'I don't think you or your daughter-in-law is responsible for your son's death. It is not because of someone's sin in the previous birth that he or she is punished in this birth. Buddha teaches that what you do in this world is all-important which requires that all human beings should be treated with compassion.'

'It is fortunate that she didn't have a child with my son. Otherwise, I would have had two lives to support with my meagre income. My younger son is a good-for-nothing drunkard. I begged Susmila to marry him but she refused. Arrogant woman!' cursed Mahishi.

'No woman should be forced to marry against her wishes. It should be on her own accord,' said Charudatta gently.

Mahishi was not impressed. 'Hmm...' she shook her head. 'This is all theoretical humbug. A woman has to be subservient to her husband and to the house she has made her home. Look at her; even her parents don't want her back.'

Charudatta stood up and politely avoiding any further curses from Mahishi, left the house. As he went out, he could see Susmila washing a huge pile of clothes near the well. He had noticed that she was beautiful with fair skin, long black hair reaching up to her waist and prominent cheek bones. A sparkle of wisdom shone from her dark oval-shaped eyes. It was a pity that she has to live the life of a widow.

❋ ❋ ❋

For Susmila, life was merciless. It was one long dreary stretch with few excitements in between. Her husband had not been a bad chap. As long as he was alive, she did all the household chores and faced her mother-in-law's taunts but there were some moments of peace with him. She looked forward to having a child who, she hoped, would definitely bring some cheer and hope to her drab existence. But before that could happen, her husband passed away. They thought that the tumour in his chest would disappear soon but she never imagined that it will turn malignant and take him away forever in a fleeting few weeks. She had heard of the dog's life that fate offers widows but never imagined that it will be this demeaning. Many times she even contemplated jumping into the well and ending her life. If she had known how her life as a widow would pan out, she would have jumped into the funeral pyre of her husband.

She was treated as an inauspicious being who can only bring ill luck to the house and her community. She was kept away from festivals, for everyone believed that her presence will only spoil the fun. For all practical purposes she lived like an ascetic. She slept on the bare floor, got up before everyone else, ate food after everyone and went to bed after cleaning the kitchen.

Even her food was restricted. She was not supposed to eat anything that can be considered tasty and sweet. She hadn't tasted salt, honey, meat or wine from the day she became a widow. Her mother-in-law took away all her ornaments even though they were given by her parents. If she had a child, her property would have gone to the child but even that was not possible now.

She remembered how her mother-in-law screamed and pulled her hair when she saw her wearing her bangles and bracelet on a festival. At just twenty-one she could not resist it. Mahishi cursed her and taunted her that she would soon turn into a strumpet if she cannot control her desires. *They are scared I will be unfaithful to the departed spirit of my husband!*

She had heard about women sages such as Gargi and Lopamudra who were revered Vedic seers, who wrote verses and were considered no less than men in philosophical debates. In one of her debates with Yajnavalkya, the well-known sage, she had irritated him so much with searching questions that he jokingly teased her saying, 'Gargi, you mustn't ask too much, or your head will drop off!'[iv]

There were many goddesses whom people flocked to visit. In the South, it seemed, such goddesses were countless. There were stories that some of the kings even hired women as their bodyguards.

But her own status was worse than that of the village donkey. She could not understand why women can be revered at one end and despised and treated as chattel at another.

She had seen the monk Charudatta visiting her house a few times and heard him give some sensible advice to Mahishi. Once he had invited everyone to a Buddhist sermon nearby. Susmila waited until her mother-in-law left the house and sneaked away quietly behind her to the sermon. A senior monk from Kaushambi spoke about Buddha's teachings and exhorted them to become upasaka or upasikas. This meant that they need not renounce social life and become a bhikshu or a bhikshuni. They can be lay followers and give alms and donations to the sangha.

The senior monk invited all of them to become followers. He said, 'We do not believe in the karma of past lives. We believe in one's karma in this life. You can improve your karma in this life if you follow the Eightfold Path. You don't have to perform rituals or give gifts to brahmanas.'

This appealed to Susmila. This meant that her sins in her past life were not responsible for her being turned into a widow in this world. That was superbly comforting!

What he said later caught her attention even more. 'We do not differentiate people because of their varna and jati. They exist in our society; we cannot wish them away. But anyone can join the sangha, even chandalas and widows,' he reiterated.

'Varna is a man-made social order,' he continued. 'It is not a divine sanction as the brahmanical system claims. Since it is man-made, it can also be changed by man.'

Finally, he concluded his sermon with the remarks, 'This universe was not created by god. It has existed forever and follows its own cosmic cycle. Once upon a time this universe was bliss. But it has now become a place of suffering because humans capitulated to desire. Until they let go of their desires man cannot liberate himself from sufferings and attain nirvana.'

* * *

For the first time in her life after widowhood, hope flowed in Susmila's veins. She made sure that when Charudatta visited her house the next time, she found a way to talk to him without her mother-in-law's knowledge.

Charudatta did not mind talking to her. He had noticed her isolation and had wanted to help her. Is that not the sacred duty of a monk?

They found a way to meet and discuss now and then, away from the prying eyes and ears of her in-laws and neighbours. Charudatta gave her a lot of comfort. He made her feel that her life is not a waste.

'It is possible to attain the highest goal of nibbana in our sangha,' he said with conviction. 'Buddha has even allowed the creation of a bhikkuni sangha exclusively for nuns. You can live with respect and peace there,' he exhorted.

'We are living in a world where women are treated subservient to men. How is it possible that in your sangha alone women will be treated well?' Susmila asked while desperate to believe that it is possible.

Charudatta had a convincing answer to that. 'Buddha himself was against establishing the bhikkuni sangha because he felt that women will be a distraction for the monks but his most beloved disciple, Ananda, convinced him that it is necessary considering that so many women are burdened by Vedic rituals and smritis. Since then women have joined us in large numbers.'

'Should I take my in-laws' permission if I want to join the sangha?' asked Susmila. 'For all you know, they may actually be happy to get rid of me. I don't mind leaving my jewels here. But she may also object just to spite me.'

'In the normal course, women have to take permission from their husbands or parents. But in your case, your husband is no more and your parents have given you up,' assured Charudatta.

Susmila's mind was made up. She requested Charudatta that when the next sermon takes place, she would like to meet the senior monk and request to be inducted into the sangha. Charudatta agreed eagerly.

When the next sermon took place, Susmila stayed in the shadows until the senior monk, Aniruddha, had talked about the life of Buddha and his path of salvation.

A few villagers went up to the monk and asked him questions about getting inducted into the sangha. They were chandalas making their living through hunting and gathering forest produce. Susmila boldly came forward and requested that she wanted to speak.

Aniruddha asked her to say what was on her mind. Mahishi and her husband Vinaya were surprised at Susmila's audaciousness. They were confused what to do but they had to keep quiet in front of this large crowd which was not ignorant of the treatment given to Susmila

Susmila came forward and said hesitatingly, 'Respected bhikshu ji, I am a widow and would like to join the sangha and serve the society just like you.' She was herself surprised at how she worked up the nerve to announce this decision.

'All those who come with a pure heart and selfless desire are welcome into the sangha,' replied Aniruddha in a kind tone.

Mahishi rushed to the front and said, 'Pardon me, bhikshu ji. She is my daughter-in-law. She has been a curse to our house. She will bring only misfortune if she joins the sangha.'

Aniruddha glanced at Charudatta who gave him a knowing smile. He had already appraised the elder bhikshu about Susmila's condition and her wish.

'How can we speak so ill of widows and chandalas?' he asked in a loud but calm voice to the crowd which had gathered to watch the scene unfolding between Susmila and her mother-in-law. 'They are no less human than we are. They have already gone through enough suffering. Instead of showing compassion should we heap more insults on them? How can you get rid of sins if you treat your own relatives and neighbours like animals to be beaten and forced to labour? If a community cannot give a decent life to its members why should it worry if a member leaves for a better destination?'

Mahishi was speechless. Except for a few in the village who considered Buddhist monks as heretics, others were open to what they preached.

Aniruddha turned towards Susmila. 'Charudatta has spoken to me about you. But I have to confirm again. Do you want to join the sangha of your own free will? There will be many restrictions on nuns. Will you be willing to abide by them?' he enquired.

Susmila had no hesitation. She had already thought about what it would mean. She had come to the decision that life outside the village cannot be worse than what it was now. She replied, 'Yes, respected bhikshu ji. I have made up my mind.'

Aniruddha looked at the assembled villagers. Except for some murmurings from Mahishi, they all seemed to accept Susmila's decision.

Aniruddha turned to Susmila and said, 'If you want to come with us you can do so right away. Don't worry about your belongings. You will be well looked after in our sangha.'

A well-built tribal youth with curly black hair and only a small waist cloth wound around his groin came forward. His face was glistening with sweat. He explained how difficult survival was for him. He had to clean the sewerage of the landlords in the village and bury the dead. He wanted to join the sangha. A few others also volunteered to join. Life in the village was a torture for them.

Susmila quietly followed them after giving the village one long look.

14

A Network Of Rebels

Satya – Vidisha – 329 BCE

It was after three months that Satya and his friends were able to make the trip to Vidisha. On horseback it was less than a day's trip from Ujjayini. This time Madanika too accompanied them. Satya had a tough time pacifying her for leaving her out of the trip to Bhrgukachha. When he narrated the adventures after he returned, Madanika became so morose that it took several days for him to get back to normal conversations with her.

As they neared the city, the traffic on the roads increased. Vidisha was an important trade junction for traders between the north and the south. As a hub for ivory carvers it attracted a lot of business.

It was almost sunset when the travellers reached the confluence of the Betwa and Bes rivers over which the city gates towered.

The Buddhist vihara at Vidisha was a spartan building. The main porch led to an open court which had open cells carved out all along its walls. The cells had stone beds and stone pillows for the monks to lay their heads on. Outside the porch there was a verandah which could be used for congregations during the warmer part of the year. Right in the middle of the back wall of the central court a small stupa housed Buddha's relics.

The vihara was a temporary resting place for monks during the severe monsoons when it was near impossible to travel on foot for spreading the message of the Buddha. Over a period of time, thanks to monks confined to a single space for months, the vihara had become a centre for discussing politics and philosophy. This was not peculiar only to Buddhist ascetics. Viharas were also built for ascetics belonging to other schools of thought such as Ajivikas, Jain and other Vedic schools. These viharas were initially built with donations from people in the surrounding villages who would also feed and clothe the monks. Later, they attracted donations from well-to-do urban traders. Many a time, kings and nobles undertook the construction of viharas to convince their subjects about their piety and generosity.

✳ ✳ ✳

When Satya and his friends entered the monastery, Ananda was engaged in an intense debate with a few other monks.

'We should not take sides between the king and his Mahamatra in this war,' he was passionately arguing. 'We should have our own plan. Neither Magadha nor the northern states are interested in our people. If we keep quiet, after the war we will be either vassals of Magadha or Sikandar, whoever wins.'

The monk sitting across from him, Shibanand, made a wry face. 'I agree we should not keep quiet. But if we don't support a side, we will get squashed like flies between two rocks,' he said vehemently. 'In this I think we should put our bet on Sikandar. If we stand on the side of our Mahamatra, then Avanti has a chance of becoming a satrapy of Sikandar. That will keep us away from the clutches of Dhanananda.'

'We should neither come into the clutches of Dhanananda nor Sikandar. There are forces throughout Bharatavarsha who are against warmongers and monarchs. Should we not strengthen their hands?' asked Ananda passionately.

About fifty monks were gathered around them participating in the debate. Many of them seemed to be on the side of Ananda who was popular in the vihara.

Ananda was tall but slight. His face had a weathered look, a product of frequent and long travels. He wore the simple monk's tunic and old sandals. He had a white scarf pinned to the tunic with a wooden clasp. Now and then he wiped his oily face with the scarf.

The entry of the visitors put a temporary halt to the debate. Ananda got up and welcomed the visitors with a warm smile.

✳ ✳ ✳

'I will get you a place to stay at the nearby inn,' he said as he led the way. 'You are not used to stone beds and pillows. Moreover, women are not allowed to stay inside the men's monastery,' he announced, grinning. 'Also, we can have a confidential chat.'

The inn was as spartan as the monastery but had comfortable cots with sheets of white linen. The visitors felt starved and the steaming hot food from the kitchen was greatly welcomed.

'There is news from Suvala,' said Ananda straightaway getting to business. 'Sikandar is encountering a lot of resistance from various tribes which is slowing down his advance into Bharatavarsha.[v] His army reached Marakanda but he had to recoup. So, in the beautiful valley of Polytimetos he spent some time replenishing his cavalry and recruited more mercenaries. He then advanced to the Jaxartes river where the Scythian tribes are valiantly confronting his huge army now. Many mercenaries are deserting his army. Also, he has to leave behind some of his trained officers and soldiers to hold onto the areas he conquered.'

Satya and others were glued to what Ananda was describing like an audience watching a magician. Ananda took a sip of hot porridge from his bowl and continued, 'Cyrus, the defeated Persian emperor, had built a number of fortified towns to keep these tribals away. Sikandar captured all these fortresses. He has even built a new town called Alexandria. In the middle of all this, Spitamenes, the Sogdian leader and his army have rebelled against him.'

'That is very heartening to hear. It shows that his army is not invincible. With courage one can confront his army. But neither the King of Avanti nor the King of Magadha are bothered,' spat Satya with bitterness.

Bala was concentrating on his soup while Madanika was looking at Ananda with awe for the massive information transfer that he was doing.

For Sajjalaka, all this sounded very interesting. He was wondering how a few blacksmiths from a corner of Ujjayini got into the centre of a political discussion that had repercussions for the entire region.

'How can we change the situation?' asked Madanika coming out of her thrall.

'Don't think that we are alone,' assured Ananda lowering his voice. 'We have built a network of rebels across many kingdoms.'

Satya wondered whom the we meant.

'We have sent our members even to the southern kingdoms to keep the people informed and mobilise them so that they don't remain bystanders in this fast-changing situation,' Ananda continued. 'There are people from all walks of life who support us. We have ascetics, artisans, traders, farmers and soldiers who are willing to join us,' he said, eyes sparkling with pride under the light of the oil lamps in the inn.

'Will crores of people spread over many kingdoms give up their ignorance and unite for a cause?' asked Satya with a healthy amount of skepticism.

'Why not?' challenged Ananda. 'Look at me. At one point in time, I was a bandit,' he announced, shocking the wits out of the small band of listeners around him. 'But one sermon changed my life. It is not that I believe in Buddhism blindly. All religions have their faults. I am constantly searching for the truth. So, I am not really worried about where I am now; I am committed to the larger cause.'

'Yes, our conviction has to come from the heart,' said Bala who now seemed to be convinced that something could be done.

'Coming back to my question,' reminded Madanika, 'what does all this mean for us?'

'All of us should stand in our place and contribute to this great cause. You can mobilise people in your colony,' suggested Ananda. 'You can organise meetings and make them political. With perseverance they will come around.'

'That is what we have already been doing,' replied Sajjalaka. 'We are already known as rebels and have entered the bad books of the Mahamatra. It is hard to say whether we are thrilled or worried about it.'

Ananda laughed along with others. 'Yes, time is short,' he said. 'I have some supporters in this vihara who have been spreading the political message among the people in this city. But there are agents of the Mahamatra in the vihara too.'

Satya and his friends exchanged knowing glances.

'You are being watched. So, be careful,' warned Ananda. 'At the same time, we have to do some propaganda. We cannot keep quiet. How about organising a public meeting in your city next month?' he proposed.

This seemed feasible to Satya. One had to take risks in these times and be courageous. This is kaliyug!

'We have been toting with the idea of holding our Agaria tribal conference soon. I have consulted many elders of other tribe. They are eager that we should have one soon. If we are able to manage a large gathering, the administration of Avanti will think twice before laying a hand on us.'

'That's an excellent idea,' responded Ananda with appreciation. 'I will also communicate to the viharas to join your efforts. Let us give a strong message to the king and Mahamatra.'

✳ ✳ ✳

Bala and Sajjalaka had already gone to sleep. They decided to stay back in Vidisha for the night and leave early morning the next day.

Satya strolled out of the monastery to the banyan tree near the central water well. He sat down on the circular stone seat built around the tree hoping to think calmly about the huge task in front of him. Was he entangling the Agarias in politics and intrigue?

He recalled the stories that his father used to tell him about the history of Agarias and their myths, magic and rituals. He loved each one of them. His father narrated stories in such wonderful way that the characters and incidents came to life and reached out to him with their joy, agony, frustration and optimism.

The Agarias were spread over the entire Gangetic basin and to the south and east of the basin. His father recalled how even at the time of his grandparents they were forest dwellers. Most forest dwelling tribes were not just hunters and brigands, as the city people were made to believe. Each one of them had a skill which they preserved and developed even under the harshest conditions of forest life.

The Agarias loved their craft and their material. Their existence was intimately tied to the roar of the bellows and the clang of hammer upon iron. Forest conditions snatched away their lives early.

When they visited cities to sell their wares, they were treated even worse than the shudras. But the huge demand for iron and steel brought about by the second urbanisation brought them nearer to the cities, even inside the city gates but on the peripheries. Peasants and artisans loved the tools made from the malleable iron produced in open smelters by the Agarias but it had been a hard battle to win recognition as a professional tribe and still was. It is time the Agarias put their stamp on the new Bharatavarsha when it was malleable and hot.

Satya and his friends left Vidisha early the next day confident that the Agarias will have a say in the future trajectory of Bharatavarsha.

15

Escape From Puhar

Madhavi – Puhar – 329 BCE

'Oh, why should they arrest a monk!?' reacted Madhavi sharply. She could not believe her ears. She had met Vallabh a few months back at the Paravar colony by chance and now he has again entered her life in another far-off place. All their meetings have been unplanned so far!

'I don't know,' said Vengayyan. 'Right now he is being taken to the quarters near our colony by a couple of highway guards. They must have arrested him on the highway.'

'Is it possible to talk to him?' asked Nandi.

'I can arrange that. I know one of the local guards in whose custody they have left him to go to the city and report to their commander. We can have a quick chat with him if we go right away.'

The three of them left immediately, walking at a brisk pace towards the quarters.

Vallabh looked exhausted but cheered up when he saw them. Vengayyan's guard friend left them alone with the instruction that they should not stay too long.

'What happened? How dare they arrest a monk!' asked Madhavi in exasperation.

'Oh, they think I am a spy from the north planning to learn the secrets about their fortifications,' quipped the monk. 'I have been travelling around and making detailed sketches of cities and forts because I am really interested in studying the history and culture of this region. But in these days of mistrust and war mongering, it is easy to pick up anyone as anti-national and a spy.'

'This may lead to serious actions; we cannot allow that!' cried Madhavi wringing her hands.

'It is not a good situation here. The commander can take any action. He may hesitate to punish a monk but you never know. No point in taking a risk,' advised Vengayyan.

'Is there a way to get him out of here?' asked Nandi in a whisper.

'This guard here belongs to our community. So, we can put pressure on him to give up the monk. But he should be able to give a possible story to the highway guards when they learn that the monk has escaped,' said Vengayyan.

The three of them looked at him with sudden respect. Madhavi would have never imagined that Vengayyan had this side to him.

'Let me speak with the guard,' said Vengayyan. He turned towards Nandi. 'Meanwhile, get your carts ready. We have to leave the city right away before the gates close for the night. Madhavi amma, you should also go with him.'

❈ ❈ ❈

Nandi and Madhavi left immediately to get the carts ready with goods and provisions for the journey. Luckily, all the purchases had been done. The sun had set and by the time they reached the gate it was already the end of the first jaamam.[vi] There was no time to lose.

Vengayyan soon arrived with the monk who looked more relaxed. He had been fed some kanji on the way. They got into the front cart and moved towards the exit gate.

'How did you manage to get him out?' asked Nandi. He felt like he was dreaming. Things were moving fast and he hardly had any time to think about the consequences.

'That was tough business,' replied Vengayyan with a tone of importance. 'My friend, the guard, has to protect his job. We had to think of a convincing story. I had to punch him in the face, tie him up and gag him. When the highway guards come back, they will find him tied up with bruises. He will tell them that he was overpowered by a deadly gang of armed assassins.'

Nandi hoped that the guards believe his story and set themselves in pursuit of a deadly gang. They would certainly not suspect a goods-laden cart.

Getting out of the gate was not difficult given the nice tip that Nandi pressed into the palms of the chief of gatekeepers. He had shown them all the tokens for duties that he had paid earlier. Hence, it was a regular affair. Moreover, there was no lookout call for an escaped prisoner.

Nandi got the carts moving quickly trying to be as far away as possible from the city gates before they had to stop at an inn for the night.

At the break of dawn they had a quick breakfast and started moving along the southern bank of Kaveri towards Uraiyur. The river flowed in a tranquil mood, the carpet of flowers floating on her waters swaying like a garland on a damsel on her way to meet her beloved. Peacocks strutted and spread their patterned plumage in the flowery groves on the banks. All along the bank, koels made their incessant mating calls perched on tall trees overlooking the river. Bright pink and white lotuses peeped out of lakes flaunting their large petals and leaves.

Madhavi and Vallabh were huddled in the leading cart driven by Nandi. Vengayyan and a couple of his friends from the fishermen's colony travelled in the cart behind.

***

'What do you plan to do now?' asked Madhavi once they were well away from Puhar. Till then they were half expecting the highway guards to come galloping after them.

Vallabh started speaking as if he hadn't registered the question. 'I have learnt a lot about your Thamizhagam in these months,' he announced. 'Yours is a very ancient civilisation. Sometimes I think it is even more ancient than that of the Gangetic Plains where I come from.' He paused here thoughtfully and drank some water out of the terracotta pot they had carried along with them.

Nandi and Madhavi waited for him to continue.

'I studied your script. There is a definite link between the Tamil Brahmi you are using now and the Indus Valley script that was used some 5000 years ago till about 1500 years ago. But I am now convinced that the civilisation and script did not vanish. People from the Indus Valley migrated to many other places in India.'

The carts were now travelling through paddy and sugarcane fields. A few black buffaloes emerged from the murky waters of the field and turned their heads around to inspect the travellers with their red eyes. Waterfowls of different types swam around in the wet field, occasionally flapping their wings noisily as they hopped from one pond to another. Sounds and chirps made by white cranes, red-footed swans, green-footed herons, water crows, fish, birds and insects regaled the travellers on the highway.

Madhavi looked at the scenes that passed by in fascination.

'I came across a lot of graffiti which resemble the Indus script. That means your language has ancient roots. Your cities are as well developed as the cities in the north. For more than 200 or 300 years now, your authors and poets have been producing written works.'

'Does it mean that at one time Dravidians were spread throughout Bharatavarsha?' asked Madhavi in a startled tone. What the monk was saying blew her mind.

'It is quite possible. But over the last 5000 years, especially from the last 1500 years, the great cities that the Indus civilisation built started withering away, probably due to change in course of rivers or a decrease in trade. Some of them might have migrated to the south too because there are also local tribes here with their own customs, gods and burial sites. Some say that the Indus Valley and Dravidian civilisations are one and the same.' Vallabh looked around him again as if he were gathering his thoughts. It seemed to Madhavi that he was just thinking aloud.

He added with caution, 'Both the Indo-Aryan and Indus civilisations have influenced each other and even use Brahmi as a common script though their languages are different.[vii] Vedic schools of thought, Buddhist and Jain philosophies, aastik and naastik viewpoints have spread to all corners of Bharatavarsha, including yours.'

Nandi was overhearing the conversation from where he directed the oxen. He chose to remain silent. The fields were agog with activity at this time of the year. Huge mounds of grain were being stored in large straw granaries from where sheaves of paddy were jutting out like the hand fan made from the fur of the kavari yak. Ploughmen were breaking ground using their ploughshares. Women cultivators sung the mugavai song with melody while they drove their cattle over paddy sheaves threshing out the corn. Minstrels stopped them on the way and entertained them with songs to the accompaniment of their tabor and flute.

As they went past villages, they could see bundles of sugar cane stems heaped outside homes and rows of ovens in the open emitting fumes from the boiling cane juice.

'Vallabh anna,' called Madhavi, addressing the monk with respect, 'if the people of Bharatavarsha are linked in some way, then why are we divided into so many parts?'

The Jain monk chuckled. 'That's a good question. Our rulers don't let us unite. They keep us divided for their own ends. Every king here wants to build an empire using public money so that they can lord over the land and the people.'

'Then what is the way out?' asked Nandi, intervening for the first time.

'It is a mammoth task, but it can be done,' replied the monk. 'There are people who are concerned about the future of Bharatavarsha, just like us, everywhere in this land. We must make them understand that while there are enemies at our gates waiting to plunder our land, there are enemies within who have kept our land divided. I have met many such people during my travels. A time will come when proper leadership will emerge to lead this movement of the people. It will have people from all regions, religions and caste. Brahmin priests will mingle with the shudras and chandalas. Buddhist and Jain ascetics will be talking to women, youth, artisans and peasants. No one will be denied entry into this movement. Let us hope that this will take place in the near future.'

Madhavi guessed that the monk knew much more about the movements in the rest of Bharatavarsha than what he revealed. Perhaps he is not yet convinced that they will be on his side. At the same time, she was not sure whether to fully trust him. There was too much he was hiding, and his actions didn't look like those belonging to the regular routine of monks. But there was something fascinating about him. He stood apart from her regular acquaintances.

On the way, Vallabh made them take a small detour after crossing Uraiyur to a hill called Sittanavasal. He spent some time at the foothills looking for entry points and trails to the top of the hill. 'This will be a good place for our monks to make their simple homes,' he murmured.

After crossing the Sirumalai hills he stopped at a hill near the Keezhakuyilkudi village, just a few kadams from Madurai.

Later, after reaching home, Madhavi tossed around in her bed thinking about her long trip. She had a hunch that it was not going to be business as usual from now on.

16

A Turning Point

Sudjata – Kaushambi – 328 BCE

The city of Kaushambi stood tall in all its splendor. From a small town established by the Kuru kingdom several centuries back, it had now blossomed into one of the greatest cities in the Gangetic belt. It was the capital of the kingdom of Vatsa situated near the confluence of the Ganga and Yamuna. Its central location on both the river and road trade routes brought prosperity and attracted the best minds of the time. It controlled trade both along the Uttarapatha and the Dakshinapatha.

Sudjata's caravan entered the eastern gate of the city. The city was fortified with numerous bastions, gates and sub-gates and encircled by a wide and deep moat. The part of the city where wealthy merchants lived boasted of many tall buildings with decorated balconies, windows and doors. The city took its name from sage Kusumba who once ran a hermitage nearby.

Sudjata knew that Chandaka had visited the monastery at Kaushambi quite often. Hence, was not surprised when he led them without any difficulty after entering the city gates. Sudjata found a lot in Chandaka to admire. He was level-headed and cool when faced with problems. He remembered how Chandaka had gathered his flock of traders and protected them when the bandits struck. Back in Pataliputra, Sudjata knew him to be an honest trader and respected in the traders' guild. His knowledge of roads and sea routes was simply first-rate. *I have found a trustworthy friend.*

The monastery at Kaushambi, like other Buddhist monasteries, had its individual existence. There was no central authority above it. In a way, it was a law unto itself, guided by the Master of the Order. The monastery was run on democratic lines. The chief monk was not appointed from above or nominated by his predecessor but elected by all the member monks.[viii]

The day to day functioning of the monastery was looked after by a committee of elder monks and the chief monk had to consult them before taking any important decision. But important decisions were taken by the entire monastery in congregations.

The chief monk, Aniruddha, was addressing one such congregation when the visitors entered.

'My dear brothers,' he appealed, 'it has become all the more important in today's circumstances when dukkha, the suffering, is increasing, that all of us need to feel boundless love for the entire world, above, below and across, unrestrained without enmity towards anyone. Our biggest treasure cannot be material things.' Aniruddha paused and looked around at his companions. They were listening intently. He wiped beads of sweat from his forehead with the edge of his robe and continued.

'We have to remember the story of the man who buried his treasure in a deep pit thinking that it will come in useful when there is a war or when the business suffers a loss or if he goes out of favour with the king. But when the real need came, he became agitated because he could not find the treasure. He was not sure whether he buried it in another place or some burglars had removed it. There is no use for such treasure. Real treasure is charity, goodness, restraint and self-control. This applies to us as well as to our sister nuns. This treasure cannot be given to others. This treasure cannot be stolen. This treasure will always be with us till we reach our graves.'

Sudjata looked around at the congregation. There were young and older monks. He was surprised to see even nuns attending the gathering. One of them looked too young and radiated peace and happiness. It appeared as if she had entered a new fascinating world.

Aniruddha now came to the main point.

'We became ascetics, not because we wanted to run away from our unhappy lives or from this world of miseries. Where can we go? The real reason why we became ascetics was that we had a thirst for knowledge. We wanted to find the truth. We were not satisfied with Vedic orthodoxy which is moving away from enlightenment and towards blind devotion and rituals.'

The monastery had a high ceiling and every word the monk spoke seemed to echo against the walls and amplify the serious tone of the message. Sudjata moved a bit closer. He could appreciate the speech.

'There is a lot of anxiety today among the people of this subcontinent. Old tribal links are breaking apart. People are now standing face to face with a new bewildering world. They have to fend for themselves. They can no longer rely on their kinsmen. Smaller republics and kingdoms are getting gobbled up by empires.

'This has been so well expressed in the Maitrayani Upanishad through the voice of a king. He says "Great heroes and mighty kings have had to give up their glory; we have seen the deaths of demigods and demons; the oceans have dried up; mountains have crumbled; the Pole Star is shaken; the Earth flounders; the gods perish. I am like a frog in a dry well.'"[ix]

There was a round of applause and nodding of heads. The audience was with the speaker.

One of the older monks put up his hand. Aniruddha gestured for him to speak.

'Respected bhikshu,' he began, 'what you are saying is true. The world has become topsy-turvy. But we ascetics have our own karma and dharma. How can we do anything to change today's world?'

Some of the younger monks smiled at each other. They were used to this older monk asking questions. Sometimes he seemed to be genuinely seeking an answer. Sometimes it looked like he did this to get the younger monks to open up.

Aniruddha continued his lecture trying to address the question. His tone was persuasive. He did not like to rabble rouse generally and certainly not this time.

'Our deeds in this life, our karma, is not determined by what we did in our earlier lives, as we are told to believe. It has come in handy to some to explain away the mystery of our suffering in this world or why men are born unequal. But we don't believe in the cycle of birth and rebirth, samsara or the transmigration of soul.'

One of the younger monks interjected and asked, 'Even if we don't believe in the cycle of rebirth, will good deeds guarantee that we attain nirvana?'

Aniruddha did not consider this as an impetuous question. He was happy that the younger monks were building the courage to ask questions without worrying whether they will be called fools. It seemed to Sudjata that the sermon which had started in a languorous pace had now gathered speed.

'There is no guarantee for anything,' said Aniruddha with a smile. 'We have to live by our conscience. There is enough speculation going on about what will happen to our soul after death. The Charvakas say that there is no such thing as a soul and when the body dies, everything dies. So, let us think about what kind of deeds are required from us in this world.'

'You also mentioned dharma,' the older monk reminded.

'Yes,' said Aniruddha. 'Both karma and dharma are connected. There is no point in doing good deeds in the abstract. How do we know they are good or bad? And that is where dharma guides us to what we need to do.'

Sudjata and Revata were huddled together and listening intently to what Aniruddha was explaining. It was new to them. They somehow felt that these concepts were relevant to them too, particularly in these times when Pataliputra was going through an upheaval. It was important to find one's bearings and stay on course. Sudjata knew of many traders who were driven to suicide by the sudden changes that were happening around them.

Aniruddha continued with the same calm tone. 'Dharma is a bit difficult to understand,' he said looking around and adjusting his robe. He seemed to be searching for the right words. 'The root of dharma is dhri, meaning to support, to sustain. So you can somewhat guess what the word means. It means that it is something which supports and sustains the functioning of society. It does so by ensuring that people's lives are in consonance with the natural law that governs the entire universe. If we were to stray from dharma, then there would exist no harmony in society. Things would go berserk.'

'This is going a bit above my head,' said another younger monk. 'In these troubled times, how does dharma help us?'

'That's good question,' appreciated Aniruddha. 'What we do today matters. In the Mahabharata war, Lord Krishna advised Arjuna that his dharma was to go to war and win over his kingdom, even if it be at the cost of his cousins. If Buddha had been the charioteer, he would have probably advised Arjuna differently. Now, is our dharma to be on the side of war or on the side of peace?' Aniruddha paused for a while to let his question sink in.

The older monk replied emphatically, 'We cannot be on the side of war. Self-seeking kings have brought a lot of misery on the people. We have to put an end to tyranny.'

There was a loud murmur of approval from the audience. Sudjata was also convinced that his life now had a larger purpose. He wanted to be a part of the effort to atop the tyranny of kings. Little did he know that he would be soon engulfed in a bitter struggle against injustice.

✻ ✻ ✻

After the sermon, Aniruddha led them to his office through a gateway shaped like an arch with a carving representing double-headed eagles at the top. The pillars and pilasters on the walls had exquisite carvings of acanthus leaf capitals.

Aniruddha was visibly happy to see Chandaka and welcomed him with an affectionate hug. He greeted Sudjata and Revata warmly. The older monk and Charudatta had also joined them. The woman whom Sudjata had noticed in the congregation was there too. Her name, as they got to know, was Susmila.

After giving a quick account of their caravan trip from Pataliputra, Chandaka informed Aniruddha about the rebellion-like situation in his city.

Aniruddha was sympathetic about the problems the trading community was facing in these times.

'Traders have been a big motive force in urbanisation and the growth of kingdoms. But they are given short shrift by the administration. They are burdened with taxes but no insurance is provided if their goods are lost. The trading community has supported monasteries enormously. In return, we have been extremely sympathetic to their cause and have even intervened with the administration on their behalf,' he said encouragingly.

'We really need your help,' Chandaka pleaded. 'When we return to Pataliputra, we don't know what kind of situation we will face there. So, we need to make a coordinated plan involving the trade guilds and monasteries.'

'The monasteries will certainly be there to help you,' assured Aniruddha. 'We need to look at the larger picture of what is happening in different parts of Bharatavarsha and act accordingly. I will put you in touch with our people in Pataliputra.'

After completing their purchases over the next few days, Sudjata's caravan returned to Pataliputra.

Book Two:
The Storm

The Interlude

Sayana – Mathura – 328 BCE

The holy city of Mathura stood at the northern part of the Ganga-Yamuna doab, the vast stretch of fertile land between the fork formed by the two rivers. Some of the ancient glory of the capital city of the Surasena mahajanapada had been rubbed off by the rapid growth of the cities to the south and south-east of the Gangetic Plains. But it was a city still to be counted, placed strategically on the Uttarapatha trade route connecting Pataliputra with the north-west frontier kingdoms.

The city had woken up early, as usual. Tall temple spires glistened under the warm rays of the dawn. People were scurrying down the steps leading to the river to do their morning prayers after a holy dip in the river. The wet stone steps reflected dully through the thin mist over the bubbling waters.

The members of Yugantar were seated on stone benches built neatly under a large banyan tree overlooking the river. Except for some casual glances, no one bothered them. They had selected the city for their next meeting since the spies of Pataliputra and Kaushambi had become hyperactive.

They had been discussing the fast-changing situation all over Bharatavarsha. Sikandar was progressing briskly towards Hindukush, the cities of Pataliputra, Kaushambi and Ujjayini had been politically active, kingdoms in the north-west were making their plans to protect their borders and the South showed increasing potential to determine the future of Bharatavarsha.

Sayana had been appraised by all other members of the group. Vallabh, the Jain monk, gave an account of his extensive travels and contacts in the regions around Madurai and Muziris. The Buddhist monks, Aniruddha and Ananda, recounted political happenings over a vast stretch of country from Kaushambi to Ujjayini and Bhrgukachha. Suvala came up with precise account of Sikandar's movements and the size of his army. Doctor Kunala, who had travelled from Toshali in the province of Kalinga all the way to Takshashila to practice Ayurvedic medicine, had many things to say about the development of science and infrastructure in the north-western region. Chandaka, the active member of the trade guild in Pataliputra, talked about the prospects of a rebellion in the city.

'We are few in numbers, but we have accomplished a lot in this short time,' observed Sayana. 'We should not worry that we are small. A small spark can ignite an entire forest. An unassuming prod in the hands of an experienced mahout can control a huge elephant. A river starts as a thin stream and builds into a massive torrent,' he said reassuringly. The others nodded their acceptance.

Aniruddha went on further. 'Firstly, we should not underestimate our strength. We have the capacity to convince the people that they need not wait for a yug purush, a mighty hero, who will bring about change. They themselves are the real heroes. If they unite into one movement then nothing can stop them.'

Vallabh too spoke up. 'We are being told we have crossed the satya, treta and dvapara yugas and have entered the kaliyuga. The Puranas say that both the duration and quality of dharma contract by one-fourth as we cross each yuga. The kaliyuga being the last is the worst period in the cosmic cycle, but it seems we have to wait for 432,000 years until a new avatar, Kalki, descends to put an end to it. While it is true that we are living in the worst times, we must instil confidence in people that they can put an end to oppression right now. That is a massive task considering the size of the sub-continent but there is no other choice for us.'

It was time for them to move on. Before proposing a closure to the meeting, Sayana informed them that he had in mind several meetings in smaller groups over the next few days to work out future strategies for each region. The work of Yugantar has succeeded in creating a groundswell of opposition to the existing state of affairs everywhere. It was not only in the political sphere that tremendous changes were happening but science, technology, medicine and statecraft were also being swamped with new ideas and innovations.

Sayana let out a deep sigh of satisfaction.

17

A New Life

Susmila – Kaushambi

'Are you ready? It's getting late!' announced Nalini as she entered the small room that had been allotted to Susmila. Already six months had gone by since she was admitted into the bhikkuni sangha, the nun's order. Their rooms were located not far from the quarters of the male monks, the bhikkus.

'Let's go,' said Susmila cheerfully. They were starting their morning rounds of the nearby colonies where they can find upasakas to give them alms.

In these short six months, Nalini had become her close friend and confidante. They went out together, ate together and spent a lot of time together talking about their past.

Nalini taught Susmila the eight conditions that nuns had to follow when they enter the sangha. They were all loaded in favour of the male monks. The nuns must rise up from their seats when a monk approaches and they cannot admonish a monk openly while he can. But life was not as bad as written in the rules. Most monks were friendly and the nuns had a certain amount of respect and freedom in the sangha.

Nalini had told her with a laugh that even the great Buddha was not keen on admitting women into the sangha. He had to finally bow done to the pressure of his favourite disciple, Ananda, and his foster mother, Gotami.

Susmila had heard that Buddhist texts still portrayed women in stereotyped roles and as submissive and pliant. They often talked about women negatively as temptresses and poisonous snakes. In a system where monks were trying to stay celibate by overcoming passion, this was perhaps an extreme reaction to keep women away. Nevertheless, the sangha made a big difference to women like Susmila. For the first time it declared that women can attain nibbana, the highest state of enlightenment, as much as men.

Technically, the sangha was not open to pregnant women and other women required the permission of their parents or husbands to join. But Susmila herself had experienced that these rules can be broken on grounds of compassion.

A commendable rule in the sangha was that nuns were never left unprotected. A large monastery usually housed both the hostels for nuns and monks within the same complex. During monsoons, when monks were forbidden to travel, nuns were also given accommodation nearby. Most importantly, nuns never went to seek alms without the monks in tow.

Community work was fun. Once their alms gathering was over, Susmila and Nalini spent time with children at the local school or helped women in the community with their daily chores.

The kingdom of Vatsa, with Kaushambi as its capital, was going through a turmoil. It had been under the domination of the Magadha empire for some time now. A few decades back, the Shisunaga dynasty of Magadha had come to a bloody end with the king and his sons murdered in a mutiny. Mahapadma, the founder of the Nanda dynasty, seized power in Magadha. He continued the same policy of domination over the kingdom of Vatsa. Now, his son Dhanananda was extracting as much tax as he could from trade routed through Vatsa.

※ ※ ※

On one of the days, Susmila, Nalini and Charudatta had gone to visit a village called Ramgarh on the outskirts of Kaushambi, bordering a forest. On entering the village, Susmila felt it was quite similar to her own village. Most villagers were farmers with small plots of land. Even with the entire family working on the land, they found it difficult to pay the huge tax which was only increasing day by day. There were a few large landholders who hired labour to till their land and paid them hardly enough to keep body and soul together. The rest of the villagers were outcasts. They were forest dwellers who had recently cleared some forests on the outskirts of the village and settled there in small wattle and daub huts. Their condition was as pathetic as mongrels living on the roadside.

Taxation was a burden on all cultivators, especially when they were faced with a bad harvest under a rapacious king. With expanding trade and agriculture, land grabbing had become a regular phenomenon. The landless labourers, the dasas, were for all practical purposes, slaves. They had to do all the menial tasks.

The tribals had succeeded to some extent in taming the wasteland and growing crops. They had hopes that with a little more luck their economic status may improve and enable them to get integrated into the village. They will be still considered shudras but it was a step above the tribal status. But just when they started nursing these hopes, a high official from Kaushambi ordered them to give up their land since a highway and a canal approved by the government were to pass through their land. The big landholders were expecting a windfall in their incomes if the development programs get going. They could use the canal water for irrigation and the highway will certainly benefit the transportation of their surplus grains to the city markets.

When Susmila's team reached the village, the situation was tense. During the last visit itself the tribals had requested them to speak to the rajjuka, the local tax collector, to give up the idea of eviction. But in Vatsa, the Buddhist order did not have as much clout as it had in Magadha. Their requests fell on deaf ears. Some of the bigger landowners and the brahmanas, who had been donated land by the king for their services, were very adamant that the eviction should go ahead in the larger public interest.

The tribal households were prepared for the worst. They had their bows and spears out and stood around their colony daring the tax collectors and their guards to enter.

Charudatta again appealed to the rajjuka. 'Please don't evict them using force. They have so far petitioned the king very peacefully. Offer them a better place to move, then they might listen. But evicting them without any compensation or alternate arrangement is adharma.'

'Who are you to teach us about adharma?' the tax official asked in the arrogant tone that came naturally to their tribe. 'Move away and let us do our duty. We have come with the king's order!' he barked, motioning them to get lost.

Susmila was rattled. 'Don't you people have families and children?' she protested loudly in an agitated voice. 'How can you mercilessly evict them?'

The tax official snorted. 'Hey bhikkuni, this is none of your business!' he shouted and made a threatening gesture at her. The monks would have none of this. They held each other's hands and formed a human chain to prevent the guards from approaching the settlement.

The rajjuka gave a sharp command to his guards to advance. 'Don't show any mercy on these outcasts!' he bellowed.

Two horse-mounted guards spurred their horses menacingly towards the bhikkus and broke the chain with their lathis.

A monk wailed when a blow landed on his wrist, fracturing his bone, and jumped with agony.

The rest of the guards entered the huts and started throwing out whatever little possessions the tribals had.

A broad-shouldered middle-aged tribal who looked like the headman of the community, gave a rallying call. 'This is our land. We have reclaimed it from the forest with our sweat and blood. Let us defend every inch of it with our blood. If we have to sacrifice our lives for it, so be it!'

The tribals let out a big whoop. One of them picked up his bow and sent an arrow flying towards a mounted guard. The arrow pierced the animal on its hind legs and made it tumble along with its rider. A melee broke out. The rajjuka and the guards screamed and cursed furiously. One of the guards speared a tribal to death. Women and children were wailing in terror. The guards in their rage set fire to the huts and beat up anyone who obstructed them mercilessly.

The rest of the village dwellers looked on helplessly. No one dared to come to the rescue of the tribals. They didn't know that this was just the beginning. The smaller landholders will be the target of the next phase of eviction.

The monks and nuns witnessed the massacre with horror. The guards cut down the men who resisted with their swords as nonchalantly as they would do to chop down a sacrificial goat. Women and children were kicked around. A ten-year-old girl who tried to save her younger brother from the guards got trampled by the horses and lay sprawled on the ground with her head smashed and bleeding.

Within half an hour, the tribal colony had been decimated. Those who were alive, a few women, older men and some children, sat huddled in a corner unable to believe their eyes. All their loved ones were gone before they could even register the events.

A few monks were hurt badly. Susmila and Nalini had bruises all over their bodies. They had fought with the guards to stop the massacre but in vain.

The rajjuka came towards them and stood menacingly with one foot raised and planted on a short stool. 'You monks should have kept away. I warned you. We are not responsible if any of you is hurt. You should be glad that you were not arrested for obstructing government officers from carrying out their duty,' he bellowed. His face did not show even an iota of remorse for taking away so many lives and burning an entire colony to ashes.

After the rajjuka and the guards left, the monks and nuns sat there for a while in dazed silence. They had never witnessed such violence before.

Susmila remembered the sermon that she had attended some time back when Aniruddha had talked about one's karma and dharma. She recalled that some traders from Pataliputra had also joined the congregation. Later they went to Aniruddha's office where he had warned that the situation all around is deteriorating and that one has to make one's own choice what they wanted to do.

Some of his words made a strong impression on her like the searing iron branding a sheep. 'The world can work without hell or heaven or even a god. But it will come to a standstill if human beings are confused about what to do. The investigation whether the soul is different from the body, whether the universe started with a big bang or it has had an infinite existence, all these can wait. Why should we worry about what will happen to us in the afterlife and try to get an entry into heaven with gifts for the god and fees for the priests? We have to proceed on the path that our conscience tells us to. We have to find our own path of salvation.'

When she was in her village, literally a slave to her mother-in-law, the world was all a hazy mist. The forest, flowers, fields lush with ripe corn, the long winding village road, the market—all seemed grey and dull. When she joined the monastery, the bright sun had swept away the mist. She could see the world in all its splendour, the trees, mountains, birds, flowers and lakes. And now suddenly, when the sun had dipped behind the mountains, those trees and mountains had turned into shadowy demons breathing fire through their ugly nostrils.

They gathered their bowls and water jugs and trudged slowly towards the monastery. When Susmila looked back, vultures were circling over the tribal colony.

18

CALL FOR REBELLION

Satya – Ujjayini – 327 BCE

'Have you come here to worry about your supply of swords or will you have some time to speak with me?' asked Madanika in mock reproach.

Satya had been sitting next to her and contemplating for the past few minutes.

He turned to her and smiled. Of late, he had been swamped, travelling to various towns around Ujjayini organising the supply of weapons to the frontier. It had to be done discreetly since the Mahamatra's spies were constantly trying to know what he was up to. He had distributed some of the work to Bala, Maitreya and Sajjalaka, his true friends. They divided the area geographically. Bala took up the northern part of Avanti and beyond, up to Mathura. Maitreya covered the southern and western portions of the kingdom and ventured south, till the Deccan.

Madanika looked extra lovely today. She had worn a blue skirt with a matching saffron coloured blouse and a pure white silk dupatta draped over her shapely shoulders. Her long eyelashes curved upwards at a bewitching angle. Her kohl-lined eyes were irresistible. Coming to think of swords and steel, Satya recalled vaguely a poem composed by a love-struck poet. He contrasted the sharpness between the kohl-lined eyes of a pretty lass and a steel-edged sword and came to the conclusion that there is no way one can parry the former.

'I should give myself a good flagellation,' Satya apologized profusely. 'You are sitting like an apsara near me and here I am, lost in another world.'

'What is worrying you?' she asked with concern, brushing his hairy right arm with her soft palm.

'It is just that the situation of our community members is worsening by the day. The economy is in bad shape and we have big inventories of farm equipment and transport accessories. If the slump continues, we are in for big trouble. Only the war in the north-west is creating some demand for weapons. Our brothers everywhere are seething with anger. They want a conference to be organised soon.'

The Agarias were spread throughout north and east India but maintained cultural and political links with all the variants of the tribe. They had a common god and celebrated rituals and festivals with small variations.

'We have to be cautious,' Madanika warned snuggling up closer to Satya. 'I overheard a lot of reports about a rebellion among the Agarias. Your name came up a few times. The Mahamatra will not hesitate to even kill his mother for money and power. We cannot expect any mercy from his guards if they decide to put us behind bars,' she said in a hushed voice. Satya could sense that she was really worried about their safety.

'Yes, I know,' he replied in an understanding tone. Discussions taking place at the Mahamatra's sounded ominous. Satya felt like he was being stalked by a blood-thirsty tiger waiting for his victim to make a mistake. 'But we need to organise the conference soon. It will be a show of strength. It is much-needed at this time. If we don't come out on the streets and show our anger, the rogues in the government will carry on looting and oppressing us even more.'

'But be careful,' Madanika again reminded him.

'I need your help,' Satya turned towards her. 'Women are very active members in our tribe. They are breadwinners as much as men. They should be in the forefront in this conference. If they play an active role then nothing can stop us. You have to mobilise them for the conference. Once we have built a strong organisation of the Agarias, even if we are not here, our struggle will continue.'

'But are you going somewhere?' Madanika asked, alarmed. 'If you are planning to go anywhere then you better don't leave me behind,' she said laying her head on his broad chest.

Satya held her closely. He would not leave her alone if it came to that.

✳ ✳ ✳

The conference of Agarias was a big affair. Tribesmen came from all over the vast Gangetic Plains and the Deccan. Indians were producing iron for at least a thousand years now, if not more. Herodotus had written that Indian soldiers recruited by the army of Xerxes used arrows of cane tipped with iron. Ctesias, the Greek physician and historian, had talked about two wonderful swords of Indian steel which were in the possession of the King of Persia. In fact, even the Macedonians were eager to learn the technology of steel making from India, once they subdued her, or so they thought.

The Agarias stood foremost in iron-making in the sub-continent. Different sections of the Asur-Agaria tribes not only had physical and cultural resemblance, but also employed the same professional technique in iron making. They believed in the same mythology, worshipped the same gods and believed in the same magic. Their technique was totally indigenous. Iron smelters dotted the whole of the Gangetic Plains. While Agarias followed their distinct technique, they were not averse to learning new ones from the Deccan or even further south, from Thamizhagam which boasted of large shipyards and manufacturing hubs requiring iron and steel.

A few hundred years back, before the rise of the big cities, the Asur-Agarias commanded respect. Many of their celebrities were mentioned in literature of those times, in the Upanishads and the Mahabharata. But a slow degeneration set in since then. Now the tribals were treated as outcasts and forest dwellers in many kingdoms. They were allowed to set up their colonies only in the peripheral areas of cities and towns as if they will pollute life at the centre. This systematic breaking of the spirits hurt the Agaria pride. They were furious that in spite of being a key force in driving the economy forward, the governments treated them like a stinkpot. This anger was writ large on their faces and in their dealings with the administration.

Satya was frankly surprised at the large turnout. The *maidan* was jampacked. Hundreds of carts, which had transported the Agarias from distant places, were lined up on the roads leading to the *maidan*. This showed that political consciousness was swelling among the Agarias. They wanted to prove a point.

✳ ✳ ✳

A burly tribal leader from the kingdom of Chedi was pouring out his anguish in a loud voice. 'Our rulers are collecting extortionate taxes from those who are creating goods for the economy. Whereas it is exempting taxes for all those up to no good like the loan sharks and the landlords. If we stop production of iron and steel, then these incompetents have to go back to the Stone Age. Let us organise a tax boycott!'

The conference was taking place in a large open ground at the edge of the city's buzzing market. Anticipating the large crowds, plenty of vendors had set up shop at the edge of the open ground. There were vendors selling fried fish and chopped mutton, fruit juice, sweet curd, skillet roasted peanuts and roasted chana. Children crowded around shops selling kites, ice creams and sweetmeats. Further down, a number of liquor shops had moved closer to the ground from inside the market lanes. A small troupe of folk artists had come from Mathura to entertain the audience.

A large dais had been set up and tribal leaders from different parts of the country were seated on it. Right below them almost reaching the dais were seated rows and rows of women who cheered whenever speakers made a key point.

Another tribal leader from Matsya stood up from his chair and recited a moving poem on the plight of the Agarias to a great applause.

'O brother, the ringing of my hammering!
Tining tining, tining tining!
By my hammering the house is filled with rice!
Tining tining tining tining!
The sparks fly out, O brother,
The showers of sparks fly out.
O the swinging of the hammer!
Who blows the bellows? Who swings the hammers?
Who shapes the iron, slowly O slowly, with the little hammer?
Little brother hammers with the *ghana*.
Big brother works with the *halaudi*, slowly O slowly!
Why were you born an Agaria?
Can you eat the iron you make?

Sansi, halaudi and ghana are hard to use.
Can you eat the iron you make?'[x]

A woman from Vatsa described her daily routine graphically. 'I get up before dawn and start gathering twigs and branches for the kitchen oven and the furnace. After that I walk to the stream, take a bath, wash my clothes and the children's and fetch pails of water for the household. My young children have to be then given a bath after which I make barley bread and a stew for the family. By that time my husband would have already fetched the iron ore, mixed it with lime and ready to start the furnace. I work with the bellows vigorously, shielding myself from the heat of the fire with a winnowing fan. I have to press the bellows so hard that I have to support myself on a rope hanging from the roof. We work till the sun sets and then put away the finished material and clean the furnace room.'

One after another, speakers made their point crystal clear. The government has to reduce the taxes and provide for a decent existence or it will face the wrath of the community.

❊ ❊ ❊

While the speakers were making fiery speeches and tempers were rising among the audience, a row of cavalry guards appeared suddenly from out of nowhere and started spreading out in a circle from the side of the market. The adults immediately picked up their children who were playing at the outer edge of the ground. Those who were seated on the ground, men and women, looked at the cavalry apprehensively.

The leader of the guards sounded a bugle to attract the attention of the tribal leaders on the stage. Satya and his friends, along with other leaders, walked towards the guards who were waiting ominously, ready to act on the signal of their leader.

'What is the problem?' demanded Satya showing his irritation at the interference. 'This is our regular annual conference. Why are you interfering?'

The leader gave an amused smile which irritated the tribesmen even more. He then arrogantly announced, 'We have come here on Mahamatra's orders. You have another half an hour to vacate this ground. If anyone is found here after that, he will go straight to the dungeons.'

One of the Agaria leaders gave a derisive laugh. 'Thousands of people have come here from all parts of India. How dare you tell us to leave now? Not only is the government incompetent, it has become intolerant too!' he said and spat on the ground.

'If you don't disperse then you will not be going back to your homes. So, decide for yourself,' said the chief of the guards pointing to a tall building at one corner of the market facing the ground. About thirty archers were lined up along the banister on the second floor of the building. They stood ready with their bowstrings stretched and arrows knocked in place.

The Agarias had looked forward to the conference and had come from such long distances that they were in no mood to go back without any concrete action from the government.

'We want a meeting with the Mahamatra. If he listens to our demands and guarantees that the administration will act, then we will go home,' said Satya giving a signal to his friends and the volunteer group.

They knew there was a good chance that their conference will be disrupted. This was happening increasingly in every city. The volunteer force formed for maintaining order in the conference had come armed with swords, sickles, spears, tridents, khurpa knives and razors. Most of them were trained to use these weapons which they themselves had manufactured. They had carried the weapons discreetly not wanting to provoke the administration but as a measure of self-defence. Some of the carts which had transported them from outside the city had false bottoms to store weapons.

The volunteers now pulled out their spears and axes. The cavalry guards hadn't anticipated a resistance. The message was not lost on the leader who grunted and left the *maidan* with his guards.

The conference resumed. It carried on into the night. The next day, a delegation of the tribal leaders gave a petition to the king to take immediate action in addressing their grievances. There was no further threat from the Mahamatra's guards, but Satya had a foreboding that the coming days will not be as peaceful.

19

INVITATION TO JOIN THE RESISTANCE

Madhavi – Madurai

It was the day of the bull fight in Madurai. The roads were packed with visitors who had come from other areas of Thamizhagam to watch the great spectacle. A large open ground had been earmarked for the sport. Bamboo poles had been erected on either side of the pathway which the bulls will take. Ropes were tied horizontally across the poles to form a temporary fence between the bulls and the spectators. Raised wooden stands had been erected for the spectators on one side of the long path that the bulls will take in the competition between man and beast.

Madhavi and Nandi had arrived an hour earlier before the start of the bull fight to get a vantage seat. Their pavilion was already crowded with traders and businessmen. Nandi had managed to get an entry pass for the two of them. The ordinary folk had to stand on the side of the bull path, below the raised stands, and watch the fight. The king and his officers had a stand with a colourful awning for themselves. This was a popular sport. The king and his entourage were there more as spectators rather than officials.

Madhavi looked back at the entrance anxiously. It was Vallabh who had suggested that they meet at the bull fight. The way he had insisted they meet soon made Madhavi wonder if he was up to something again. After they had saved him from the highway guards at Puhar, they had not seen each other. It had been few months since.

Meanwhile, she had been thinking about the highly illuminating conversations they had on their way back to Madurai. He seemed to be particularly knowledgeable about the connection between the Indus Valley civilisation and Thamizhagam. But some of his activities worried her. He had stopped frequently on the way back to draw maps of rivers and forts. He had also made a note of natural caves on hilly terrains. He even inspected one or two of them, delaying their journey back to the city. But he didn't seem worried that the highway guards can catch up with them.

The crowd was already roaring in anticipation. People were milling around behind the bamboo cordon meant for spectators trying to get a vantage position. Festoons of mango leaves, thoranams, and flower garlands decorated the arena. The bulls and their owners were assembling at one corner of the arena. The bulls looked well-fed and intimidating. They belonged to a special breed with huge humps and a menacing forehead. The fresh red paint on their horns dazzled in the morning sun.

The *eru thazhuvuthal*, literally meaning 'embracing the bull' was an extremely popular sport in the south. The aayars, cattle owners, considered it a family honour to train bulls for the event and the owner of the best performing bull could even expect an award from the king.

Unlike the bull sport in other countries, the odds were not against the bulls but against the young tamers who entered the arena. They tried to embrace the bull rather than kill it. The bulls were not infuriated before they entered the arena, but the huge crowds and earsplitting roars certainly enraged them.

** * **

Just when Madhavi gave up on the monk, he entered their section of the stand and came directly to them. It looked like before entering he had made sure that there were no spies looking around for a certain monk who had escaped from Puhar.

Vanakkam, he greeted first Madhavi and then Nandi, who was watching the start of the bull fight intently. They greeted him back warmly.

'I have to be a bit careful. Since my return, I am being watched here. Looks like there are spies here connected to Pataliputra. They seem to be having some influence in the king's court,' he announced settling down beside them.

The first bull was ready to be let into the narrow winding path. Young, unarmed competitors waited with bated breath inside the cordoned area. They were bare-chested and had their dhotis tightly bound around their waist and above their knees. They wore garlands of sapphire-coloured kaya flowers and the bright red kodal flowers. Occasionally they glanced at the beautiful girls who stood near the balustrade of one portion of the raised platform. The bull fight was one kind of an ordeal that young men took up to prove their masculinity. The competition was practically a syamwara where girls decided on their life mates based on how they handled the bulls or the other way about.

The first bull had now entered the arena and was getting accustomed to the deafening roars from the stands. It didn't show its annoyance and calmly measured its young adversaries. The tamers approached the bull, gingerly circling around the animal, looking for a hold.

'Do you know that this kind of bull fight sport has been there for about 2000 years?' Vallabh asked breaking their trance. 'I have come across old rock paintings in Karikkiyur in the Nilgiri hills depicting bull fights. And the way it is practiced here has a lot of resemblance to the sport in the Indus Valley and the religious ceremonials among the Cretans in the Mediterranean.[xi] This shows that different cultures have mixed and spread far and wide in Bharatavarsha. No culture has tried to dominate the others. There has been space for all cultures and languages to grow.'

It was news for Madhavi that a sport could unite civilisations thousands of kadams away.

The sport was well under way now. Another bull had been let into the arena and a crowd of young men ran towards it to try their luck. There was dust all around. When the bull veered towards the bamboo fence to evade the tamers, the spectators on the other side of the fence fell back in fear that the bull will cut through the fence and gore them. After a while it was difficult to know whether it was the red paint or the blood of the young tamers which was glistening on the horns. Some of the tamers had been thrown off violently. Some had been gored on the thigh or the shoulders. There were shouts, yells and moans all around.

Madhavi looked away. She wondered whether the sport is good for the bull or the tamers. The spectators were certainly excited and were yelling for more blood safely barricaded away from the bulls

Vallabh now lowered his voice. 'There is something confidential I want to discuss with you both,' he said in a conspiratorial tone. Both Madhavi and Nandi turned towards him forgetting the bull fight.

❊ ❊ ❊

'I have come to know you both well. So, I guess I can trust you. There are many things happening in the north and north-west which will impact the course that Bharatavarsha will take in the future. The biggest question is whether people will have a better deal than now or will things get even lousier. But no one is going to answer this question because it is people like you and I who should be concerned and not believe in fatalism. If we act fast then the answer will be something favourable to the people.'

The usually circumspect Nandi asked, 'How does a few people like us matter to the future of a nation?'

'It matters a lot,' said Vallabh emphatically. 'There are thousands and lakhs of people like us who want to be in the forefront of change. Several sharp minds have already been trying to understand our past and mould the future taking the best from it. Would you both like to join this initiative?' Vallabh stopped here and waited anxiously for a response.

For Madhavi, this was a dream come true. Here was a man proposing something that could liberate her from her humdrum life and take her to exciting places. She had been quite fed up with practicing her medicine in a small colony in Madurai like a frog in the well. She wanted to explore the beyond, find medicines hitherto unknown, and learn techniques that can revolutionise the field. But she wanted to be sure whether she understood Vallabh's proposal well.

'What do you really mean when you say that we should join your initiative?' she asked.

'It means that you have to get out of this place and travel with me to those parts where things are happening and circumstances are opening up enormous opportunities. You can practice medicine with the most advanced practitioners in Takshashila if you so wish.'

Madhavi cried out in delight. 'Do you really mean it?' she asked excitedly.

Nandi was fidgeting. He could not really understand where the conversation was leading to. He could see that Vallabh was serious and Madhavi was ecstatic.

'I am damn serious,' Vallabh said. 'I understand it is a big decision, but it will be an unforgettable experience. *That* I can vouch for,' he said with a broad smile.

✳ ✳ ✳

The bull fight was coming to a close. Each bull had a gold coin wrapped in a cloth and tied to one of its horns. The bull tamer had to hug the hump of the bull and untie the cloth to become the winner and get the gold coin. A couple of young muscular cowherds had untied the cloth and received a huge roar of applause. They soon vaulted over the fence and joined their gang of friends who had come to cheer them. Others, who had faced the wrong end of the bull, were being helped to get back to the pavilion. One of the tamers was being carried out on a stretcher. The crowd had had a field day.

Vallabh turned to Nandi and asked, 'How about you, sir?'

Nandi was nonplussed. 'What will I do if I come with you?' he asked a bit bemused.

'You are a trader with excellent experience in dealing with different kinds of customers including the foreign ones. You have a more than adequate idea of road and sea routes and about imports and exports. We need help to cartograph our trade routes and document them well. You can be of great assistance in this.'

This gave Nandi a lot of satisfaction. Looked like he too had an important place in the larger mysterious plan.

'We need some time to think about this. How much time do we have?' he asked.

'Not much. A month or two at the most. Sikandar will soon enter

Hindukush. And Pataliputra is on the verge of rebellion,' said Vallabh getting up. 'I will not be able to hang around here for too long. The noose is tightening around me. I will have to leave but will try to get in touch soon. I have to make a lot of arrangements.'

Madhavi and Nandi too got up. They had a lot on their minds now.

'You can call your fishermen friends too to join us,' Vallabh said as he got down the stand and disappeared.

* * *

The nightmare occurred again. She ran for her life along a narrow path in the forest used by hunters and forest dwellers. Sharp pebbles and stones cut her feet. The pain was getting unbearable. She kept running, avoiding the sharp thorny branches which stretched out into the path like poisonous snakes flicking out their tongues.

She recalled what her father had taught her about them. 'Snakes are generally harmless. They may appear threatening when it flicks its tongue out, but they are simply trying to taste the air to get a better sense of their surroundings. Their excellent sense of taste and smell compensate for their poor eyesight. When a snake flicks its tongue, it collects odors which are processed by the sensory organ located inside the roof of the snake's mouth. Through smelling and tasting the air it can locate a prey such as a mouse.'

Madhavi wondered how she could recall this even when she was running with chafed and bleeding feet and burning cuts across her forearms and shoulders. Her blouse and pavadai were in tatters. She kept running and punishing herself. She was not sure how long or how far away she had come from the cart. She stumbled and went headlong into a small stream that appeared out of nowhere. The cool water embraced her and she must have laid there for some time before a hand pulled her out.

She woke up with a start in the middle of the night. The forest in the Siddhar colony sounded muted and ominous. There was an occasional howl of wolves or the clatter of wings of a bird disturbed in its sleep.

She thought about Vallabh's offer to join his efforts in the north. Will she be wrenched away from her near and dear ones yet another time in her life? Or will her leaving the Siddhar colony liberate her from her nightmares and propel her to a higher destiny in life? She was now a grown-up woman, not the vulnerable girl anymore. She need not be dependent on anyone. She can take care of herself. She had a skill which will help her to survive anywhere. She decided to take up Vallabh's offer.

It was already dawn. She resolved to meet Nandi to make plans for the future without wasting any more time.

20

REVOLT IN PATALIPUTRA

Sudjata – Pataliputra

Sudjata had never witnessed such a huge rally on the streets of Pataliputra in his lifetime of two and a half decades. It looked like the entire city was up in arms. Lakhs of people had gathered in support of the trader's guild which had called for the massive rally. Slogans rent the air: *Down with the tyrant Dhanananda!; Let us put an end to the back-breaking taxes!; You have not followed rajdharma, you have no right to rule! and Death to the sadist Minister, Amatya Rakshasha!*

The history of the Magadhan empire had been a history of political ambitions, unprincipled plots, loot of the people and bloodshed. Many of them were believed to be patricides including Ajatashatru and the four kings who succeeded him. This, despite the fact that they were followers of Buddha and Mahavira! Dhanananda, the current ruler, had accumulated such astronomical wealth through taxes levied on the people and tributes from vassal states that even the Greek writers considered him to be far richer than the Persian king Darius. He was rumoured to have hoarded his wealth in under-sea vaults, safely tucked away from rivals and thieves.

When Sudjata returned from his caravan trip to Kaushambi, he could sense that the political situation had deteriorated immensely. There was simply no section of the people who was not dissatisfied with the current regime on one count or another. The trader's guild took the lead in organising the protest because of the heavy taxes that they had to pay for their goods at the manufacturing point, at the market, at the city gates when the goods were taken out for export and in the highways at toll booths. Increasing highway robberies, thanks to lax highway patrols, further added to the misery of traders.

Artisans, students, farmers, fishermen, tribals, transport workers, and even the army soldiers were disgruntled and came out on demonstrations and protests frequently. The response of the administration to these demonstrations was brutal and clinical. The demonstrators were immediately picked off the roads by the security guards and thrown into dungeons. The leaders were taken to torture chambers whose administrators excelled in experimenting with the most gruesome tortures on the hapless victims. Magadha's jails were overflowing and torture chambers resonated with blood-curdling screams and pitiful cries. Dhanananda had even thrown out his Minister Vishnugupta for criticising his administration, who had then vowed to overthrow his regime. It was rumoured that Vishnugupta escaped an assassination attempt and fled the kingdom to raise an army.

Women had no security. Kidnappings and rapes were increasing by the day. The worst offenders were the palace officers, high ranking security officials and wealthy merchants. The king, his brothers and sons considered the entire kingdom as their harem. Crime on the streets of the city was at its peak.

Pataliputra's location at the confluence of the Ganga and Son in the south, and the Gandak and Gogra to the north, gave it control over the booming trade routes from the east to the west. The kingdom's fertile soil filled the granaries year after year. Nearby forests yielded huge amounts of quality timber. Thousands of elephants captured from the forests and tamed, served in the army and in the transportation and construction sectors. The kingdom also had huge reserves of minerals and raw materials. But the biggest factor for Magadha's rise was the police and military power, necessary for any kingdom to have imperialist visions.

✳ ✳ ✳

Sudjata recalled the meeting of the trade guild, the sreni, a month ago, from where all this started. The guild was an industrial and mercantile organisation. The guilds played a predominant part in the economy of the Magadhan kingdom. Pataliputra being the largest city boasted of countless guilds. They represented all trades and industries. Sudjata chuckled to himself when he remembered that there was also a guild of thieves in the city.

The guild had members from both the craftsmen's cooperatives as well as individual artisans and workmen. It determined wages, work rules, prices and quality standards. Its regulations had the force of law approved by the king himself. The guild was not only an economic power but a social regulator as well. It resolved disputes between guild members and even took up disputes between husband and wife. Temples and monasteries respected the guild since it was an important contributor to their funds. The Buddhist order did not allow women to become nuns until they could obtain permission from their husbands and the guild. An important factor that bound members to the guild was that it took care of the widows and orphans of its members and also provided them with some sort of health insurance. Members were even offered loans by the guild.

Chandaka was making a fervent appeal to the Jyeshthaka, the chief of the guild. He was the richest member and the post being hereditary, his arrogance seemed to be natural.

'The taxes have become unbearable. We have given several memorandums to the king, but they have only fallen on deaf ears. The administration has forced us to take to the streets. I talked to many members and they are all for it. We cannot delay this any further. Let's call for a rally in two weeks,' Chandaka argued passionately.

The hall in which the guild meeting was taking place was large. Sunlight entered through the many windows and cast a gleam on the portraits of previous chiefs of the guild hung on the smoothly painted walls. The current chief sat on the pillow-lined diwan with his other council members. He was a ruddy faced, round-shaped middle-aged man. He leaned on a large cushion and had his legs stretched out as sitting with legs folded put too much pressure on his overflowing belly. He was dressed in an immaculate silk dhoti and kurta and had a gold-lined silk turban wound around his bald head.

The Jyeshthaka was a very practical man. He followed the rules of Vedic orthodoxy to the hilt. He wanted no blemish in his observance of the four ashramas of the Vedic order—the brahmacharya (student life), the grahasthya (family life), vanaprastha (retired life) and sanyasi (ascetic life). He was in stage two and had no doubts that when the time came, he will graduate to stage three without much effort. He also accepted his position in the Vedic order without quarrels. After all, who was he to quarrel? Indra and Kubera and all other gods in the Vedic pantheon could not have been kinder. He knew that he was in the third position in the varna system, after the brahmanas who were born from the mouth of Brahma and the kshatriyas who were produced from the shoulders. He himself was a vaishya which appeared from the thighs of the Creator. He was on good terms with the two higher castes. The fourth one, the shudra, he treated them with disdain, as the caste which came out of the feet of the Creator needed to be.

He carefully followed all the rituals and gave ample gifts to the brahmanas to wash away his sins, which kept multiplying by the minute. He had found a perfect way to balance the spiritual part of his life with the sinful part. Of late, the Buddhist sanghas offered some more redemption from his sins if he were to contribute a small amount to their maintenance, which he gladly did. It was double insurance for his soul in the afterlife. But currently his mind was far away from his spiritual responsibilities. He looked forward to the evening appointment with one of the most highly paid and hard-to-get courtesans in the capital city of Magadha. But this Chandaka was spoiling his mood. As Chandaka spoke, the Jyeshthaka's face got redder by the minute.

'How can we annoy the king and take out a rally?' he interjected in a querulous voice. He was furious inside but tried to maintain an equitable stance knowing the mood of the members. 'I have been talking to the king and his ministers. They have asked for some more time. The economy is in a bad shape as you all know. The government is anxious that it does not go into a deficit. Let us not screw up the negotiation process. We all have to tighten our belts for some more time.'

Sudjata was aware that the Jyeshthaka had enough money to support the next twenty generations of his family. The king had allowed him to monopolise issuing licenses and permits to new enterprises. He also controlled all exports and imports. A share of the customs duty and highway tolls flowed into the pockets of all the members of the trade guild council. His message to tighten belts was directed at the ordinary members of the guild. So he was not surprised at his opposition to a rally. *Such a pretentious loaf who never tires saying that he has given his life for the guild!*

Many other traders were enraged by the flippant remark of the Jyeshthaka.

One member stood up hurriedly. 'If we wait for some more time my family will go bankrupt and I will have no option but to commit suicide. Better to give my life on the streets protesting rather than hang myself,' he said passionately.

A few council members supported the Jyeshthaka to remain calm and follow the petition route, but majority of the ordinary members rejected the suggestion outright.

One member who had a handlebar moustache and a trimmed beard said, 'Ours is not the only guild thinking about a protest. Other guilds like those of washermen, physicians, metalsmiths and cart drivers are also with us. Peasants and students will also be taking part in the rally.'

The Jyeshthaka had had enough. He removed his persuasive mask and bared his fangs. 'You stupid idiots! I want all of you to behave like good citizens. We are not going out on any rally-*bally*!' he barked. 'If anyone violates the decision of the guild they will be expelled and asked to appear before the guild court.' He, however, did not care to explain how the decision was made.

The entire gathering hooted and howled at the council members. Sensing that it was not safe to remain in the building anymore, the council members made a quick exit.

✳ ✳ ✳

When the trade guild council leadership refused to agitate for the lowering of taxes, Chandaka and Sayana, who had been mobilising other trade guilds, were left with no option but to go ahead with the protest rally. The Buddhist and Brahmana councils of the court at Pataliputra, who had substantial influence with the king, refused to intervene. They did not want to forego state support to their religion. Criticising the king will only provide an advantage to the competitor to get closer to the king's council.

Chandaka and Sayana had used their networks to the maximum potential. Sudjata had given Chandaka a lot of help in reaching out to traders in the city. Revata had also pitched in and done a lot of propaganda among his friends who were in the private security service.

The demonstration wound like a giant python through the streets of Pataliputra. The protestors had wisely decided to start from the crowded marketplace and go through the main streets of the working-class part of the city. As they advanced through the colonies of weavers, textile dyers, washermen, ironsmiths, pottery makers and butchers, the numbers swelled. Younger men and women from the communities joined the demonstration and raised loud slogans.

Chandaka was in the forefront of the demonstration along with other guild representatives holding a large cloth banner with the slogan: Abide by rajdharma, Listen to the voice of people! Sudjata and Revata walked a little behind the main banner. Revata had organised a group of volunteers to provide security for the protestors. People lined up all along the streets and cheered the protestors lustily.

A troupe of artists staged a short street skit when the demonstration paused at an intersection. Actors dressed in garish costumes imitated king Dhanananda, Prime Minister Rakshasha and their flunkeys.

As the demonstration reached the city square, the king's guards erected a barricade and prevented the demonstrators from advancing towards the palace. Some of the protestors made an attempt to climb over the barricades and were repulsed by sword wielding guards. Just then a couple of empty carriages at one corner of the square were set on fire by a few masked mercenaries who were clearly sent by the city administration to disrupt the rally. From out of the blue, a cavalry force of twenty riders entered from one of the side streets and approached the leading contingent.

Revata was quick to recognise that a trap had been set for them. The fire was an organised provocation to justify the deployment of the cavalry. Anticipating this he had come with a few other ex-soldiers armed with swords and daggers. He signalled to them to move to the front and protect the leaders of the demonstration.

The cavalry swung towards the leaders carrying the large banner. They plucked the banner and tore it. They then advanced ferociously trampling all who stood in their way. Revata and his friends formed a chain around the leaders from the guilds and deftly warded off the vicious attacks of the cavalry. Sudjata quickly led Chandaka and Sayana away from the melee.

The demonstrators did not give up. They were enraged at the unprovoked attack by the king's guards. This only proved that the administration had decided to suspend all rights of the people and impose their rule with an iron hand. Several demonstrators were killed in the scuffle. The king's guards also suffered losses.

The site of the protest soon looked like a typhoon ravaged area. Carts had been overturned, flags and banners trampled down in the mud and slippers, shoes and turbans littered around. The king's guards had gone after the hapless demonstrators like a pack of lions charging a herd of deer.

Sayana and Chandaka, along with Sudjata and Revata evaded arrest and reached an inn on one of the side streets whose owner had provided space many times for their activist meetings.

Sayana drank some water out of a pitcher and sat down motioning the others to sit near him. They were a little out of breath.

'The situation has changed dramatically,' he started in a tone that could hardly hide his excitement. 'Even I didn't anticipate such a huge rally. The rebellion has started. It is not going to take much time for it to spread to other cities and kingdoms. Dhanananda's downfall is near.'

'What is our next move?' asked Sudjata.

'We cannot stay in this city any longer. They will soon have us thrown into the dungeons. I have made arrangements to leave for Kaushambi tonight. We have a massive task ahead of us. If we don't act now, the rebellion will not go in the direction we want,' Sayana said resolutely.

What Sayana said was a bit ambiguous for Sudjata and Revata but they did not want to ask questions. They thought they were already into too much action. So Sayana's suggestion that they should act immediately was puzzling but then the most immediate thing to do was to get as far away from the city as possible. Sudjata wondered whether they would be able to return at all till the rogue Dhanananda was ruling the city.

Sudjata and Revata got the feeling that tremendous forces were at work at different places in India and the days of Dhanananda were numbered.

21

STUBBORN RESISTANCE

Suvala – Swat Valley – 327 BCE

Suvala stood on a small hillock on the left bank of the Swat river. He had come with a contingent of twenty riders to get advance information on Sikandar's movements. The Macedonians had overrun Takshashila and signed a peace treaty with Ambhi, the King of Gandhara. They were now headed towards the Hindukush. If they are not weakened and slowed down here then it will be a cakewalk for Sikandar's forces to cross Punjab, even taking into account the huge army of Paurus, the King of Kekaya.

The cool breeze from the river made him shiver. It was a beautiful sight from where he stood. The Swat valley lay in the lap of mountainous ranges, the offshoots of the Hindukush. The larger part of the valley was bordered with mountains and hills whose crests were sparkling like freshly cut diamonds in the morning sun. The valley ran for about 90 kos. Two narrow strips of plains ran along the banks of the river. The Swat river took its name from the Sanskrit root, *Suvastu,* meaning 'clear azure water'. *Soon it will be bloody with the corpses of men and animals.*

Suvala had already observed how the Greek phalanx worked. It was crucial to take advantage of its weakness. That would mean the battle with the Macedonians should not be on their terms.

The main body, the phalanx, was a unit of 18,000 men which was distributed into six brigades of 3000 each. The phalangist soldier wore the usual defensive armour of the Greek heavy infantry—helmet, breast-plate and greaves, and almost the whole front of his person was covered with the long shield called the aspis. His weapons were a sword long enough to enable a man in the second rank to reach an enemy who had come to close quarters with the comrade who stood before him, and the celebrated spear, known by the Macedonian name, sarissa, twenty four feet long. The sarissa, when couched, projected eighteen feet in front of the soldier. The space between the ranks was such that those of the second rank were fifteen; those of the third, twelve; those of the fourth, nine; those of the fifth, six; and those of the sixth, three feet in advance of the first line, so that the man at the head of the file was guarded on each side by the points of six spears. The ordinary depth of the phalanx was of sixteen ranks. The men who stood too far behind to use their sarissas. Therefore, they kept them raised until they advanced to fill a vacant place. As the efficacy of the phalanx depended on its compactness, and this again on the uniformity of its movements, the greatest care was taken to select the best soldiers for the foremost and hindmost ranks. The army had many such units. The bulk and core of the phalanx consisted of Macedonians, the rest being foreign mercenaries.

The only resistance standing between Sikandar and Bharatavarsha were the Kamboja and Gandhara tribes known for their superb horse-riding skills, fierce independence and battle readiness. They were called the Ayudhajivin Sangha, the war-like republics. Suvala himself belonged to the Ashvakayana tribe and had been trying to get the other tribes like the Ashvayanas and the Hastinayanas into a confederation.

But tribal enmity was proving very difficult to overcome. He was resigned to the fate that each tribe must fight its own battle.

✳ ✳ ✳

Realising that these tribes are going to be a big threat, Sikandar himself personally took command of the army which included a select force of shield-bearing guards, foot-companions, archers, Agrianians and mounted javelin-men. He knew that if these highlanders are not subdued then his march into India would neither be secure nor effective.

The Ashvayanas were the ones who first challenged Sikandar. Suvala led a big contingent of his tribe, Ashvakayanas, and joined the fight. At the head of the Kunar valley they offered stubborn resistance to the Macedonian army.

Suvala had been organising a regular supply of high-quality swords, daggers, and iron-tipped spears through the Agaria network coordinated by Satya from Ujjayini. The tribesmen loved the swords for their light weight and flexibility. That was one reason why the tribals could make a dent in the Macedonian army even when they were vastly outnumbered.

Sikandar was seriously wounded in the right shoulder by an arrow and his officers Ptolemy and Leonatos were also injured. This infuriated him so much that he burnt the city of Andaka to the ground.

It was in this battle that Suvala and his companions noted the weakness of the phalanx. The phalanx could only operate effectively on level and open ground. It was unfit for rapid advance and rough terrain, and useless if its ranks were broken. It was thus helpless in the face of an active enemy like the horse-borne tribals unless well-supported by cavalry and light troops. So, the phalanx has to be separated at all costs from the light cavalry. The tribal army never confronted the Macedonians in the plains. They harassed the army by organising lightning strikes from the hills and quickly disappearing back into the forests. This had considerably weakened the Macedonian army and their morale was depleting by the day. Many mercenaries decided to drop out, forcing Sikandar to recruit new mercenaries from the captured towns.

* * *

With the capture of Andaka, the Ashvayanas joined another part of their tribe at the city of Arigaon. Though they put up a stiff resistance, the city was captured by Sikandar's forces and put to fire. While the tribes continued their warfare from the mountains, they made the tactical mistake of descending onto plain ground, underestimating the Macedonian forces and too confident of their numbers. The Macedonians captured a large number of ordinary tribal people and confiscated their bullocks. Besides warfare, the Kambojas were good at agriculture and cattle rearing, belying the historians of the Greeks that they were barbarians.

Suvala and his companions along with the survivors of the Ashvayanas retreated to the Swat valley and awaited the arrival of the Macedonian army. They were not strong enough to stop and turn back the army, but at least they could weaken and demoralize it. With each passing day Sikandar was having trouble to egg his army forward. His soldiers were intoxicated with the initial victories over the Persians. But now, as they advanced towards India, every city put up resistance. It hurt Sikandar that after having conquered the rest of the known world, India was slipping out of his grasp.

* * *

The winter was bone chilling in the valley. Gusts of wind combined forces with the snow and scattered sharp snowflakes across the valley which made life miserable for the tribal warriors. The hills echoed with their loud hissing like that from a pit filled with snakes.

Now and then the hissing stopped for a few moments and the entire valley stood still as if nature paused to think. As the snowflakes cut into the uncovered parts of their faces, they felt that the enemy's blades would have been more soothing. The forest trails on the hills were slimy with snow and mud making the movement of horsemen and foot soldiers grueling. The long branches of trees drooped low as if weighed down with the knowledge of an impending bloodbath.

Suvala had organised to strengthen the strongholds of the Ashvakayanas at Massaga, Ora, Bazira, and Aornos. The scouts had informed Suvala and the commander of the tribal army, Assacanus, that Sikandar will be besieging their fort at Massaga in a matter of days. The commander seemed to be a bit overconfident.

When Suvala had advised him to be cautious he had said defensively, 'We have mustered an army of 30,000 cavalry, 30,000 infantry and 30 elephants. Seven thousand soldiers had joined from Abhisara as reinforcements. We are on firm ground.'

Suvala sighed. He knew that Assacanus was grossly underestimating the enemy. But he was the commander of the army and Suvala cannot prick his ego. He said in a measured tone, 'Let us be cautious. We are facing the world's best army. Frankly, we cannot defend this citadel for long because their army is superior to us in the plains. Let us defend the city as long as we can. After that we may have to retreat to the hills.'

Assacanus did not argue but gave a half-hearted nod.

The battle at Massaga was fierce when it came. After besieging the fort, Sikandar feigned a retreat to lure the Ashvakayanas out of their fort. In spite of Suvala's warnings, 7000 tribals pursued the Macedonian army assuming that it had given up. Sikandar suddenly turned back and engaged the tribal army, but the damage was contained. Only 200 men lost their lives. The rest retreated safely into the citadel.

The next day, Sikandar attacked the fort walls using his phalanx. But they were repelled by arrows shot from the citadel towers by the tribal marksmen.

The third day, Sikandar attacked the fort walls with his war engines, the ballistas. A small breach was created but when his soldiers tried to rush through it, the Ashvakayana defenders repelled them from the safety of the citadel.

The following day the Macedonians wheeled in the huge wooden tower they had been building for the past many days to the fort wall and sent arrows into the defenders on top of the citadel. But the tribesmen still held out. So far so good.

Another day passed. The Macedonian engineers brought a wooden bridge close to the breach in the fort wall hoping to get their soldiers into the fort. But as the soldiers stormed over the bridge, it gave way under their weight. It was a disaster for the Macedonians. The tribals rained arrows on the retreating soldiers killing many of them.

On the eleventh day, the tribesmen faced a major loss. When the commander came out to supervise his troops on the roof of the citadel, a stray missile from the ballista felled him. The Ashvakayanas didn't lose their wits. The commander's mother Kripa took over the operations. Suvala was surprised to find that she rallied all the women in the city to defend themselves.

The battle continued for several days. Both sides suffered heavy losses. Kripa offered the Macedonians a peace agreement against the advice of Suvala. That proved to be a costly mistake. Suvala had seen Sikandar repeatedly violating peace agreements and setting entire cities on fire. Moreover, Sikandar offered safe exit provided they joined his army as mercenaries.

The Ashvakayanas would die rather than fight against their countrymen. Suvala and his comrades waited until midnight and quietly exited the fort through the back door.

The next day when Sikandar learnt that the fighter men and women had left the fort, he let his fury descend upon the hapless women and children left behind. After raping the women, his army cut them to pieces. Even children were not spared. All the buildings were torched. For days after, the fort smouldered while forest animals and vultures feasted on the corpses.

❊ ❊ ❊

Sikandar was a vengeful man. He could not digest the escape of the tribals, whom he had planned to massacre anyway once they signed the peace treaty. His army pursued the Ashvakayanas into the mountains.

Suvala led the remaining warriors to Ora and they put up one more bold stand against the ravaging army. The King of Abhisara sent a military contingent to relieve the Ashvakayanas at Ora. Hearing this, Sikandar, who had sent a part of his army to Bazira, recalled them and rushed with his entire force to Ora.

Suvala's heart bled. They had lost thousands of their best warriors. Their women and children had been raped and burnt alive. Their towns were up in smokes. But they were weakening the Macedonian army which would overrun India if given a free passageway. The battle at Ora and Bazira again went on for days and inflicted heavy casualties on both sides. *Will these sacrifices be remembered by future generations of Indians?*

The tribal army then moved to the high fortress of Aornos. Sikandar had suffered such massive losses that he recruited more mercenaries, strengthened his defences at the captured forts and set up a base near Aornos at a place called Embolima.

The fortress at Aornos was highly formidable and strategic. The Greek army discovered a narrow path up the fort. This was fortified with a palisade and trench by Ptolemy, the Macedonian commander. But the Ashvakayanas did not let the Greeks come up to the fort. They gave a tough fight and pushed the Greek army back.

After many days of fighting, the Greeks could finally find a ravine over which they erected a wooden bridge to reach a spot that was on level with the Aornus fort.

As the Greek army advanced towards the fort, the defenders rolled down massive stones which pummeled hundreds of Greek soldiers into the ravine below. After many days of fighting, the defenders evacuated the fort and escaped through a hidden path behind the hill. The story of Massaga was repeated here. Sikandar stormed into an unarmed fort and massacred those who were left behind.

The Ashvakayanas did not give up yet. Suvala joined forces with Afridi, the son of Kripa. They raised an army of 20,000 and a fleet of 15 war elephants. They again gave a good fight to the Macedonian army but met with heavy losses.

As Sikandar's army advanced much more slowly than anticipated and considerably weakened, the Ashvayanas and the Ashvakayanas whose forts had been taken, did not give up. As soon as the Macedonian army went ahead, they regrouped and captured their forts killing the governors appointed by Sikandar. Nicanor, the governor of Massaga was assassinated.

❖ ❖ ❖

When Suvala returned from the battlefield to meet the Yugantar, they analysed what went wrong. The Kamboja and Gandhara kingdoms were among the strongest republics at an earlier time. But infighting between the kingdoms of India left these two republics at the mercy of the invading Achaemenid army. Because of their

Indo-Greek and Indo-Iranian culture, the orthodox kingdoms of the Gangetic Plains shunned them, calling them *mlechcha*, the foreigners. The mahajanapadas of Kamboja and Gandhara slowly disintegrated and their confederacies fell apart. Every tribe was left to fend for itself. Each one of the tribes put up tremendous resistance but since there was no confederacy, the Macedonian army could defeat them one by one with their well-organised army and superior numbers.

But in the final reckoning the tribals had succeeded in inflicting heavy casualties on the Macedonian army. It had to pause to lick its wounds, its morale ebbing away.

22

A TRIP OF BONDING

Nandi – Madurai to Ujjayini – 327 BCE

The trip to Ujjayini required a lot of preparation. Madhavi had to hand over her patients to her fellow doctors and pack some of the palm leaf manuscripts that will come in handy when she reached her destination, about which she barely knew anything. Nandi had to make temporary arrangements for a couple of his trade partners to handle his existing customers. Vengayyan had the least problem. He did not have any business as such to hand over. He packed his sparse belongings and took leave of his friends and family.

Vallabh had advised Nandi that they should take the sea route from Korkai, the Pandyan port, to Bhrgukachha from where they can switch over to the land route. He had warned them that it is a long route but a safe one as it was a busy trade route with a lot of ships plying back and forth. The land route through Suvarnagiri and Pratishthana was not safe. Bandits lurked in the mountains and rivers were often in spate during monsoons. In fact, Vallabh had even made their bookings in a reliable ship which regularly plied on this route. He had told them to get in touch with Captain Mano as soon as they boarded.

The first part of the trip from Korkai port in the Bay of Bengal to Muziris in the Arabian sea was a bit tricky. They took the shorter route through the Mannar Straits which separated the Indian peninsula from the island of Lanka. The ships travelling through the Gulf of Mannar had to tackle the winds of both monsoons. Vessels had to carefully avoid the sandbanks, coral reefs and rocky islets. This required expert navigation.

The waterway was neither deep nor wide. Vessels laden with heavy goods had to transfer their cargoes to smaller boats at the entrance to the Gulf and then get them back on board after crossing to the other side. For this reason, some of the larger ships were built with prows at both ends so that they could easily manoeuvre back and forth in the narrow channel. Local seafarers used huge dugout canoes held together by a yoke called sangara to navigate this channel.

Fortunately, Madhavi's ship was steered by an expert captain and helmsman. Mano turned out to be an expert on the sea route as well as a good conversationalist. He was from the Chera port of Muziris and had travelled both east and west of the Indian subcontinent. His knowledge of languages, culture and food across the route was phenomenal. He was about the same age as Nandi, looked generally cheerful and was respected by his teammates. He had a thick lock of black hair tied behind in a ponytail with a black band and wore a locket with a pendant shaped like a ship.

Mano loved Sangam poems and recited some of the verses he loved as a mariner. They were awesome in their rhyme, meter and content. One of them struck Madhavi as particularly graphic. It was the song of a fisher woman who was pining for her lover to return from the high seas.

'Before I united with the lord
of the shores with powerful waves,

..........where the sand is like white moon,
..........punnai trees grow with tall branches,
..........many kinds of goods are brought by
..........the wind in ships from various
..........countries, and a white heron
..........pregnant with eggs moves away in
..........fear of the roaring ocean waves,
it was a pleasant sight to see gnālal trees
with small flowers on the shore of the cold
backwater, where a small white seagull
that searches the dark expanse and catches
shrimp, calls his tender-legged mate,
and shares his catch with her.
Now, with a distressed heart, I have
become sad like this with many thoughts!'[xii]

Nandi and Mano spent a lot of time discussing the trade routes and the mind-blowing stories told by the yavanars who came from different regions of the world to Indian shores.

One evening as the two of them stood in the deck watching the dusk spread over the sea like an inky blue fog and the waves gently lapping against the side of the ship, Mano said, 'Do you know that more than 2500 years back Indian traders carried copper, timber, ivory, pearls, carnelian and gold to Mesopotamia? Harappans were bulk-shipping timber and lapis lazuli to Sumer. Later on, there was trade between Lothal in Gujarat and Oman, Bahrain and Mesopotamia.'

'Yes, I have heard many stories about Indians doing trade by sea from many centuries back though not in the kind of detail you have described,' responded Nandi.

Madhavi just then sauntered onto the deck. 'Looks like you have nothing else to talk other than sea trade and shipping,' she chided playfully.

'We sailors can talk only about the sea and women,' Mano said laughingly. 'They are both alike in some ways,' he taunted.

'How is that?' asked Madhavi throwing a glance at Nandi who was smiling away.

'The sea is as unpredictable as a woman. You never know when a tempest will break out and when it will calm down.'

Nandi burst into laughter. Madhavi threw a nasty scowl at him.

He said in a placative tone, 'We were discussing about our glorious maritime history. Mano here is very well informed.'

Mano took the cue and continued, 'Even the boat building and coastal trade from Kalinga in the east along the Indian coast to Sind in the west must have been happening for centuries. But there is one thing lacking.' He paused here and gave a command to his helmsman to steer away from the coral reef ahead.

'And that is?' prompted Madhavi.

'Our cartography is primitive and our navy is literally non-existent. I have seen the Greeks, Chinese and Persians use a lot more documentation of sea routes than we do,' said Mano. The other two nodded in agreement.

'Maybe we have all the maps in our head,' said Nandi. 'We Indians are known for our oral memory.'

'But somewhere down the line we have to record our knowledge. We Siddhars too carried our knowledge in our head and handed it down from generation to generation, but once we learnt the Brahmi script we started recording everything. That has come in handy so many times.'

'That is the one thing we have to crack,' said Mano adjusting the sails. 'There are some big plans being made.'

Madhavi looked at Nandi with a mystified expression. He simply shrugged.

✻ ✻ ✻

They reached Muziris early morning the next day. The wharves were alive and buzzling with shouts of sailors and workmen. Madhavi wondered whether Muziris was as big as Puhar or even bigger. It was the capital of the Chera kingdom in the west coast. So it had stronger linkages with Sind, Persia, Greece and Africa than the eastern ports of South India. It had one of the best harbours on the Indian coastline. The harbour spread out behind the offshore bar where the lagoon, formed by the estuary of the Periyar river, opened.

Large ships with their sails fluttering in the monsoon wind were making their way towards the harbour, their massive wooden hulls steering them through the busy route across the Periyar river basin until they dropped anchor at the shallow waters.

Sailors from yavanar ships were giving instructions to the local headload workers to load or unload rolls of silk, gunny bags full of spices, cartons of gold and other exotic stuff. A row of traders had set up shops along the sides of the neatly laid market streets. As in Puhar, Madhavi noticed that many foreigners were wearing local clothes and were even speaking the local dialect. They had become permanent residents of the city and acted as interlocutors and representatives of foreign traders.

Mano noticed how Madhavi and Nandi were absorbing the scene around them. 'Ships come here from 40 countries from around the world,' he informed, his face beaming with pride.

Vengayyan was helping the sailors to unload material from the ship. While Mano got the ship cleaned and goods loaded, Madhavi and Nandi went around the city markets.

✻ ✻ ✻

Since they left Korkai, Nandi hardly had a chance to speak with Madhavi in private. Madhavi had a bout of sea sickness the first couple of days on the ship. The trip to the market gave her and Nandi some time to reflect on the adventure they had embarked upon.

'This is going to be a long trip,' said Nandi as they sat under the shade of the awning of a shop selling fried fish. 'Do you think we have taken the right decision?' he asked.

Once Madhavi took the decision to make the arduous trip she was grateful when Nandi decided to join her without hesitation. He trusted her judgement. She felt his question was sincere.

Madhavi gently took his hand in hers. 'Nandi, I am incredibly grateful that you decided to join me; you had to make a hard decision. I am convinced this is going to be an eventful trip. I was fed up with the monotonous life in Madurai. Mostly though, I wanted to escape from my nightmares,' she confided.

When she took his hand in hers Nandi felt an exciting tingle. This was the first time that Madhavi had taken his hand for a reason other than to check his pulse. He was also moved by her wish to escape from the mundane life she was leading. He had never been adventurous, always cautious in his trade dealings to a fault. But the decision to team up with Madhavi had not been a business decision. For the first time in his professional life he forgot to think about profit and returns.

Nandi had read many of the agam poems describing a lover's fanciful imagination of his love. He had thought they were very far-fetched but now that he was in love, he could appreciate some of those lyrics. The Tamil bards excelled in this area. A poet had imagined that even Lord Siva had been convinced to part with the crescent moon entangled in his knotted hair so that it became the forehead of a beautiful nymph. Nandi tried to picturize the crescent moon adorning Madhavi's forehead. It didn't seem that far-fetched now. Another bard had admitted that the Lord of Love, Kama, had let go of his sugarcane bow to become the two dark eyebrows of a hero's lover. One poet went even further—he had the audacity to say that just like a foe surrenders his arms when defeated in the battlefield, Lord Indra had surrendered to the lure of a beautiful maiden and sacrificed his thunderbolt, which had the power to secure even the immortal gods, to serve as her waist. Another highly imaginative suggestion was that the six-faced Lord Murugan let his fiery lance turn into the two dark glowing eyes of a beautiful damsel so that her beloved can writhe in pain. *How women have made men's minds so fertile!*

He chuckled to himself and squeezed her hand. 'I think I took a good decision. After all, life should have a meaning.'

They sat there together for some more time enjoying their proximity and the bustle of the streets. Finally, the shop-keeper reminded them to pay up and give their seats to new customers. Madhavi giggled and they got up and started walking towards the ship and their unknown adventures.

❊ ❊ ❊

Mano had completed his business in Muziris and they all set sail for Bhrgukachha. With the wind helping them and the sea placid, they crossed Tyndis and reached Bhrgukachha on the tenth day.

They were happy to see Vallabh waiting for them at the wharf when they reached the port. He greeted them with a broad grin. He seemed to know Mano for ages. They all chatted up about their trip and the huge market at Muziris.

'I am very happy to see South Indians joining our effort,' he said and continued with a hint of humour, 'I hope you have overcome your doubts about North Indians. Not all of us are Aryans and certainly we did not drive all the Dravidians to the South.'

Madhavi knew that he was just teasing them. 'The northerners think that they constitute India. But we have decided not to give up,' she said. All nodded and laughed.

'That's true,' Vallabh said suddenly turning serious. 'India is not just the North or the North-west or the South. If we don't stay together, then India will be up for grabs. We are like a mighty elephant but the question is: are we aware of it?'

Madhavi and Nandi were pleasantly surprised to know that Mano will be handing over the charge of his ship to a fellow captain and joining them on their trip to the North.

'We will be leaving for Kaushambi as soon as possible,' informed Vallabh. But we are going to have trouble passing through Ujjayini.'

'Why?' asked Mano.

'The King of Avanti has been murdered,' replied Vallabh matter-of-factly.

23

MURDER

Satya was waiting impatiently at the usual meeting spot at the Pushpakaranda park. He had come well before time. Madanika had sent a message that she had some important news. He looked around to see whether any suspicious character had followed him into the park. Since the day of the Agaria conference and the standoff with the Mahamatra's guards, he was in the wanted list. But the administration was looking for the right opportunity to roundup the rebels. The security apparatus knew that the Agarias were a very well-knit community and they didn't want to buy trouble by arresting prominent members without making detailed plans.

It was getting a bit cooler in the nights. The children who were playing near him had themselves covered with spun woolen garments. The pond in the centre of the park was covered with leaves and flowers shed from the gigantic trees all around. The crisp air and the fallen leaves reminded Satya that life is ever-changing and one has to move on. Suvala had sent adulatory messages on the usefulness of the steel weaponry dispatched to the frontier. He had even requested him to consider coming to Takshashila and interacting with the best minds there on steel technology, warfare and weaponry. It was an irresistible offer.

Lost in thoughts, he did not notice that Madanika had entered the park and had spotted him. She sat next to him with a smile but Satya could sense a certain tenseness in it. He had known her since childhood. They had studied and played together. Since her family could not afford to set up a furnace on their own, she had decided to serve the royal courtesan. Luckily, her community did not look at her employment as an embarrassment.

'How have you been these days?' asked Satya as he put a hand around her shoulder and pulled her closer.

'It has been very tough,' she replied resting her head on his shoulder.

'You had sent an urgent message. I was quite worried,' said Satya tenderly.

'Yes, I am worried too,' said Madanika and looked at him. 'There are secret meetings going on every day at Vasantasena's palace. They are now careful and don't say anything when I am serving them food and drinks. But I could hear some snippets of conversation here and there. It looks like the Mahamatra is planning something terrible soon to capture power.'

Satya guessed that she didn't want to talk about the increased debauchery and wickedness that accompanied these secret meetings. The Mahamatra did not hesitate to bribe his supporters with the choicest liquor and women apart from a share of the tax money. He kept them literally under house arrest, no doubt with exotic privileges, to keep them away from the king's overtures. And Vasantasena knew exactly how to keep these scums who masqueraded as nobles under her full control. She imported or bought the most beautiful slaves from different parts of India to cater to the different tastes of her customers. They went through rigorous training on conversational skills required to keep their customers engaged and loyal for a long period. She even devised innovative sexual games to keep her clients satisfied. Madanika had hinted bashfully about a new game of chess that she had innovated where women of the harem were used as pawns, rooks and bishops.

'What makes you think that?' asked Satya referring to Madanika's premonition of terrible things.

'There have been more late-night meetings than usual and the security has been doubled. But what really made me suspicious is that a delegation came from Takshashila. Some names like Ambhi and Vishnugupta figured in their discussion.'

'That's serious,' said Satya sounding alarmed. 'It looks like something is brewing.'

'I am not worried about these schemes. What I am worried about is you,' said Madanika tightening her grip on his arm.

Satya looked at her with some apprehension. 'What is it that worries you?' he asked her tenderly. Her concern wasn't news to him.

'One of my friends heard your name along with a few other Agaria leaders being mentioned in a meeting last night. She sent a message asking me to meet at her quarters. She was positive that it was your name. She knows about us.'

'Wow, looks like I am getting popular!' he said lightly. 'Soon they will label me as a traitor and extremist. But it doesn't surprise me since their spies have been following me for months now.'

'We should not take this lightly,' entreated Madanika. 'Anything can happen anytime so we should be prepared to leave the city at short notice.'

'I have also been thinking about this and making arrangements,' replied Satya comforting her by holding her hand. 'Suvala and Ananda have invited me to visit the north.'

'Only you?' she asked, looking at Satya from the corner of her eyes.

'Of course, it means all of us,' he replied. 'I am nothing without my friends and my sweetheart. We should all be getting ready to leave.'

'Something tells me it would be very soon.'

'You sound so sure.'

'Yes,' said Madanika emphatically. 'There was also talk about murder at one of the meetings.'

'Who will be that poor bloke?' asked Satya.

'It looks like it will be the king,' replied Madanika.

24

THE CARAVAN TO KAUSHAMBI

Vallabh – Takshashila – 326 BCE

The Greek linguist Scipio was giving one of his boring speeches on the influence of Greek language and culture in the Indian subcontinent. As usual he was disgustingly pompous. He wore a dark grey suit over black slacks and an old bluish cap covered his bald head. Vallabh had a big urge to kick him on the shin to make him stop but restrained himself with effort. The loudmouth had actually mellowed a bit after the standoff between Sikandar and Porus and the quick retreat of the Macedonian army. If Gandhara had become a vassal of the Macedonians then such a discussion would have been unimaginable. Many Greek documenters, traders, artists and other professionals had been left behind in Takshashila to keep up the pretence that the Greeks still had control over the city. But they were quickly becoming irrelevant in the tremendous changes happening in the rest of India.

The Department of Linguistics at the Takshahila University, where the debate was going on, was an old structure built of stone and timber. The debating hall had a barrel-vaulted high ceiling resting on strong stone pillars. Through the square glass windows the yellow glow of sunlight seeped in and made grotesque shadows of the furniture and people inside. There were just twelve of them, the most brilliant minds in the university on languages and scripts.

Scipio continued in his high-pitched voice. 'The Greek language and script have greatly influenced the Indian languages and scripts. As you are all aware, Sanskrit is an Indo-Aryan language and the Brahmi and Kharosthi scripts have close links with the Semitic and Greek scripts of the west. It is no wonder that Greek is getting exceedingly popular in India. It may even soon replace Sanskrit and the unsophisticated languages like the Prakrits.'

The Chair of the debating forum signalled politely that he should wind up soon.

Vallabh started his presentation in a cheerful tone. 'Brahmi is read from left to right while Semitic scripts are read from right to left. So, there is very little chance that Brahmi came from the west. Brahmi must have its beginnings in the Indus civilization script though, as yet, we don't have conclusive proof but it is unambiguous that it is an Indian product. It has adapted very well to the sounds of Indian languages.'[xiii]

Vallabh knew that he had captured the attention of other members of the forum. He paused a little, studying the manuscript in front of him. 'There are many other facts about Indian languages. The scripts of the south have their own history. Graffiti in the south show that the Indus script had penetrated far south making a great connection between the languages of the north and the south.[xiv] The Tamil Brahmi has developed wonderfully. Other scripts like the Grantha and the Vattezhuthu also developed. They look superficially different but every Southeast Asian script has its source in Brahmi. So how can we accept that Greek and Semitic scripts of the west have influenced Indian languages? I think this is a ruse of the western conquerors to make Indians think that they are using borrowed languages and scripts.'

Many in the room nodded vigorously. Scipio snorted.

Aniruddha had been listening attentively and he now made a signal to the Chair that he had something to add.

He had a deep tone which made an immediate impact on the listeners. 'Old Vedic Sanskrit is considered to be an Indo-European language. Maybe so. But since Vedic times, Sanskrit has evolved. Its grammar has become simple. It has borrowed a lot of words from other Indian languages. Panini, the great grammarian, developed the Ashtadhyayi, the book of grammar, sitting in this very room at least a century back. Our alphabets have been so scientifically classified that the West borrowed the science of phonetics from us.'

'Hear, hear!' exclaimed many in the audience. The debate was simply taking the wind out of the western argument that India is indebted to the west for its culture and civilisation.

Ananda too joined the debate. 'Ladies and gentlemen,' he began, for there were two women linguists in the august gathering. 'Just as the Brahmi script is an Indian product and Sanskrit and the Prakrits have evolved in Indian conditions, the South also has made tremendous strides. The Tamil Brahmi script is certainly a relation of the Indus script. The Tamil language has been in existence probably for as long as Sanskrit. It has a wonderfully structured grammar called the Tolkappiyam, which is as great a work as the Ashtadhyayi. The sad part is that when different sections of Indians start to prove that their language is better than others, then foreigners try to exploit these differences.' Ananda glanced at Scipio whose face was getting redder as the debate proceeded.

One of the professors with a heavy beard and a pointed nose butted in. 'I have proof that when Sanskrit evolved from the Vedic to the classical stage it started using compound nouns with many members influenced by Tamil. In the same way, Tamil has borrowed many Sanskrit words. This happens all the time when people speaking different languages live near each other and have a common history and culture.'

The debate continued for a while and finally the professor in the Chair observed, 'This debating forum totally debunks the theory that Indian languages have evolved under the influence of western languages, scripts and grammar. We are not able to find the science of phonetics more advanced than here in any part of the world. Cultural colonialism has to be condemned as much as military colonialism.'

✳ ✳ ✳

The kingdom of Gandhara was the western-most part of India and had been for centuries the eastern-most frontier of the Persian empire. Takshashila, the capital, was at the crossroads of the main trade route between India and West Asia and beyond. It was also perched on a branch of the Silk Road that connected China to the West. The sprawling university in the city fortunately survived the scorched earth policy of the Macedonian army since King Ambhi had signed a no-war pact with Sikandar. A large number of students studying at the university, enraged by Ambhi's refusal to join the war against Sikandar, travelled to Jhelum to support Porus in his resistance. They were no match for a well-trained army but their numbers and energy made a difference. After Sikandar's retreat, the university was back to its usual business. It was perhaps the largest university in the world at that time with thousands of students vying for admission from as many as 40 countries.

After the long debate, Vallabh and his friends reached the open-air restaurant at the side of the fabulous park in the university. The restaurant served a sumptuous meal at student prices. The friends ordered the Buddhist meal package the restaurant specialised in. The city had many monasteries and the university admitted Buddhist monks and nuns into its exalted portals. Vallabh too could find some Jain monks in the city.

He sipped slowly on his hot vegetable soup spiced with herbs and pepper.

'You know what the problem is?' he asked wiping his lips with the edge of his robe. 'We have fantastic languages and script. We write tons and tons of material but we are writing on palm leaf manuscripts and wood strips which don't last. How do we record our science and culture and political thought so that future generations can judge us for what we are?'

'That's true,' replied Aniruddha. 'Perhaps there is a solution but it may be very cumbersome.'

'What is that cumbersome solution?' asked Ananda.

'You can see the graffiti on cave walls; they have been there for millennia. But it is not just Stone Age hunters who carved on stone. I heard that the Persian king, Darius, made a lot of stone inscriptions. It may not be just the administration using stone inscriptions, even poets, writers and lovers might be using stone as a medium.'

'It is a cumbersome solution,' admitted Vallabh. 'But until we discover another easy-to-use medium to record our writings, stones and rocks are the most enduring. I think we should propose to our linguistics committee that we should make a plan to initiate stone inscriptions soon.'

'Our university doesn't have that kind of reach or funds. We are just incubators. Large administrations like Magadha should take this up,' suggested Ananda.

'Our fellow professor, Vishnugupta, and his protégé have been raising an army to capture Magadha,' pointed out Vallabh. 'They are open to novel ideas. Our friend Sayana has been working with them on economy and statecraft. We should certainly get together on this.'

❊ ❊ ❊

It was by chance that Vallabh and Aniruddha noticed the fire in the library building of the Linguistics Department that night. After dinner they had come out for a stroll on the lawns of the university. Flickers of light shot up from the right corner room of the library. Wisps of dark sooty smoke rose against the background of the night sky like the flickering tongues of poisonous snakes. Silhouetted by the flames, they could see a couple of masked men running away in the opposite direction. Just then the moon hid herself behind dark clouds, as if wanting to shield the arsonists. The fire was clearly no accident; it was an act of arson.

They ran towards the building shouting for help. The night guards patrolling the university grounds reached the building swiftly and ordered the building attendants to start dousing the fire with water. Takshashila was still under the shadow of war clouds due to which security forces and patrolling had been beefed up.

The masked men were quickly apprehended by Vallabh and the security guards. It did not take much convincing to get them to confess that they were Scipio's hired henchmen at the university. The Greek governor and Magistrate of Takshashila, who were Sikandar's representatives in the city, tried to cover up Scipio's crime under the cover of diplomatic immunity. Fortunately, the damage to the library was minimal and only a few scrolls were lost, for which duplicates could be found.

The arson was just a reflection of the imperialist thinking of the Macedonian invaders that all other civilisations, other than them, were barbarians who required to be domesticated. Scipio was unrepentant at the inquiry. Justifying his act, he had the audacity to say, 'Alexander has brought civilisation to this part of the world. He has built over several cities in the provinces he conquered among the barbarian tribes. He has seeded them with Greek magistrates in order to emancipate them from their undomesticated and beastly way of life.'[xv]

Aniruddha and others in the court room were appalled by this pretension and he could not hold back himself. With the court's permission, he explained, 'It's a lie that Sikandar rebuilt a lot of cities, most of them called Alexandria after his name. Major settlements already existed along these trade routes. Neither did the Greeks open up a new maritime route in the Persian Gulf and Red Sea because Sikandar wanted to make the Persian Gulf as prosperous as Phoenicia. So, it is a lie that Sikandar brought civilisation to this part, which was already the centre of civilisation and trade for centuries.'

Vallabh added, 'Rather than being a land of barbarians, there have been human settlements in Bactria, Gandhara and other areas of the north-west of Bharatavarsha for centuries. The Persians have had a lot of influence in this route. The Indus river has been an artery which connected many regions of the north-west with western and eastern India. Maritime trade has been happening all along between this region and the rest of the world. This professor wants to bring Bharatavarsha under Hellenistic influence. That's why he has been trying to establish that Greek is the source of all languages in India and that even the Brahmi script was borrowed. He was defeated in this debate so he has become rabid and wanted to erase all our research work on scripts and languages by burning down the library. Sikandar burnt Persepolis for the same reason. He wanted to erase all Persian influence in the region.'

Vallabh recalled how the kingdoms in the South looked at his activities with suspicion. Initially, he had felt that he was a stranger in a foreign land but once he understood the language and customs, he had learnt a lot. There was such a dichotomy. The South traded more with the Greeks and Arabs than with the cities of the Gangetic Plains. India was a land of paradox.

Vallabh continued in a serious tone. 'We have to learn our lessons from the narrow thinking of these westerners. We ourselves should respect all languages and cultures in our Bharatavarsha. There is no one superior language or culture. If we succumb to this Hellenistic bigotry then we can get easily divided by external aggressors.' *But are we capable of preventing history from repeating itself?*

In spite of threats that Indo-Greek trade relations might plummet, Professor Scipio had to pack his bags and leave for his country. The administration of Takshashila had no choice but to bow to the will of the people.

25

CARTOGRAPHY

Mano – Takshashila – 325 BCE

The huge library at the Trade Department of Takshashila University gave one the feeling of walking through a crypt. The walls had gathered dust which stuck to them like moss glued to wood. The air smelled of leaf manuscripts and old age. Huge and tall wooden shelves fitted into recesses rose right up to the ceiling filled with bound manuscripts, scrolls, maps and other documents. Oil taper candles were not allowed since there was so much of inflammable material. Skylights on the roof and walls allowed some sunlight to filter in.

Mano, Sudjata and Nandi were seated on stone benches arranged around a stone table that protruded from the wall. They were poring through miscellaneous manuscripts and maps.

'I have never seen thousands of books and maps under one single roof!' exclaimed Mano. 'I wonder how the university managed to get so many of them from so many different regions. There are Persian, Greek, Chinese and even Sumerian manuscripts.'

Nandi nodded vigorously. 'Why, I even came across Tamil manuscripts. Someone here told me that our grammarian Tholkappiyar had met Panini in this university. It was hard to believe that Tholkappiyar would have taken the same route as I took to come here a couple of centuries back. But after seeing Tamil manuscripts here I have started to believe the story.'

'Have we been able to locate some maps of trade routes?' asked Sudjata who had joined them a bit late.

'Sure,' replied Mano waving his hand across the table. 'There are quite a few of them here. Most interesting is a map from the time of the Indus civilization.'

'Wow, that's extraordinary!' commented Sudjata with genuine astonishment. 'Hard to imagine how these maps have been preserved for a millennium or more.'

Mano unfolded a fairly large crumpled map gingerly. 'The Indian Ocean has been the birth of shipping and sea trade. The Indus Valley people knew spinning, weaving, pottery-making, metallurgy and other crafts. So, it is natural they knew about boat-building and sailing on the high seas. There is also a book here which talks about their flourishing maritime trade with various countries.' He fetched the book from the next table and opened a page. 'See, there is a drawing of a boat on terracotta from Mohenjodaro. It is dated at least 1500 years back. It seems that Lothal was not only an excellent port built with remarkable engineering ingenuity and skill, but it also doubled up as a boat-building centre. It could handle ships at both high and low tides. It had sluice gates.'[xvi]

Both Sudjata and Nandi bent over the table to look at the drawings.

'That's fantastic,' said Nandi. 'When I went to Puhar last time I looked for maps in the library there. The library wasn't as big as this one but there were a huge number of documents and maps. We have been exporting fine muslin and timber, aromatic spices, sweet incenses, ivory and sandalwood from the Malabar coast. The lengthy voyage and the bulky nature of the cargo would have meant that the steady trade would have been established many centuries ago.'

'What all this means,' said Sudjata looking at the drawings spread over the table, 'is that land and sea trade had never slackened from the time of the Indus civilisation, the time of the first urbanisation, to the period of second urbanisation that is happening now. The goods exported have been similar, the ships and sea routes used have been similar. So trading, ship-building and sailing—all must have been a continuous activity smoothly developing from one generation to the next.'

'The Silk Route was not only a land route but a sea route as well. It connected Sumer, India and China,' announced Mano. He picked up a scroll marked 'Silk Route' gently and blew on the dust and unrolled it. The edges of the scroll were frayed. He spread it over another table and examined it for a few minutes.

The old librarian was getting impatient. These visitors had now been coming regularly to the library and dusting as many books and opening as many scrolls as possible for a full-time researcher in a day. They occupied no less than 3 or 4 tables. He had to invariably remind them when they were about to leave to kindly clear the tables and put the scrolls back in their appropriate bins.

It was time to go for lunch. They put back the scrolls and cleared the table of books. When they walked out of the library their clothes had a thin coating of dust and their faces were grimy from knowledge and wisdom.

As they washed their hands and sat down for lunch, Mano continued from where he had left. 'In one of the books I came across remarkable similarities between techniques and materials used for building Sumerian ships 1500 years ago and the traditional techniques and materials used in Muziris and Tyndis on the western coast of south India. This may very well be true of ships built in Puhar as well.'

'One thing is certain,' said Sudjata emphatically, 'Other than Indians, no one else could have mastered sailing in the monsoon winds. Once they understood the monsoons, it made sailing on the high seas so much easier. For them, the ocean was nothing to be scared of. It became a highway of a different sort to travel to other lands and transport their goods.'

26

AYURVEDA – THE SCIENCE OF LIFE

Madhavi – 326 BCE

As Madhavi's cart steadily approached Jhelum she could see the smoke from the campfires even when they were still an hour's drive away from the river. The fields were barren. As they made progress, she started hearing a low murmur, as if Jhelum were in spate. A little further ahead, voices of men floated towards them. Soon she could hear horses whinnying and elephants trumpeting. This was the first time in her life that she would be visiting a battleground. As she heard the shouts and clash of steel, she prepared herself for what she was about to witness. But when she finally got a view of the battlefield it shook her to the bones.

She motioned to the cart driver to stop and stepping down from the cart, beckoned her friends Susmila and Nalini to follow her. She had been introduced to them at Kaushambi by Vallabh and had since become attached to them. Their honesty and simplicity charmed her. Their narratives about their life before joining the monastery made her cry in her bed. Vallabh and Aniruddha had organised a cart and security for them to reach the battle ground at Jhelum.

It was early evening. Thousands of cookfires had already been lit to provide warmth as well as prepare food for those who had survived the battle. The cavalry horses were tied to hundreds of poles in a long line stretching into the horizon. Huge elephants were tethered to iron weights sunk into the ground with iron chains looped around a ring. Thousands of trees had been felled and cut into logs for constructing rafts or for building the siege engines.

They were met by a senior captain wearing a helmet and a mail shirt. The seal that Aniruddha had given them seemed to be welcome at the camp. The captain took them to a large tent where some officers were having a serious discussion. Madhavi was surprised to see that there were officers from both the Greek army and the kingdom of Purus.

One of the commanders stood up and welcomed them. 'You have made such a long trip from Kaushambi, you must be spent,' he said politely. 'Doctors and nurses are always welcome in a battlefield. I also hear that you are from South India?'

'Yes,' said Madhavi. 'And with me are Susmila and Nalini. I hope we are not too late.'

'As you might have heard,' replied the commander motioning them to sit down, 'the battle at Jhelum was a stalemate. Both sides lost heavily. There were many casualties so King Sikandar and King Porus decided to call a truce. It would have surprised you to see Macedonian commanders in this tent. Till yesterday we were sworn enemies but now we have decided to get together and attend to our dead and wounded.'

He introduced them to the Greek commanders through an interlocutor.

The Greek commanders welcomed them once they heard that they had come to provide health services to those wounded. One of them commented, 'It will be great to see both Greek and Indian medicine at work.'

They were taken to their tents and provided a hot meal.

'I think we should get some sleep tonight,' said Madhavi as they undressed for bed. 'We would have our hands full tomorrow.'

❇ ❇ ❇

When Madhavi and her friends ventured out of the tent next morning, they were greeted by a colossal scene. There were thousands of soldiers, helpers, cooks, washer women and others busy at their work. The two massive armies had set up their tents on the right bank of Jhelum not far from each other. The dark green banners of the Puru army were flapping in the wind while the Greek camp sported white and red banners. The tents were also decorated with the same colours. The siege engines were all lined up in a row away from the tents as if they were unwanted beggars. Their work of destruction had been done and no one cared for them now. The neighing of horses, the trumpeting of elephants and the heady smell of the preparations for the breakfast mixed with dung and human excreta made Madhavi's head spin.

As they approached the tent put up for the wounded, cries and moans added to her discomfort. Attending to the wounded and dying was an essential part of her profession but she had not prepared herself for such a large-scale version of a hospital ward. There were doctors and nurses scurrying around to check a pulse or change a blood-soaked bandage or provide medicines and water to crying and groaning patients. There were no partitions, so surgeries and amputations were done in full view of others in the camp. Blood-curdling cries and groans came from different corners of the tent from patients whose limbs were being amputated or open wounds surgically closed and stitched.

Susmila and Nalini were stunned for a while but soon joined the nurses to help them with their huge load of work. Madhavi went over to a group of doctors who were discussing about prioritising treatment and making a requirement plan for medicines and equipment.

'Hello,' greeted a senior doctor. 'I am Kunala. I have been expecting you. Aniruddha informed me that you and your friends will be joining us here to help. You must be under a shock; it's not every day that you treat patients after a devastating war. We are trying to do our best under the circumstances.'

Kunala looked to be about 50 years old. He was of medium height and broad shouldered. Madhavi looked at his shining bright black eyes and felt comforted. Those eyes reminded her of her father's eyes which cared for the world and created an instant feeling of trust in the person they rested upon. Madhavi could feel the restlessness in those eyes, the anxiety that even five minutes should not be wasted in life.

Madhavi greeted him warmly in return. 'I am happy to be of help. I think you are short of anaesthetics and sedatives. I can help there,' she offered.

'Oh, that will be a great help,' he said with a sigh. 'We do lack these drugs. That's why you can hear cries of pain. We have been doing the cauterization with fire and alkali without anesthetics. Also, we follow the Sushruta Samhita procedure for letting out of some blood as the first step in treatment of wounds.'

Madhavi had heard of this treatise on medicine which was perhaps the first of its kind in the world. Sushruta had written the first volumes of his treatise at least three centuries back and it was being continuously revised.

Kunala turned out to be one of those excellent conversationalists, those who easily removed the initial hesitation between strangers to open up. He involved Madhavi in a conversation straightaway, not in a one-way dialogue but in an eager exchange of views.

'There are very few here trained in the shalya tantra, which is actually surgical science,' the doctor continued earnestly, 'but we are trying to do our best. With limited equipment we have done rhinoplasty and lithotomy. We are also making arrangements to transfer some of the patients to the hospital at Takshashila.'

'I have heard of Sushruta Samhita as well as Charaka Samhita which deals with medicine. I am myself a Siddha doctor and know that the basic principles of diagnosis and treatment are the same. Only the medicine varies,' said Madhavi.

'It makes one sad. The way astrologers thrive on bad omens, we learn from a patient's suffering. And a war provides doctors the most difficult patients and the most complex challenges. This is a good place to test your theories too. We have some Greek doctors as well working with us. Often we have debates over what is best.'

Madhavi laughed. 'Yes, we learn from the miseries of other people but we also provide them with a cure. It will be interesting to see what the Greeks know.'

'Well, not much, in my opinion,' said Kunala with some satisfaction. 'They may have a good war machine but their doctors are no good. They have not even been able to treat their king, Sikandar, who has a severe wound and some kind of food poisoning.'

Madhavi was amused. 'Is that so!' she exclaimed. 'They claim to have the world's biggest army but you say they are not good at curing their injured?'

'There is a misconception that Ayurveda is just about humoral pathology, a treatise on the three doshas. In fact, the Greeks believe in the tridosha principle dogmatically but Ayurveda is more than just the interpretation of body humors.'

Madhavi had also believed in this viewpoint but she waited for the doctor to continue.

He moved on to the next patient and Madhavi followed him like a medical student anxious to please her guide.

'The Greeks believe that Humoral Pathology explains all diseases as caused by the mixture of the cardinal humors, the blood, bile, mucus or phlegm and water. These are the vata, pitta and kapha that we talk about, except that vata looked too complex for them so they replaced it with their theory of 'water'. But this is so obnoxious,' commented the doctor.[xvii]

'That's fascinating,' commented Madhavi with genuine interest.

'At Sikandar's request some surgeons from India are accompanying him to Greece. This is a definite indication that surgical science is advanced here. Susruta and Divodasa have contributed a lot to it.'

'Yes, we also practice surgery in the South and have been quite successful in removing cancerous tissues and infected tissues. But I hear incredible stories about north Indian surgeons. Is it true that we are so good in plastic surgery that we can replace a severed head with another?' asked Madhavi innocently.

Kunala roared with laughter. Other doctors and nurses in the hall glanced at him with a smile. They could guess that Kunala was enjoying his conversation with the beautiful doctor from the South.

'That is absurd!' sputtered Kunala in between bouts of laughter. 'We neither replace heads nor do we have that kind of genetic science where we can grow babies outside the mother's womb, like Kunti giving birth to Karna before marriage. Neither are we able to use stem cells to grow body parts. We are proud of our achievements but not jingoists. We should not let pseudo-science dominate our research.'

'Sorry, you were talking about the difference between our approach and the western approach to curing diseases,' reminded Madhavi.

'Yes, we got a bit diverted. What I was trying to explain was that Ayurveda is not an encyclopaedia of the Indian system of medicine. So, you may not have a big chapter on human anatomy in the Sushruta Samhita but it is the Science of Life in its entirety,' explained Kunala.

'Can you elaborate that point more?' requested Madhavi.

'Sure,' said Kunala with a satisfied smile. All the time while he talked, he moved from patient to patient. advising the nurses about medication. 'It is customary and convenient to group apart such phenomena that are termed mental, that is related to psychology and sociology. But there is no such demarcations in nature. In the entire Science of Life, which Ayurveda is, psychology and sociology are inseparably linked with Anatomy and Physiology. Even more, I would say, with Pathology and Hygiene and above all, with Treatment. Don't you think so?' he asked.

Madhavi nodded and added, 'You are saying that Biological Sciences must deal with whatever phenomena are manifested by living matter in whatever condition it occurs.'

'You have put your finger on it,' said Kunala patting her shoulder. 'Life in health, sukhayuha, as well as life in disease, dukkhayuha, therefore, fall within the scope of Biology—even life exhibited by man in Society, hitahitam, is not exempted from it.'

हिताहितं सुखं दुःखं आयुस्तस्य हिताहितम् ।

मानं च तच्च यत्रोक्तं आयुर्वेदः स उच्यते ॥

***

The next few weeks were hectic for Madhavi, Susmila and Nalini. They worked from morning to night assisting the medical contingent. With the help of Doctor Kunala, Madhavi took a squad of helpers with her to the nearby forest to collect herbs, barks, leaves and flowers for preparing her medicines. They were greatly appreciated by the Indian and Greek doctors alike and added to the dwindling stock of emergency medicines.

Another aspect endeared Madhavi to the doctors even more. Using her knowledge of the Varma kalai, the art of understanding and manipulating vital pressure points in the body, she could cure many patients with a non-surgical approach. Her treatment combined massage, alternative medicine and yoga. Doctor Kunala and a host of Indian and Greek doctors acknowledged this as a very useful addition to the existing treatment.

Patients who could be transported were taken to the hospital at Takshashila which also had a medical college attached to it. After taking care of emergencies and discharging patients with non-serious wounds, Doctor Kunala made arrangements to take Madhavi and her friends to Takshashila.

❋ ❋ ❋

Takshashila University was the most organized learning center of ancient India which was funded by the rulers of almost all the kingdoms of India and abroad. It had a variety of disciplines to offer its students from all over the known world—art, philososphy, medicine, linguistics, political and military science. The university campus hosted about ten thousand students. Not so tall buildings were spread out over a large area. It had some of the world's most reputed professors. Panini the grammarian, Jivaka the physician and Sushruta the founder of Ayurveda were amongst its prestigious alumni. It was no wonder that students flocked to the university. The cosmopolitan ambience of the university encouraged research and debate among different schools of thought, languages, religions and cultures.

The campus had regular departments and lecture rooms. But a novelty was that some professors conducted their courses in large houses with students staying as paying guests. This helped to bring down the tuition costs for the students.

There were considerable leeway given to teachers to design their own curriculum. Students were from a mixed background—there were children of kings and nobles paid for by the state treasury, and then there were poorer students who received scholarships on the basis of their merit. Many students worked part-time to sustain themselves.

Madhavi liked the ambience of the university. She looked forward to working with Doctor Kunala and other eminent professors in the department of public health. She also looked forward to meeting Nandi and his newfound friends. *I wonder what Nandi is doing now. Does he miss me as much as I miss him?*

* * *

The Department of Public Health, like other departments in the campus, was a spartan building made of fired brick, square windows with wooden frames, high ceiling, stone tables carved into niches on the walls and comfortable wooden chairs. The hospital where the students interned was within walking distance. Now, it had patients from all over the area where the Macedonian army had cut and trampled their way through. There were patients from the tribal areas of Khamboja, from Gandhara and from the recent battles in Punjab. A good number of Greek soldiers and mercenaries, who could not return with the retreating army of Sikandar, were also admitted. The enemy soldiers had now become guests. The kingdom of Gandhara did not treat them as refugees without rights. They were treated in the best Indian traditions of *atithi devo bhava,* guest is God.

Madhavi could again have many more interactions with Doctor Kunala and other specialists in the department. She spent hours in the medical library poring over manuscripts and diagrams. The more she listened to Kunala, the more fascinated she became of his knowledge.

Right now, they were discussing the real essence of Ayurveda and Indian thought on health and medicine.

Kunala was saying, 'What we need to explain to the world is that Ayurveda is not just a list of medicines for various diseases. It is not an encyclopaedia on medicine, to be dogmatically followed by physicians. Rather we should look at it as a guide, as the philosophy of health.'

'How so?' commented Madhavi. 'Everyone thinks that Sushruta Samhita is a book on medicines.'

'Precisely the problem,' reacted Kunala biting away at a piece of peacock meat. 'The very name Ayurveda indicates ayus—life! It is a treatise on Biology dealing with the general truths of life. The special truths of life and their practical sides are also dealt with in the treatise but that is only a corollary.'

'But will it be practical then?' asked Madhavi.

'Practice has to come from the mind's eye and not just from the body's. We should not let Ayurveda deteriorate into a system of Medicine and Surgery which has neither Biology nor Anatomy Physiology or Pathology—but is a systematised empiricism or quackery. We should understand the principal structures of the human body, but more important is our understanding of the molecular construction of an organism. Only this can help us as a reliable guide to treatment.'

'What you are saying is really going above my head,' admitted Madhavi humbly. 'But I guess I will begin to understand some day.'

'Not to worry,' said Kunala. 'It took me years to comprehend this. What has become clear to me is that a knowledge of the anatomical structures of the body is of great value, at least so far as it helps the surgeons in their operations. But as far as Biology is concerned with medicine, Sushruta emphasises on the knowledge of the molecular construction of the body. The protean work of the protoplasm, its constant ever-changing nature, cannot be detected by the body's eye; to know its work, mind's eye is necessary along with that of the body.'

Madhavi said a bit hesitantly, 'I have studied in our Siddhar manuscripts that the psychological and physiological functions of the body need to be understood to treat patients. We also look at the three humors in the body and check whether they are in equilibrium. We check whether there is an equilibrium in the external factors influencing the patient like environment, climatic conditions, diet, physical activities and stress levels. Our concepts of pathyam and apathyam, the dos and don'ts are not only to do with food but with the psychological and physiological state of the body.'

'Your observations are interesting,' said Kunala with genuine appreciation. 'It adds to the theory that the body has to be understood in its whole. What we have learnt from your system and from the Greek system can very well be added as a layer to the Samhita. Our Indian treatises are collective works. Though an author is mentioned, many others add their knowledge to the treatise as knowledge advances. So, we should add our knowledge to the existing corpus.'

Madhavi smiled with satisfaction. Here she was from a city far south discussing with the best minds in medicine and working in one of world's renowned universities. What more could she want!

27

THE WONDER STEEL

Satya – Takshashila – 235 BCE

'He conquered half the world and yet he wants a gift of steel from us?' asked Satya incredulously.

Suvala laughed and said, 'He is fascinated with our sharp swords. King Porus gave him a gift of two cartloads of steel swords, daggers, ploughs and blades. He even promised to import more steel from us.'

'Our steel is world renowned now,' said a beaming Bala. Maitreya, Sajjalaka and Madanika were all smiles.

'What exactly makes our steel so great?' asked Suvala with genuine wonder.

'The steel we make is an alloy of iron and carbon,' said Satya. 'I learnt this technology from a group of blacksmiths who had come north from Kodumanal in Thamizhagam. What we do is heat black magnetite ore along with carbon in a sealed clay crucible inside a charcoal furnace to completely remove slag. The carbon comes from bamboo chips and leaves from plants such as the winged bean.'[xviii]

Satya and his friends had been busy since they arrived in Takshashila. They set up a model furnace there near the technology centre in the city. It was funded partly by the government and partly by the university. They now had plans to set up one in Mathura and Kaushambi.

Satya took Suvala into the room housing the model furnace. A hot blast of air welcomed them when they entered. It was unbearably hot, but the bare-chested and sweating technicians worked at the red-hot furnace without a quibble. There were two furnaces, one in each far corner. The air stank of iron ore, burning leaves and red-hot clay. There were both men and women technicians and apprentices, though women had to work fully clothed and were drenched in sweat. In Ujjayini they had many open-air furnaces. Here in Takshashila there were strict restrictions on pollution. So, the furnaces were provided with adequate ventilation and tall chimneys to puff out the exhaust gases.

Bala took Suvala nearer the furnace. 'It seems the Tamil have been producing this steel for some 300 years now. Their ports have been exporting it to Rome, Egypt, Arabia and China. It is exported as cakes of steely iron. They call it urukku which has become distorted into Wootz steel.'

Satya pointed to one of the furnaces. 'This is the first step. The alloy is made by hammering porous iron while it is hot. Then, the metal is sealed in a clay container with wood chips. At high temperatures, the wood turns to carbon. It then bonds with iron to make steel. Of course, all this can only be done with experience. For every new batch of iron ore, the process has to be tweaked.'

'Why have the foreigners not been able to master this technology?' asked Suvala.

This time Madanika gave an explanation. 'We have a long history of working with metals. Indians have been working for centuries on bronze alloys. We had mastered mixing a high percentage of tin in the bronze alloy at extremely high temperatures. This technology has also helped us to master steel production.'

'That's true,' reiterated Satya. 'We can produce intensely high temperatures in our furnaces. To withstand such temperatures, even our crucibles are made of alloy steel. I think we are the world's best at hot-forging.'

'I don't have any doubt,' confirmed Suvala.

***

At dinner time, Suvala was all praise for the steel weapon consignments that Satya and his friends managed to send to the war front.

'That was simply awesome,' Suvala gushed. 'The weapons made a lot of difference in the hands of our tribal fighters. They had the advantage of making quick forays on the Macedonian army. This, coupled with the sharp swords and blades, put the world's largest and most organised army on the back foot many times. We made enormous sacrifices, but we slowed down the army and demoralised it. This showed how Indians, if they put their heads together, can take on the world's best.'

Satya looked at his friends. It was unbelievable that such a small force as a bunch of blacksmiths from Ujjayini could make a big impact.

'Though there was talk that Sikandar had won the battle but he was impressed by Porus's valour and returned the kingdom. Is that true?' enquired Madanika.

Suvala shrugged. 'In the battle of Jhelum we used this superiority even more to our advantage. We used the steel to make protective armour for the elephant cavalry. That is why we could achieve a deadlock. Sikandar's scribes were reporting that Porus surrendered and Sikandar was magnanimous enough to give him back his kingdom. But everyone knows that Sikandar had never been compassionate with those he conquered. He put them to death and torched their cities.'

'Why would he do the opposite now?' muttered Madnaika. 'The fact is he did not win.'

'Now, what next?' asked Suvala.

'We should be happy that we sent back the invaders. But what pains me is that the steel swords and weapons we sent you have cut more heads and limbs. If only the steel could be used to make people's lives better.' Satya sounded dejected.

'Well,' sighed Suvala. 'It looks like peace comes only after war and devastation. After the Macedonian army left, the kingdoms in the north-west and west of Magadha are rallying together to escape from being swallowed by Dhanananda. So, the demand for steel weapons is going to spurt once more.'

'When will all this end?' asked Bala mirroring Satya's mood.

'Until the *praja* learns to rule by itself, there is a need for a raja, even if he is a despot. Till then there will be a race for domination and larger kingdoms will swallow the smaller ones.'

'But with despots like Dhanananda, the Magadhan empire may even disintegrate into pieces,' observed Madanika.

'True,' agreed Suvala. 'We have to hope for the best in this situation. I heard that Chandragupta Maurya has assured of a stable regime if others assist him to topple Dhanananda. He has support inside Pataliputra but the crucial factor is that people should also be organised enough to demand that the raja follow his dharma. What is the guarantee that Chandragupta will keep to his work?'

28

STATECRAFT

'The raja should follow rajdharma and the people should have foolproof guarantee to ensure that. If rajdharma is violated, people should have a mechanism in their hands to punish the ruler,' demanded Sayana emphatically.

The best minds in political science were gathered to discuss the constitution of the new empire that was coming into being, the empire of the Mauryas. This was not the first meeting. Chandragupta had still not seized power but from the time that Sikandar had retreated, he and his mentor, Vishnugupta alias Kautilya, were making all efforts to string together the armies of the north and north-west to overwhelm the Magadhan empire.

Sayana both admired and hated Kautilya. He admired him for his intelligence and political acumen. He hated him for his nose-in-the-air attitude and his unscrupulous methods to achieve his aims. He was tall, dark and had a scraggy face. His untied tuft of hair reached his shoulders; his hands and palms were calloused indicating that life had treated him roughly. He was known to travel widely and had contacts in high places. Sayana knew Kautilya was helping his protégé to raise an army with the help of several kingdoms. King Porus had been killed by Seleucus, the Greek commander. His son Malayketu had taken charge and it was rumoured that Kautilya was stirring up old animosities between his kingdom and that of Gandhara.

There were a few professors in the university who looked at Kautilya with awe and others with some degree of aversion. In any case, he was a colourful figure and had a lot of stories floating about him. Sayana had heard that Kautilya wanted to dethrone Dhanananda because he was insulted in his court but did not believe it to be the only reason. Kautilya went about his work methodically and was a well-read man. It did not look like his motive was only revenge. His tuft of untied hair, which he was twirling with his index finger now, had another story attached to it. It was said that when he was insulted by Dhanananda, he had vowed not to tie up his tuft until the latter was dethroned. It seemed suspiciously close to the story of Draupadi, the wife of Pandavas, who vowed not to tie her hair until she washed it with the blood of those who disrobed her in the Hastinapura court. So, Sayana didn't give much credence to it.

Sikandar's invasion had necessitated a seminar on developing the theory of statecraft. Not that this was the first time the scholars were thinking about statecraft. Investigation on the science of statecraft had started some 300 years back. There were already five different schools of thought—those of Brihaspati, Ushanas, Prachetasa Manu, Parasara and Ambhi. There had been great teachers of the science like Vishalaksha and Bharadwaja. The library at the department already had documents on four different schools and thirteen individual teachers of Arthashastra.

The professors at the university had gathered to form a working group to develop an advanced constitution that will befit a large nation and advances made in various sciences. They were hands-on professors in the sense that they were all political activists from different areas of India.

There was a lengthy discussion on the term Arthashastra itself. Several professors wanted to give a narrow meaning to the term, that it meant the science of generating wealth in individual hands, in the hands of the nobility, the setthis and the owners of large manufactures. They argued that there are four great aims of human endeavor classified as dharma, artha, kama and moksha. For them, these terms meant moral behaviour, wealth, worldly pleasures and salvation.[xix]

Both Sayana and Kautilya had to present a strong case for the correct interpretation of the term, which had a much wider significance than just wealth.

Sayana explained passionately to the group that 'the material well-being of individuals is a part of the term *artha.*'

Kautilya also elaborated on the term. 'The source of the livelihood of people is wealth. The corollary is that the wealth of a nation is both the territory of a state and its citizens who may follow a variety of occupations and produce material wealth.'

Sayana took this on further. 'The state has a crucial role to play in maintaining the material well-being of the nation and its people. Therefore, it is the "science of economics", including the duty of the state to start productive enterprises, provide capital to run the enterprises and ensure that they contribute to creating livelihoods and also to the wealth of the nation.'

Finally, the working group accepted the larger meaning of the term.

❋ ❋ ❋

Sayana did not trust Kautilya for various reasons. He did not have clinching evidence but it was an open secret that Kautilya and Chandragupta advised Sikandar to cross the Beas river and attack the Magadhan empire of Dhanananda. They had assured him that it will be easy pickings since the emperor was very unpopular and there was an uprising in his capital city. But in return Chandragupta had demanded to be installed as the new emperor, which Sikandar could not digest.

After the breakdown of talks with Sikandar, Kautilya had advised Chandragupta not to make a direct attack on Pataliputra since the Magadhan empire had an empire which even the Macedonian king feared. Instead they raised an army of mercenaries, made pacts with the provinces surrounding Magadha and took advantage of the hatred of the vassals of the Magadhan empire towards their exploiter.

Kautilya was very appreciative of the efforts of Yugantar to weaken Sikandar's army with their hit and run tactics and the superior steel weapons. He was eager to learn from their study of Sikandar's battle strategy. He also admired their work in cartography, knowhow to build a capable navy, understanding of steel technology and advances in preventive and curative medicine.

But Sayana suspected that all this knowledge will be used to build an invincible empire where people can get even more pushed to the margins of political power. So, he wanted to do his best in developing a constitution that could guarantee rajdharma and which would provide people with mechanisms to overthrow the raja if he becomes an oppressor. It doesn't matter how kind-hearted a king is to start with but power corrupts and absolute power corrupts absolutely.

* * *

It was almost a year later that Sayana and Kautilya again locked horns on the question of rajdharma. The working group had continued its reading and discussions. They had even consulted the Greeks and Persians about their administrative structure. Kautilya had been busy with his maneuvers to oust the Magadhan king. Sayana had been strengthening the presence of Yugantar in several towns.

Kautilya put forward the point that 'an essential constituent of the state is its treasury, kosha. A king with a depleted treasury eats into the very vitality of the citizens and the country. Therefore, the state needs ruthless tax collectors backed by the army and administration.'

Sayana cautioned with, 'A king who impoverishes his own people or angers them by unjust exactions will also lose their loyalty. So, the state has to first create livelihoods and put money into the hands of people.'

Kautilya emphasized a lot on *dandaniti*, the science of law enforcement. A copy of the book by the same name, written at the time of the Mahabharata was there in the library of the department. Kautilya argued that the state should have powers to detect and punish criminals. The anti-social elements, 'the thorns of society' must be removed.

Sayana countered this saying. 'At the same time the fabric of society has to be maintained by the state by ensuring peaceful relations between citizens and rights of various sections of people including women.'

Kautilya had worked out details of law enforcement and a voluminous and comprehensive set of fines and punishments for all kinds of crimes. Sayana demanded that there should be mechanisms in the hands of people to protest if their rights are violated and demand action against officials who violated their rights.

There was a lot of discussion on a strong state and a weak state. After multiple heated exchanges the professors came to the conclusion that a king meting out unjust punishment is hated by the people he terrorizes while one who is too lenient is held in contempt; whoever imposes just and deserved punishment is respected and honoured.

❋ ❋ ❋

The working group met in Kaushambi after a few months when war against Magadha was imminent. The attempt to give divine status to the king came up for discussion.

The members agreed that from the Vedic times kingship was thought to be based on human needs and military necessity. The most intelligent and brave person in the community was chosen as the king or queen. But in the kingdoms of the Gangetic Plains, Vedic orthodoxy was forcing rituals such as the rajasuya, the Royal Consecration, to declare the king as a divine being. The three steps a king took on a tiger's skin was equated to the three steps that god Vishnu took to cover the earth and heaven. And lo! The king acquired divine powers. But Buddhism and Jainism looked at kingship as a trusted relationship between the king and his people.

Kautilya was obviously thinking about the Mauryan empire that was coming into being. He said, 'Of course, I have no illusions about the king's human nature and I do not believe in mysticism. But when the need arises, legends about the origin of kingship have propaganda value. So, there is no harm in using these legends when there is anarchy.'

Sayana disagreed. 'Our legends say that when anarchy prevailed at the dawn of the aeon, men elected the mythical first king, Manu Vaivastavata to kingship. So where did god come in here?'

'People don't have any respect for a peer. A king should be given some mythical powers. People should be told that the king fulfils the functions of Indra, the King of gods, as well as that of Yama, the god of death upon earth. So, in order to create an authority whom all will obey without question, we should make it clear that all who criticise him will be punished not only by the secular arm of the state but also by heaven.'

'This is preposterous!' exclaimed Sayana. 'Have we not heard in our Vedic texts that when a king harangues his troops before battle he should tell them that he is a paid servant just as they are, in order to win their trust?'

'Well, a king needs to adopt different tactics,' explained Kautilya. 'He should also have a strong spy system. Some of his secret agents should be disguised as gods during the consecration. He should be seen by all people welcoming these gods and having a feast with them, so that at least some of the gullible subjects will believe that he mixes with gods on equal terms.'

Sayana scoffed at the suggestion. 'In India gods can be got for a dime a dozen. Every brahmana is a god when he performs rituals. So, if a king is a god on earth, he is only one god among many. Do you think his divinity is going to be taken seriously?'

Kautilya did not give up. 'This is necessary,' he reiterated. 'Indian people are steeped in mysticism and religion. If the country is not to fall into chaos, you need to appeal to these sentiments now and then. You have to make a set of rules and stipulate various classifications, even if they sound sterile. We must keep the continuity with what was advised by Bhishma in the Shanti Parva of Mahabharata. People may say there is a lot of pedantry and contradictions in our srutis and dharmashastra, but they keep empires going.'

Many other members in the group also rejected the idea of royal divinity as the preferred ruse of sycophants who want to befuddle simple people as well as stupid monarchs. But there was a lot of confusion on how to provide mechanisms for people to dislodge a king if he turned into an oppressor.

The discussion was long and each one stuck to his stand. Sayana gave up with a huge sigh. *The Arthashastra will be probably the world's first treatise on statecraft but it is going to be pockmarked with contradictory statements.*

❋ ❋ ❋

Sayana had come to Pataliputra to attend the rajasuya of Chandragupta Maurya. It was not an extravagant ceremony with the king preferring a minimum of rituals. Priests and ascetics from all religions were invited.

The final touches were being given to the Arthashastra. Many working group members had come all the way from Takshashila, Muziris, Madurai, Ujjayini, Mathura, Kashi and other centres of learning in India.

Sayana had a question troubling him. 'It is clear that the job of a king is not to legislate. It is to protect, not only his subjects from invasion, but also of the order of society, harmony among its citizens, ensuring the right way of life for all people. But then he can be an autocrat, as we have seen very often, not answerable to anyone. So, what kind of practical checks can we have? What if he starts promoting himself as divine?'

Kautilya laughed. 'Firstly, the brahmana priests will not allow that. If a king takes his divinity too seriously and declares that he doesn't need any rituals, then they will be out of their jobs.'

Sayana threw his head back in disapproval. 'A king can very well become an autocrat. Even the Mahabharata explicitly sanctions revolt against a king who oppresses people or who fails to protect them. It says that such a king should be killed like a mad dog. Cannot we introduce some of these concepts here. After all, if a king himself is guilty then who will punish him?'

Kautilya was a bit taken aback. His protégé had just been declared the king and he didn't want to antagonize him so soon.

'I guess we have to build some controls without undermining the sovereignty of the king,' said Kautilya in a persuasive tone. 'We can insist on minister's councils and open assemblies of people in the king's court. We have to build pressure groups to compel the king to abide by his rajdharma.'

Sayana's frustration was mounting. 'All I can see are many paragraphs in the current draft advocating all kinds of deceit and duplicity that kings can resort to acquire and maintain power. You have argued that they should all be there because our greatest enemy is internal anarchy and external attack. But there is nothing binding on the king. There is no guarantee that the rights of our subjects will be protected.'

'What do you suggest?' asked Kautilya backing down a bit.

'I think we must clearly define the duty of a king. We should keep reiterating this in many places in the document, lest our king and lawmakers forget their accountability to the people.'

Sayana had come prepared with many formulations. He put forward the first one.

> *'In the happiness of his subjects lies the king's happiness,*
> *In the welfare of his subjects, his welfare.*
> *The king's good is not that which pleases him,*
> *But that which pleases his subjects.'[xx]*

After several arguments and drafts, Sayana felt he was not making much progress. But, little did he know that not even one among the many contemporary civilizations in the world could boast of the lofty ideals that the Arthashastra expounded in a methodical style.

EPILOGUE

Aniruddha was in the middle of his morning sermon when Sayana entered the Kaushambi monastery. They had a lot to share. After the sermon they sat down under the Bodhi tree away from the daily bustle of the monastery.

'After all our efforts, have we created a centralised state of the rich?' enquired Aniruddha.

Sayana chuckled. 'It is not yet as centralised as Chandragupta would wish. The empire has been established by merging various janapadas with the earlier Nanda empire. So there is some degree of autonomy which I can see still existing. For the time being, the empire has to deal with different economies, customs and polities. But it will soon be enlarging its core area and establishing its sway over all the trade routes.'

'That's already happening,' endorsed Aniruddha. 'The bureaucracy is expanding rapidly and more tax collectors are being hired. You had yourself mentioned many times that Arthashastra, while talking about a king's duty, also had an imperial ideology and vision.'

'There were so many pulls and pressures in the working group,' reminisced Sayana. 'There was a debate between centralisation and delegation of powers, between expenditures on social development and the army. The empire was built through people's movements and uprisings in several cities and the coming together of the north and north-western kingdoms against external aggression. So, it is bound to have some democratic features, but only so long as people can defend them.'

'I can see some sharp differences between the Mauryan and the Magadhan empires. This new empire is not insular, the way

Dhanananda was. It has a global outlook extending beyond the subcontinent. Chandragupta has welcomed ambassadors from many countries. Books and research studies on Indian philosophy, medicine and technology are reaching Greece and Rome through Persia.'

'All the discussions we had on the relationship between economics and politics will not go in vain,' commented Sayana, as if reassuring himself. 'At least we are not in a political vacuum now. We can still play a role in shaping the administration and politics of this empire.'

'I sincerely hope so,' responded Aniruddha. 'They say that *uneasy lies the head that wears the crown* and that is exactly what is happening to Chandragupta. It seems that he doesn't sleep in the same room every night, doesn't trust his ministers and employs food tasters to sample his food before he eats. He has to understand that he can get his sleep back if only he cares for the protection and well-being of his subjects.'

❖ ❖ ❖

'You both look wonderful,' greeted Vallabh as he settled down on the low cot in the small apartment that Madhavi and Nandi had rented in Takshashila. They were married in a simple ceremony and surrounded by friends in the university.

Vallabh had sent a message to Madhavi and Nandi a few weeks back that he would like to drop in when he visited the city next time. When he arrived, Nandi was washing the vessels and Madhavi had been preparing the batter and a vegetable stew for a south Indian style breakfast.

'I still recall how we met the first time in a shady alley in Madurai,' he said and chuckled.

Madhavi and Nandi recalled the amusing encounter and joined him in the laugh.

'Do you have any plans of going to the South?' asked Vallabh casually.

'Yes, we have been toying with the idea for a month now. It's just that we don't know what we are going to do once we reach there,' said Madhavi.

'I can solve the problem for you,' said Vallabh with a twinkle in his eye. 'There is a project that we can work on together.'

'I thought the South was out of bounds for you. Who will rescue you when you get arrested next time?' teased Nandi.

'Oh no, this time I need not go clandestinely. The Yugantar have entrusted me with connecting the trade and artisan guilds in Pataliputra with those in your cities,' Vallabh replied confidently.

'Where do we fit in your next grand scheme?' asked Madhavi.

'Many things are involved in this. We need to complete the documentation on trade routes between Pataliputra and the South as well as between Korkai in the south east and Muziris in the south west.'

'That sounds interesting,' remarked Nandi. It was a mammoth task but he was sure that Yugantar had some resources who can help.

'What about me?' asked Madhavi. 'Do I go back to my good old Siddhar colony and start holding the wrists of patients?'

'There is something for you too,' said Vallabh hurriedly. 'The Greeks have sent their ambassador here to build relations between the two countries. They are keenly interested in exchanging notes on the health system and medicine. You can establish a collaboration between the health departments in Takshashila and Pataliputra and the college in Madurai.'

'What will you be doing?' they almost asked in chorus.

'Well, there are lots of gaps in our understanding of the various Brahmi scripts and their connection with the Indus script. I am going to work on it. After all, we have to understand where our oral and writing systems came from. And, of course, I need to scout for more hill caves for the Jain bhikshus to live in!'

They continued to discuss various possibilities and the preparations that required to be done for the long trip back late into the night.

❊ ❊ ❊

Satya and his friends were busy setting up a steel furnace in Mathura. They had been working on technology transfer for the past three years. Madanika had been broaching to Satya about returning to Ujjayini, tentatively at first and now more persistently.

'That's a good idea,' responded Ananda when they told him their decision. 'In fact, I had been waiting for the right time to meet you and plan for the future,' he admitted.

'Plan for the future?' asked Bala. He had been helping in the forge and when he noticed that Ananda had arrived, had joined them at the anteroom, along with the rest.

'Yes, don't think your work is over after setting up the forges in a few cities. The real work starts now,' he announced enjoying how his audience had turned edgy. 'The Agarias have been having their annual conference. It is time to include other steel manufacturing tribes in the east and south in the conference too. Their customs differ but not much. I have observed that most of them worship Asur in his many forms. So they were all probably related at one time until they dispersed. Why not we plan for a large conference this year? It is important for workers to have a voice in the affairs of this country.'

Satya thought it was a good idea and looked at his friends who seemed to be in agreement.

'How can we do this alone?' asked Sajjalaka.

'The Yugantar will be connecting you to others. It will also arrange for representatives of trade guilds to attend the conference from various cities. Maybe a few years from now, we can think of an all-India confederation of manufacturers, artisans and trade guilds.'

The task looked mammoth to Satya but it also sounded exciting.

'What is the situation in Ujjayini?' asked Madanika. 'Remember, we can get arrested for sedition and murder.'

'That's no worry,' laughed Ananda. 'Avanti is more or less a province of the Mauryan empire now. The Mahamatra is now counting bars in the state prison for the murder of the king. So, nothing can stop the Agaria conference.'

'Suvala has been wanting to meet you. He wants to consult you on building a blacksmiths guild in the North West,' informed Ananda before taking leave.

❊ ❊ ❊

Susmila and Nalini were back at the monastery at Kaushambi. The time spent at the war front and the hospital at Takshashila, helping the doctors and taking care of the sick, had given them a lot of confidence. Susmila had heard that from the time of the Buddha, nuns had been composing verses in Magadhi. The collection was called Therigatha and it was expanding. The verses reflected stories and situations from the lives of the nuns before they were ordained into the sangha. They were about marriage, motherhood, betrayal and women's position in society.

'I want to contribute to this collection of verses,' announced Susmila to Aniruddha one day.

'How do you plan to do that?' asked Aniruddha. 'Are you going to write about your life?'

'I have heard shocking stories and incidents from other nuns. The pain I went through is nothing compared to what they have experienced. I want to help them compose the verse,' said Susmila sounding eager.

Aniruddha could see that she had an honest sentiment for the proposal. The composition would be an assertion that women were equal to men in wisdom and spiritual attainment.

At the next congregation at the monastery, Susmila requested that a verse she had compiled based on the life story of Chanda be read out. Aniruddha promptly agreed. Chanda was a widow without children, cast aside by society, who became a nun.

The composition beautifully brought out what women had to endure in a patriarchal society.

> 'Before, I had fallen on evil times: no husband, no children,
> no relatives, friends,
> no way to obtain clothing & food.
> So, taking a staff & bowl in hand,
> begging for alms from house to house,
> feverish from the cold & heat,
> I wandered for seven full years.
> Then seeing a nun
> obtaining food & drink,
> I approached her & said:
> "Let me go forth into homelessness."
>
> She, Patachara, from sympathy,
> let me go forth;
> then, exhorting me,
> urged me on to the highest goal.
> Hearing her words,

I did her bidding.
Her exhortation was not in vain.
I'm a three-knowledge woman,
fermentation-free.'[xxi]

❄ ❄ ❄

The revolt of the traders and manufacturers in Pataliputra was one of the important factors that pulled the Magadhan empire down. The new regime of Chandragupta treated the guilds with more respect.

Chandaka and Sudjata had become active leaders of the trade guild at Pataliputra after Dhanananda was defeated.

At the next meeting of the guild, Chandaka assessed the new situation. 'The state has given us considerable autonomy,' he explained, 'not as a favour but because of our assertion of rights. Though whatever be the current disposition of the state, it will be dealing with us warily. We are a unique form of organisation which can safeguard the interests of traders and craftsmen against any oppression by the administration. So, we need to codify our rules and demand that the guild be given statutory powers to deal with problems faced by members.'[xxii]

Sudjata also made a point. 'There are attempts to equate the sreni with a caste-based organisation. We should oppose these attempts. The leader of a guild should be elected democratically. Also, it should not become a caste-based organisation. No one will have hereditary rights in the organisation. Membership should be open to all strata of traders and producers.'

A senior member made a request. He said, 'In Dhanananda's regime there was no protection for traders and their caravans. He and his ministers looted all the membership money and taxes. We cannot allow that to happen now.'

'Good point,' agreed Sudjata. 'We have to ensure that the guild spends money on maintenance of guards in the markets and on highways. Forest guards have to be appointed for guaranteeing safety for caravans. We must put in place an insurance scheme so that manufacturers and traders are compensated during calamities.'

One of the members stood up and asked, 'How can we win the trust of people?'

Chandaka was glad the question came up. 'Earlier the guilds were controlled by the rich setthis who were worried only about filling their pockets and entered into all kinds of corrupt deals with the administration. We now have democratically elected office bearers. We are demanding that the guilds also be given powers as courts of justice so that people in towns and villages need not come all the way to the capital for justice. A part of our expenditure will also go towards construction of roads, watersheds, traveller's rest houses, and other things which can make the guilds popular among the people.'

KEY ACTORS

The Yugantar leadership

Sayana: the priest, philosopher and expert in statecraft based in Pataliputra who inspires the brotherhood and engages Kautilya in the debate on Arthashastra

Vallabh: the roving Jain monk who mobilises Madhavi and Nandi and who is an expert in Indian languages and scripts

Aniruddha: the Buddhist monk at the Kaushambi monastery

Suvala: the fiery warrior from the north-east who tries to unite the tribals in the Swat valley to weaken the Macedonian forces

Kunala: the doctor practicing Ayurveda and an expert on the Sushruta Samhita

At Ujjayini

Satya: a talented blacksmith and leader of the Agaria tribe

Bala, Maitreya and Sajjalaka: friends and members of Satya's gang of rebels

Madanika: Satya's lover and key informant

Vasantasena: the courtesan in Ujjayini

At Vidisha

Ananda – a senior monk at the monastery

Shibanand – another monk at the monastery

At Madurai

Madhavi: the Siddha doctor who wants to discover the world

Nandivarman (Nandi): a carefree trader who loves Madhavi and trusts her judgement

Vengayyan: the fisherman from the Pparavar colony

At Kaushambi

Susmila: the widow who escaped from the brink of death

Mahishi: Susmila's vile mother-in-law

Vinaya: Mahishi's husband

Charudatta: the Buddhist monk who saves Susmila

Nalini: Susmila's friend at the nun's quarters

At Pataliputra

Sudjata: the young trader who wants to get away from his financial troubles

Chandaka: the seasoned leader of the caravan, the Sarthavahaka and a prominent member of the sreni, the trader's council

Revata: the fearless caravan security guard

SELECT GLOSSARY

Angadi – a bazaar

Angavastram – a piece of white cloth traditionally worn by men over the shoulders like a shawl or stole

Arthashastra – an ancient treatise on statecraft

Ayurveda – an ancient system of medicine that has survived till today, the science of Life

Avanti – an ancient Indian mahajanapada, roughly corresponding to the present day Malwa region

Lohasur – god of iron, worshipped by the Agaria tribe who specialize in smelting iron ore and steel

Brahmana – the highest caste of priests in Vedic orthodox system

Bhrgukachchha – lies along the Narmada River near the Gulf of Khambhat (Cambay) of the Arabian Sea

Charpai – a light bedstead used in India consisting of a web of rope or tape netting

Chera – ancient kingdom in south-west India with Muziris as the capital

Chola – ancient kingdom in south India with Uraiyur as the capital

Dakshinapatha – the great southern trade route

Dhoti – a garment worn by males in south India, made of cotton or silk, tied around the waist and extending to cover the legs

Gandhara – a kingdom located around present-day Kandahar in Afghanistan

Indra – king of the gods, the *devas*

Janapada – ancient republics and kingdoms

Kadam – a unit of distance in ancient Thamizhagam, roughy 1.2 kms

Kamboja – a kingdom in the north-west frontier of ancient India located around present-day Kabul

Kolam – an intricate floor drawing made from flour, white or coloured

Kos – a unit of distance, about 3 km

Kshatriya – the second caste in the varna system associated with warriors

Kuzhal – a traditional double reed wind instrument popular in south India

Mahajanapada – larger ancient republics and kingdoms

Muhurtha – a time unit equal to one-thirtieth of a day, 48 minutes.

Muziris – an ancient port city on the south-western coast of India, near present day Cochin

Pandya – ancient kingdom in south India with Madurai as the capital

Puhar – short form of Poompuhar, an ancient port located in the south-eastern coast of India at the tail end of the Kaveri river

Sangha – in Buddhism, it refers to the monastic community of bhikkhus (monks) and bhikkhunis (nuns)

Shudra – the lowest caste mentioned in the varna system referring to manual labourers and peasants

Siddha – an ancient system of medicine that has survived till today

Upasaka – a male lay follower of Buddha's teachings

Uttarapatha – the northern high road, along the river Ganges crossing the Indo-Gangetic watershed, going through the Punjab to Takshashila (Gandhara) and further to present-day Balkh in Afghanistan (Bactria)

Vaisya – one of the four castes mentioned in the varna system usually denoting traders, moneylenders and farmers.

Varna – the caste system of Vedic orthodoxy

Vatsa – a kingdom corresponding to the territory of modern Allahabad in Uttar Pradesh, at the confluence of the Ganges and Yamuna rivers

Vihara – a Buddhist monastery

Yajna – sacrifice

Yavanar – originally used to denote Greeks but later extended to Romans and other foreigners

Yaazh – a harp-like instrument popular in ancient Tamil music, the ancestor of modern-day veena

SELECT REFERENCES

I have depended on many books, papers, texts and reports for writing this novel. They gave me a wealth of information on and insights into ancient India. I welcome readers to experience the journey I went through.

The Cilappatikaram: The Tale of an Anklet, Penguin Classics, is an excellent English translation by R. Parthasarathy of one of the world's masterpieces and perhaps India's finest epic in a language other than Sanskrit. I relied on the original as well as the translation for the description of life in ancient South India and the magnificent city of Madurai and the port of Puhar.

Romila Thapar's *History of Early India: From the origins to AD 1300*, brings to life ancient India, the second urbanization, its diverse kingdoms, landscapes, languages and beliefs. It has debunked the theory of the Aryan invasion and has provided good insights into Vedic orthodoxy and the naastik schools of thought.

A.L. Basham's *The Wonder That Was India* published by Rupa is an excellent study of Indian history, culture, literature and languages. His translations of Sanskrit and Tamil poems are exquisite. His understanding of the origins of languages and scripts is marvelous. I have borrowed some of his translations in this novel.

R.S. Sharma's *India's Ancient Past* is also an excellent read on the origins and growth of the Indian civilization, empires and schools of philosophy.

A History of Ancient and Early Medieval India: From the stone age to the 12th century by Upinder Singh, gave me an excellent introduction to original sources of documentation of the history of ancient India. It has a clear and balanced explanation of several historical developments.

The maps given at the beginning of this novel have been adapted from this text.

An English Translation of the Sushruta Samhita edited by Kaviraj Kunjalal Bhishagratna is wonderful reading for those who want to delve into the wonders of medical science in ancient India. I have tried, to my best ability, to present the correct understanding of Ayurveda as an encyclopaedia of the Indian system of medicine in all its departments, but as a "science of Life entire".

Indian Shipping: A Historical Survey by Baldeo Sahay is a scholarly and unique work written in a style which is not only highly informative and educative but also immensely readable. For those who wish to understand the complete history of India's many-faceted maritime activity, this book is a must. I consulted chapters in this book on sea routes at the time of the Indus civilisation as well as during the 4th century BCE, the period of this novel.

Alexander's Campaign (327-326 BC): A Chronological Marker In The Archaeology Of India by Himanshu Prabha Ray, debunks the colonialist theory that the invasion of Alexander set in motion major developments in India.

Iron Making in Ancient India - Acritical Assessment brought out by the National Metallurgical Laboratory of India is a well-researched paper on steel making and furnaces in ancient India.

The excellent translation of Mrichchakatika, The Little Clay Cart, edited by M.R. Kale inspired me to choose Ujjayini as one of the key locations in the novel. The drama by Sudraka is dated later than 4th century BCE but the description of the park and the murder of the king have been adapted in the novel.

Likewise, *Pattupattu: Ten Tamil Idylls,* translated beautifully by J.V. Chelliah are among the best poems in the Sangam literature. The chapter on Maduraikanchi gives a beautiful account of ancient Madurai city and has added flavour to the chapters relating to Madurai in the novel.

Finally, for an accurate account of Alexander's invasion, I referred to the great compendium called *The Invasion of India by Alexander the Great*. It is one great collection of the accounts of various Greek authors like Arrian, Curtis, Plutarch, Diodorous and Justin. It is a biased account of the invasion by Greek historians but nevertheless a great read.

I have referred to many other papers, journals, articles, monographs and the like. There is no space to describe them here but they have all contributed immensely to the novel. I am greatly indebted to the authors.

END NOTES

i   The Wonder that was India, A.L. Basham, - A translation from Kalidasa's Megha-duta, P. 422

ii   Ancient iron making in India, B Prakash

iii   The Silappadikaram, translated by Ramachandra Dikshitar

iv   The Wonder that was India, A.L.Basham, P. 181

v   The invasion of India by Alexander the Great, as described by Arrian and others, Westminster, 1892

vi   https://medium.com/welcometoindia/ancient-indian-measurement-of-time-for-a-day-b70b6c650b3e

vii   https://www.ancient.eu/Brahmi_Script/

viii The Wonder that was India, P. 285

ix   Ibid., P. 248

x   The Agaria, P. 171

xi   The Wonder that Was India, P. 211

xii   Nattrinai 31 - https://learnsangamtamil.com/%e0%ae%b1%e0%af%8d%e0%ae%b1%e0%ae%bf%e0%ae%a3%e0%af%88/

xiii The wonder that was India, P. 398

xiv Dravidian is the language of the Indus writing, Clyde Winters, Current Science, Vol 103, No. 10

xv   Trade Networks in North-West India and Bactria: The Material Record of Indo-Greek Contact: Himanshu Prabha Ray

xvi Indian Shipping – A Historical Survey, Baldeo Sahay, P. 13

xvii Sushruta Samhita, Introduction to the Translation

xviii   https://en.wikipedia.org/wiki/Wootz_steel

xix   Kautilya: The Arthashastra, edited by L.N. Rangarajan, Penguin Books

xx   The wonder that was India, AL Basham

xxi   https://tipitaka.fandom.com/wiki/Thig_5.12_PTS:_Thig_122-126-_Canda:_The_Beggar

xxii   Guilds in Ancient India, KK Thaplyal, http://iks.iitgn.ac.in/wp-content/uploads/2017/01/Guilds_in_Ancient_India.pdf